Spells

APRILYNNE PIKE

Spells

HarperCollins *Children's Books*

First published in Great Britain by HarperCollins *Children's Books* 2010
HarperCollins *Children's Books* is a division of HarperCollins*Publishers* Ltd,
77-85 Fulham Palace Road, Hammersmith, London W6 8JB

Visit us on the web at
www.harpercollins.co.uk

1

SPELLS
Text copyright © Aprilynne Pike 2010

Aprilynne Pike asserts the moral right to be identified
as the author of this work.

ISBN-13 978 0 00 731437 9

Printed and bound in England by
Clays Ltd, St Ives plc

To Kenny – for all the little things.
And the big things.
And everything in between.
Thank you.

Chapter One

Laurel stood in front of the cabin, scanning the tree line, her throat constricting in a rush of nerves. He was there, somewhere, watching her. The fact that she couldn't see him yet meant nothing.

It wasn't that Laurel didn't want to see him. Sometimes she thought she wanted to see him too much. Getting involved with Tamani was like playing in a roaring river. Take one step too far and the current would never let you go. She had chosen to stay with David, and she still believed it was the right choice. But it didn't make this reunion any easier.

Or stop her hands from shaking.

She had promised Tamani she would come see him when she got her driver's licence. Though she hadn't been specific about a date, she *had* said May. It was now almost the end of June. He had to know she was avoiding him. He would be here now – the first one to meet her – and she wasn't sure whether to be excited or afraid. The feelings mixed into a heady blend of something she'd never felt before – and wasn't sure she ever wanted to feel again.

Laurel found herself clutching the tiny ring Tamani had given her last year, the one she wore on a thin chain around her neck. She had tried not to think about him these last six months. *Tried*, she admitted to herself, *and failed*. She forced herself to unwrap her fingers from around the little ring and attempted to make her arms swing naturally, confidently at her sides as she walked towards the forest.

As the shadows of the branches fell across her, a streak of green and black swung down from a tree and scooped Laurel up. She screamed in terror, then delight.

"Did you miss me?" Tamani asked with that same bewitching half-grin that had entranced her since the first time she'd met him.

Instantly, it was as though the last six months had never happened. Just the sight of him, the feel of him so close to her, melted every fear, every thought. . . every resolve. Laurel wrapped her arms around him and squeezed as hard as she could. She never wanted to let go.

"I'll take that as a yes," Tamani said with a groan.

She forced herself to let go and step back. It was like trying to make a river flow the other direction. But after a few seconds she managed and settled for standing silently, drinking in the sight of him. The same longish, black hair, his quick smile, those mesmerising green eyes. A cloud of awkwardness descended and Laurel stared down at her shoes, a little embarrassed at her zealous greeting and unsure of what to say next.

"I expected you earlier," Tamani said at last.

Now that she was here with him, it felt ridiculous that she had been afraid. But Laurel could still recall the cold pit of fear in her stomach every time she'd thought about seeing Tamani again. "I'm sorry."

"Why didn't you come?"

"I was afraid," she answered honestly.

"Of me?" Tamani asked with a smile.

"Sort of."

"Why?"

She took a deep breath. He deserved the truth. "It's too easy to be here with you. I don't trust myself."

Tamani grinned. "I guess I can't be too offended by that."

Laurel rolled her eyes. Her long absence certainly hadn't dampened his bravado.

"How is everything?"

"Fine. Good. Everything's good," she stammered.

He hesitated. "How are your friends?"

"My friends?" Laurel asked. "Could you possibly be more transparent?"

Laurel unconsciously touched a silver bracelet on her wrist. Tamani's eyes followed the movement.

Tamani kicked at the dirt. "How's David?" he finally asked.

"He's great."

"Are you two... ?" He let the question hang.

"Are we together?"

"I guess that's it." Tamani glanced again at the intricate silver bracelet. Frustration clouded his features, transforming the glance into a glare, but he dispelled it with a smile.

The bracelet was a gift from David. He had given it to her just before Christmas last year, when they officially became a couple. It was a delicate silver vine with tiny flowers blooming around crystal centres. He hadn't said as much, but Laurel suspected it was to balance out the faerie ring she still wore every day. She couldn't bear to put the tiny ring away and, true to her promise, every time she thought of the ring, she thought of Tamani. She still had feelings for him. Torn and uncertain feelings, mostly – but strong enough to make her feel guilty when her thoughts wandered in that direction.

David was everything she could ask for in a boyfriend. Everything except what he wasn't, what he never could be. But Tamani could never be what David was, either.

"Yes, we are," she finally answered.

Tamani was silent.

"I need him, Tam," she said, her tone soft but not apologetic. She couldn't – wouldn't – apologise for choosing David. "I told you before how it was."

"Sure." He ran his hands up and down her arms. "But he's not here now."

"You know I couldn't live with that," she forced herself to say. But it was barely a whisper.

Tamani sighed. "I'm just going to have to accept it, aren't I?"

"Unless you really want me to be alone."

He slung one arm around her shoulders – friendly now. "I could never want that for you."

She put her arms around him and squeezed.

"What's that for?" Tamani asked.

"Just for being you."

"Well, I certainly won't turn down a hug," he said. His

tone was casual, joking, but he wrapped his other arm around her tightly, almost desperately. Before she could pull away, however, his arm dropped, then pointed down the path. "Come on," Tamani said. "It's this way."

Laurel's mouth went dry. It was time.

Pushing her hand into her pocket, Laurel felt the embossed card for what was doubtless the hundredth time. It had shown up on her pillow one morning in early May, sealed with wax and tied with a sparkling silver ribbon. The message was brief – four short lines – but they changed everything.

Due to the woefully inadequate nature of your current education, you are summoned to the Academy of Avalon.

Please report to the gate at mid-morning, the first day of summer. Your presence will be required for eight weeks.

Woefully inadequate. Her mom hadn't been too happy with that. But then, her mom hadn't been too happy with much of anything involving faeries lately. After the initial revelation of Laurel being a faerie, things had been surprisingly OK. Her parents had always known there was something different about their adopted daughter. As crazy as the truth actually turned out to be – that Laurel was a changeling, a faerie child left in their care to inherit sacred fae land they had accepted it with surprising ease, at least at first. Her dad's attitude hadn't changed, but over the last few months her mom had grown more and more freaked out by the idea that Laurel wasn't human. She'd stopped talking about it, then refused to even hear about it, and things had finally come to a head last month when Laurel got the invitation. Well, more like a summons, really. It had taken a lot of arguing from Laurel – and a fair bit of persuasion from her dad – before her mom had agreed to let her go. As if, somehow, she would come back even less human than when she'd left.

Laurel was glad she'd neglected to tell them anything about the trolls; she had no doubt she wouldn't be standing here today if she had.

"Are you ready?" Tamani pressed, sensing Laurel's hesitation.

Ready? Laurel wasn't sure if she could ever be more ready for this. . . or less.

Silently, she followed him through the forest, trees filtering the sunlight and shading their trek. The path was scarcely a path at all, but Laurel knew where it led. Soon they would come to a small, gnarled tree, a unique species in this forest but otherwise ordinary in its appearance. Though she had spent twelve years of her life living here and exploring the land, she had seen this tree only once before – when she brought Tamani back from fighting trolls, wounded and barely conscious. Last time she had witnessed the tree's transformation and gotten a tiny glimpse of what lay beyond. Today she would go through the gate.

Today, she would see Avalon for herself.

As they walked deeper into the forest, other faeries fell into step behind them, and Laurel forced herself not to crane her neck and stare. She wasn't sure she'd ever get used to these beautiful, silent guards who never spoke to her and rarely met her eyes. They were always there, even when she couldn't see them. She knew that now. She wondered briefly how many of them had been watching her since she was just a child, but the mortification was too great. Her parents watching her juvenile antics were one thing; nameless supernatural sentries were quite another. She swallowed, focused forward, and tried to think of something else.

Soon they arrived, emerging through a stand of redwoods clustered protectively around the ancient, twisted tree. The faerie sentries formed a half-circle and, after a sharp gesture from Shar – the leader of the sentries – Tamani dislodged his hand from Laurel's vicelike grip to join them. Standing in the middle of the dozen or so sentries, Laurel clutched the straps of her backpack. Her breathing quickened as each sentry laid one hand against the bark of the tree, right where its stout trunk split into two thick limbs. Then the tree began to vibrate as the light of the clearing seemed to gather around its branches.

Laurel was determined to keep her eyes open this time, to watch the entire transformation. But even as she squinted resolutely against the glow, a brilliant flash forced her eyelids shut for the briefest of instants. When they opened again, the tree had transformed into the arching gate of tall, golden bars, laced with curling vines dotted with purple flowers. Two sturdy posts on either side anchored the gate into the ground, but otherwise it stood alone in the sunlit forest. Laurel let out a breath she hadn't realised she was holding, only to hold it again as the gate swung outward.

Tangible warmth rolled forth from the gateway, and even ten feet away Laurel caught the aromatic scent of life and growth she recognised from years of gardening with her mom. But this was stronger – a pure perfume of bottled summer sunlight. She felt her feet begin to move forward of their own accord and was nearly through the gate when something tugged at her hand. Laurel tore her eyes away from the gateway and was startled to see that Tamani had stepped out of formation to wrap her hand gently in his own. A touch on her other hand prompted her to look back through the gate.

Jamison, the old Winter faerie she had met last fall, lifted her free hand and set it on his arm like a gentleman in a Regency movie. He smiled at Tamani cordially but pointedly. "Thank you for bringing us Laurel, Tam. I will take her from here."

Tamani's hand didn't fall away immediately. "I'll come see you next week," he said, quiet but not whispering.

The three of them stood there for a few seconds, frozen in time. Then Jamison tilted his head and nodded once at Tamani. Tamani nodded back and returned to his place in the semicircle.

Laurel felt his eyes on her, but her face was already turning back to the bright glow pouring from the golden gate. The pull of Avalon was too strong to linger even on the sharp regret she felt at having to leave Tamani so quickly after their reunion. But he would come see her soon.

Jamison stepped just inside the golden archway and beckoned Laurel forward, releasing his hold on the hand lying on his arm. "Welcome back, Laurel," he said softly.

With her breath catching in her throat, Laurel stepped forward and crossed the threshold of the gate, her feet stepping into Avalon for the first time. *Not really the first time,* she reminded herself. *This is where I came from.*

For a moment she could see nothing but leaves on a huge overhanging oak tree and dark, loose soil at her feet, lined with plush, emerald grass. Jamison led her out from under the canopy of foliage, and sunlight shone down on to her face, warming her cheeks instantly and making her blink.

They were in some kind of walled park. Trails of rich, black earth snaked through the vibrant greenery that ran up against a stone wall. Laurel had never seen a stone wall so tall before – to build such a thing without concrete must have taken decades. The garden was dotted with trees and long, leafy vines snaked up their trunks and wound around their branches. She could see flowers all over the vines, but they were tightly closed against the warmth of the day.

She turned to look back at the gate. It was shut now, and beyond its golden bars she could see only darkness. It was in the middle of the park and wasn't connected to anything at all – it was just standing upright, surrounded by about twenty sentries, all female. Laurel tilted her head. There *was* something. She took a step forward, and broad-bladed spears with tips that seemed to be made of crystal crossed in front of her vision.

"It's all right, Captain," came Jamison's voice from behind Laurel. "She can look."

The spears went away and Laurel stepped forward, sure her eyes were tricking her. But no, at a right angle to the gate was another gate. Laurel continued walking until she had circled four gates, linked by the sturdy posts that she recognised from the other side of the gate. Each post attached to two of the gates, forming a perfect square around the strange blackness that persisted behind them, despite the fact that she should have been able to look right through the bars to the sentries standing on the other side.

"I don't understand," Laurel said, coming to stand by Jamison again.

"Your gate isn't the only one," Jamison said with a smile.

Laurel vaguely remembered Tamani talking about four gates last fall, when she had come to him battered and bruised after being thrown in the Chetco River by trolls. "Four gates," she said softly, pushing back the unpleasant part of the memory.

"To the four corners of the earth. One step could take you to your home, the mountains of Japan, the highlands of Scotland, or the mouth of the Nile River in Egypt."

"That's amazing," Laurel said, staring at the gate. *Gates?* "Thousands of miles in a single step."

"And the most vulnerable place in all of Avalon," Jamison said. "Clever, though, don't you think? Quite a feat. The gates were made by King Oberon, at the cost of his life, but it was Queen Isis who cloaked the gates on the other side – and only a few hundred years ago."

"The Egyptian goddess?" Laurel asked breathlessly.

"Only named after the goddess," Jamison said, smiling. "As much as we'd like to believe otherwise, not all the major figures in human history are faeries. Come, my *Am fear-faire* will worry if we tarry too long."

"Your what?"

He looked at her then, his gaze questioning at first, then strangely sorrowful. *"Am fear-faire,"* he repeated. "My guardians. I have at least two with me at all times."

"Why?"

"Because I am a Winter faerie." Jamison walked slowly down the earthen path, seeming to weigh his words as he spoke them. "Our gifts are the rarest of all fae, so we are honoured. We alone can open the gates, so we are protected. And Avalon itself is vulnerable to our power, so we must never be compromised by an enemy. With great power—"

"Comes great responsibility?" Laurel finished.

Jamison turned to her, smiling now. "And who taught you this?"

Laurel paused, confused. "Uh, Spider-Man?" she said lamely.

"I suppose some truths truly are universal," Jamison laughed, his voice echoing off the great stone walls. Then he sobered. "It's a phrase we Winter faeries use often. The Briton King, Arthur, said it after witnessing the terrible revenge the trolls took on Camelot. He always believed that destruction was his fault, that he could have prevented it."

"Could he have?" Laurel asked.

Jamison nodded to two sentries, who stood at either side of an enormous set of wooden doors that led through the walls. "Probably not," he said to Laurel. "But it is a good reminder nonetheless."

The doors swung open soundlessly, and all thoughts were chased from Laurel's head as she and Jamison walked out of the enclosure and on to a hillside.

Verdant beauty flowed down the hill and as far as she could see in every direction. Black paths snaked through masses of trees, interspersed with long, flower-speckled meadows and rainbow clusters of something Laurel couldn't identify – they looked like gigantic balloons of every imaginable colour, sitting on the ground and sparkling like soap bubbles. Farther down, in a ring that appeared to spread all the way around the base of the hill, were the roofs of small houses, and Laurel could make out brightly coloured dots moving about that must be other faeries.

"There are... *thousands* of them," Laurel said, not quite realising she had spoken aloud.

"Of course," Jamison said, mirth colouring his voice. "Almost the entire species lives here. We number more than eighty thousand now." He paused. "That probably sounds small to you."

"No," Laurel said quickly. "I mean, I know there are more humans than that, but... I never imagined so many faeries all in one place." It was strange; it made her feel both normal and very insignificant. She'd met other faeries, of course – Tamani, Shar, the sentries she glimpsed from time to time – but the thought of thousands upon thousands of faeries was almost overwhelming.

Jamison's hand touched the small of her back. "There will be time for sightseeing another day," he said softly. "We must take you to the Academy. Continue."

Laurel followed Jamison down the perimeter of the stone wall. When they rounded the side of the enclosure, Laurel looked uphill and her breath caught in her throat again. About a quarter mile up the gentle slope an enormous tower rose against the skyline, jutting from the centre of a sprawling building straight out of *Jane Eyre*. It didn't look like a castle so much as a grand library, all square, grey stones and steeply pitched roofs. Massive windows dotted every wall, and skylights glittered among slate shingles like caches of faceted prisms. Every surface was veined with creepers, framed by flowers, glimpsed through foliage, or otherwise host to plants of innumerable variety.

Jamison's words answered the question Laurel was too amazed to ask. He gestured towards the structure with one arm as he spoke. "The Academy of Avalon."

Chapter Two

As they walked towards the Academy, Laurel glimpsed another building through breaks in the forest. At the very top of the tall hill, just a bit higher than the towering Academy, sat the crumbling ruins of a castle. Laurel blinked and squinted; perhaps *crumbling* was not the right word. It was definitely falling to pieces, but ropes of green wound through the white marble as if sewing the walls together, and the canopy of an enormous tree spread out above it, shading half the structure beneath its leaves. "What's that building?" Laurel asked the next time it came into view.

"That is the Winter Palace," Jamison said. "I live there."

"Is it safe?" Laurel asked dubiously.

"Of course not," Jamison replied. "It is one of the most

dangerous places in all of Avalon. But *I* am safe there, as are its other occutrousers."

"Is it going to fall down?" Laurel asked, eyeing one corner that was done up like a corset with viridian laces.

"No, indeed," Jamison replied. "We Winter faeries have been caring for this palace for more than three thousand years. The roots of that redwood grow with the castle now, as much a part of the structure as the original marble. She would never let it fall."

"Why don't you just build a new one?"

Jamison was silent for a few moments, and Laurel worried that her question had offended him. But when he responded, he didn't sound upset. "The castle is not only a home, Laurel. It also safeguards many things – things we cannot risk moving simply for convenience or for satisfying our vanity with a fancy new structure." He gestured back at their stony grey destination with a smile. "We have the Academy for that."

Laurel looked back up at the castle with new eyes. Instead of the haphazard loops of green she had seen at first glance, she could now pick out the order and method in the latticework stripes. Careful braces on the corners, a web of roots supporting large expanses of wall – the tree really had become part of the castle. Or perhaps the castle had become a part of the tree. The whole structure seemed to lounge contentedly in the embrace of its sprawling roots.

Around the next bend they came upon what Laurel first thought was a wrought-iron fence. A closer look revealed that it was actually a living wall. Branches wound and curved and wrapped about one another in complicated curlicues, like an impossibly complex bonsai tree. Two guards, one male, one female, stood at a gate, both in ceremonial armour of a vibrant blue, complete with shiny, plumed helmets. They both bowed low to Jamison and reached for their side of the gate.

"Come," Jamison said, beckoning Laurel forward when she hesitated at the gate. "They are waiting for you."

The grounds of the Academy were bustling with life. Dozens of faeries were at work around the yard. Some were dressed in fine, flowing dresses or light silken trousers and had books in their hands. Others were clad in more homespun cottons and busied themselves digging and pruning. Still others were picking flowers, searching the many heavy-laden bushes for perfect specimens. As Jamison and Laurel passed, most of the faeries paused in their work and bowed at the waist. But everyone at least inclined his or her head respectfully.

"Are…" Laurel felt silly asking. "Are they bowing to me?"

"It's possible," Jamison replied. "But I suspect they are mostly bowing to me."

His casual tone caught Laurel off guard. But clearly being bowed to was commonplace for Jamison. He did not even stop to acknowledge it. "Should I have bowed when you came to the gate?" Laurel asked, her voice a little unsteady.

"Oh, no," Jamison said readily. "You are a Fall faerie. You bow only to the Queen. A slight nod of respect is more than enough from you."

Laurel walked in silent confusion as they passed several more faeries. She watched the few who only inclined their heads. They caught her eye as she passed and she wasn't sure quite how to take their expressions. Some seemed curious; others glared. Many were simply unreadable. Ducking her head timidly, Laurel hurried forward to keep pace with Jamison.

As they approached the towering front doors, a set of footmen pulled them open and Jamison led Laurel into a spacious foyer with a domed ceiling made entirely of glass. Sunlight poured through it, nourishing the hundreds of potted plants adorning the room. The foyer was less busy than the grounds, though there were a few faeries sitting on loungers and at small desks with books out in front of them.

An older faerie – *not as old as Jamison*, Laurel thought, though it was hard to tell with faeries – approached them and inclined her head. "Jamison, a pleasure." She smiled at Laurel. "I assume this is Laurel; my, how you've changed."

Laurel was startled for a moment, then remembered that she had spent seven years in Avalon before going to live with her parents. The fact that *she* couldn't remember anyone didn't mean they couldn't remember her. It made her strangely uncomfortable to wonder how many of the faeries she passed on the grounds could remember a past she would never recall.

"I'm Aurora," the faerie said. "I teach the initiates, who are both ahead of and behind you." She laughed, as if at some private joke. "Come, I'll show you to your room. We've freshened it up – traded outgrown things for new ones – but other than that we have left it undisturbed for your return."

"I have a room here?" Laurel asked before she could stop herself.

"Of course," Aurora said without looking back. "This is your home."

Home? Laurel glanced around at the austere foyer, the intricate banisters on the winding staircase, the sparkling windows and skylights. Had this really been her home?

It looked – felt – so foreign. She glanced behind her where Jamison followed, but there certainly wasn't any gawking from him. His surroundings in the Winter Palace were probably even more grand.

On the third floor they approached a hallway lined with dark cherrywood doors. Names were painted on each in a glittering, curly script. *Mara, Katya, Fawn, Sierra, Sari.* Aurora stopped in front of a door that very clearly said *Laurel.*

Laurel felt her chest tighten and time seemed to crawl as Aurora turned the knob and pushed the door open. It glided on silent hinges over a plush, crème-coloured carpet and revealed a large room with one wall made completely of glass. The other walls were draped in pale green satin that stretched from ceiling to floor. A skylight opened over half the room, shining down on to an enormous bed covered with a silk spread and enclosed by sheer curtains so light they ruffled in the hint of a breeze that came through the doorway. Modest but obviously well-constructed furniture – a desk, dresser, and armoire – completed the room. Laurel stepped inside and gazed slowly around, searching for something familiar, something that felt like home.

But though it was one of the most beautiful rooms she had ever seen, she didn't remember it. Not a wisp of a memory, no trace of recognition. Nothing. A wave of disappointment crashed over her, but she tried to hide it as she turned to Jamison and Aurora. "Thank you," she said, hoping her smile wasn't too tight. What did it matter that she didn't remember? She was here now. That was the important thing.

"I'll let you unpack and freshen up," Aurora said. Her eyes flitted over Laurel's tank top and jean shorts. "You are welcome to wear whatever you like here at the Academy; however, you might find the clothing in your wardrobe a bit more comfortable. We guessed your size, but new clothing can be tailored for you as early as tomorrow, if you like. Those… breeches… you're wearing – the fabric looks like it would chafe terribly."

A small chuckle from Jamison made Aurora stand a little straighter. "Ring this bell," she said, pointing, "if you need anything. We have a full staff to attend you. You may do as you will for an hour, then I will send one of our fundamentals instructors up to begin your lessons."

"Today?" Laurel asked, a bit louder than she had intended.

Aurora's eyes darted to Jamison. "Jamison and the Queen herself have instructed us to make full use of the time you have with us. It is far too brief as it is."

Laurel nodded, a thrill of excitement and nervousness

shooting through her. "OK," she said. "I'll be ready."

"I'll leave you then." Aurora turned and looked at Jamison, but he waved a hand at her.

"I will stay a few moments more before I return to the palace."

"Of course," Aurora said with a nod before leaving them alone.

Jamison stood in the doorway, surveying the room. As the sound of Aurora's footsteps faded down the hall, Jamison spoke. "I haven't been here since I escorted you to go and live with your parents thirteen years ago." He looked up at her. "I hope you do not mind the rush into your work. We have so little time."

Laurel shook her head. "It's fine. I just… I have so many questions."

"And most will have to wait," Jamison said with a smile that softened his words. "The time you will spend here is too precious to be wasted on the manners and mores of Avalon. There are many years ahead for you to learn things like that."

Laurel nodded, even though she wasn't sure she agreed.

"Besides," Jamison added with a sly look in his eye, "I am sure your friend Tamani would be more than happy to answer every question you have time to ask him." He started to turn to go.

"When will I see you again?" Laurel asked.

"I will come for you when your eight weeks are up," he said. "And I will make sure we have some time to discuss things," he promised. With a brief farewell he left, pulling the door shut behind him, leaving Laurel feeling starkly alone.

Standing in the middle of the room, Laurel turned in a circle, trying to take it all in. She didn't remember this place, but there was a comfort to it – a realisation that, on some level, her tastes had not changed. Green had always been a favourite colour, and she generally chose simplicity over ornate patterns and designs. The canopy was a little girlish, but then, she had chosen it a lifetime ago.

She walked over to the desk and sat down, noting to herself that the chair was just a little too small. She pulled out drawers and found sheets of thick paper, pots of paint, quill pens, and a composition book with her name on it. It took Laurel a few seconds to realise that the name looked so familiar because it was written in her own young-girl handwriting. Hands shaking, she carefully opened the book to the first page. It was a list of Latin words Laurel suspected were plants. She flipped through the pages and found more of the same. Even the English words didn't make much sense. How utterly discouraging to realise that she had known more at seven than she did now, at sixteen. *Or twenty,* she corrected herself, *or however old I'm supposed to be now.* She tried not to think about her actual age too much; all it did was remind her of the seven years of her faerie life now lost to her memory. She felt sixteen; as far as she was concerned, she *was* sixteen. Laurel put the book back and stood to walk over to the wardrobe.

Inside were several sundresses and a few ankle-length skirts made from a light, flowing material. A column of drawers revealed peasant-style blouses and fitted tops with cap sleeves. Laurel rubbed the material against her face, loving the silky soft feel of it. She tried on several and settled for a light pink sundress before continuing her exploration of the room.

She didn't get far before she walked to the window and caught her breath at the view below her. Her room overlooked the biggest flower garden she had ever seen; rows of flowers in every imaginable hue spread out below her in a cascade of colour almost as big as the grounds in front of the Academy. Her fingers pressed against the glass as she tried to take in the whole sight at once. It struck her as a waste that a room with such a magnificent view had just been sitting, empty, for the last thirteen years.

A knock on the door startled Laurel and she hurried to answer it, adjusting her dress as she did. After taking a moment to smooth her hair, Laurel opened the door.

"Laurel, I presume?" the tall faerie said with a smooth, deep voice. He studied her. "Well, you haven't changed all that much."

A touch taken aback, Laurel could only stare blankly up at the faerie. She had seen pictures of herself as a child; she had changed immensely!

The tall faerie wore what looked like linen Yoga trousers and a dark green shirt made of silky fabric that hung open at the chest in a way that did not seem the least bit sensual. Laurel considered her own tendency towards tank tops to expose more of her photosynthetic skin and decided this was similar. His demeanour was distinguished, formal. A look almost completely contradicted by his lack of shoes or socks.

"I am Yeardley, professor of fundamentals. May I?" the faerie said, inclining his head.

"Oh, of course," Laurel blustered, opening the door wider.

Yeardley strode in and the faerie behind him followed closely. "There," Yeardley said, pointing to Laurel's desk. The other faerie stacked the pile of books on Laurel's desk, bowed low to both Laurel and Yeardley, and backed out of the doorway before turning to walk down the hall.

Laurel turned back to the professor, who hadn't looked away.

"I know Jamison is eager for you to begin classes, but, to be quite frank, I cannot start you on even the most basic lessons until you have some sort of foundation on which to build."

Laurel opened her mouth to speak, realised she was in completely over her head, and closed it again.

"I have brought you what I believe to be the most basic and essential information that is requisite to beginning your true studies. I suggest you start immediately."

Laurel's eyes swung over to the stack of books. "All of those?" she asked.

"No. This is only the first half. I have one more batch when you have finished. Trust me," the faerie said, "these were as few as I could possibly justify." He looked down at a piece of paper he had pulled from a shoulder bag. "One of our acolytes" – he looked up at her—" that's the level you would be at, by the way, under more favourable circumstances – has agreed to be your tutor. She will be available to you during all daylight hours, and explaining such basic concepts to you will hardly be a strain, so feel free to use her. We hope you spend no more than two weeks relearning the things you have forgotten since you left us."

Wishing she could disappear through the floor, Laurel stood with her fists clenched.

"Her name is Katya," Yeardley continued, paying no attention to Laurel's reaction. "I suspect she will come introduce herself soon. Don't let her social nature distract you from your studies."

Laurel nodded stiffly, her eyes fixed firmly on the stack of books.

"I will leave you to your reading then," he said, turning on his bare heel. "When all the books are read, we can begin regular classes." He paused in the doorway. "Your staff can summon me when you are finished, but don't bother until you have read each book completely. There simply isn't any point." Without a goodbye he strode through the doorway and pulled the door shut behind him, a loud click filling the deep silence of Laurel's room.

Taking a long breath, Laurel walked over to the desk and looked at the spines of some of the ancient-looking books: *Fundamental Herbology*, *Origins of Elixirs*, *The Complete Encyclopedia of Defensive Herbs*, and *Troll Anatomy*. Laurel grimaced at the last one.

She had always enjoyed reading, but these books weren't exactly light fiction. She looked from the tall stack of books to the picture window across the room and noted that the sun had already begun its descent into the western sky.

She sighed. This was not what she had expected of today.

Chapter Three

Laurel sat cross-legged on her bed with a pair of scissors, cutting sheets of paper into makeshift note cards. It had taken her less than an hour of reading to realise that the situation demanded note cards. And highlighters. A year of studying biology with David had apparently turned her into a neurotic method-studier. But the next morning she was dismayed to discover that the "staff", as everyone called the soft-spoken, plainly dressed servants who scurried around the Academy, had no idea what note cards were. They were, however, familiar with scissors, so Laurel was making her own note cards out of a fine card stock. The highlighters, unfortunately, were a lost cause.

A soft rap sounded at the door. "Come in," Laurel

called, worried that she would scatter bits of paper everywhere if she tried to actually get up and open it.

The door swung open and a small, blond head poked in. "Laurel?"

Having given up trying to recognise people, Laurel simply nodded and waited for the stranger to introduce herself.

The short, pixie-style haircut was followed by a bright smile that Laurel found herself automatically returning. It was a relief to see a smile directed at her. Dinner the evening before had been a complete disaster. Laurel had been summoned around seven to come down for the evening meal. She had hurried downstairs behind a faerie who had showed her the way to the dining hall – Laurel should have gotten a clue when she heard *dining hall* instead of *cafeteria* – in her sundress and bare feet, her hair still pulled back in a ponytail. The moment she entered the room Laurel realised she'd made a mistake. Everyone was dressed in button-down shirts and silk trousers, or floor-length skirts and dresses. It was practically a white-tie formal affair. Worse, she'd been pulled to the front of the room by Aurora to be welcomed back and presented to the Fall faeries. Hundreds of Fall faeries with no one better to look at than her.

Note to self: Dress for dinner.

But that was last night, and now here was a genuine smile, aimed at her.

"Come on in," Laurel said. She didn't particularly care who this faerie was or why she was here, just that she looked friendly.

And that she represented a reason for Laurel to take a break.

"I'm Katya," the faerie said.

"Laurel," she said automatically.

"Well, of course I know that," Katya said with a little laugh. "Everyone knows who *you* are."

Laurel looked self-consciously down at her lap.

"I hope you've found the Academy to your liking," Katya continued, sounding like the perfect hostess. "I know I am always a bit unsettled when I have to travel. I don't sleep well," Katya said, coming to sit beside her on the bed.

Laurel avoided her eyes and made a noise of agreement without actually saying anything, wondering how far Katya could really have travelled within Avalon.

In truth, Laurel *hadn't* slept well. She hoped it was the new environment, as Katya had suggested. But she'd been ripped awake several times by nightmares, and not just the usual ones of trolls, guns pointed at Tamani, pointing a gun at Barnes, or icy waves closing in over her

39

head. Last night it wasn't her running from Barnes, her feet in slow motion; it was her parents, David, Chelsea, Shar, and Tamani.

Laurel had risen from her bed and walked to the window, pressed her forehead against the cool glass, and looked down at the twinkling lights scattered throughout the darkness that spread below her. It seemed so contradictory, coming to Avalon to learn how to protect herself and her loved ones, and in so doing, leaving them vulnerable. Though if the trolls were hunting *her*, maybe her family was safer when she wasn't around. The whole situation was out of her control, out of her very knowledge. She hated feeling helpless – useless.

"What are you doing?" Katya asked, pulling Laurel from her dreary thoughts.

"Making note cards."

"Note cards?"

"Um, studying tools I use back at ho—in the human world," Laurel said.

Katya picked up one of the homemade cards. "Are they just these small pieces of carding or is there something else I'm not seeing?"

"No. Just that. Pretty simple."

"Then why are you doing it yourself?"

"Uh?" Laurel shook her head, then shrugged. "I needed note cards?"

Katya's eyes were wide and innocently questioning. "Aren't you supposed to study like mad while you're here? That's what Yeardley told me."

"Yes, but note cards will help me study better," Laurel insisted. "It's worth the time to make them."

"That's not what I mean." Katya laughed then walked over to the silver bell Aurora had pointed out yesterday and rang it. Its clear peal rolled around the room for a few seconds, leaving the air feeling almost alive.

"Wow," Laurel said, earning a puzzled look from Katya.

A few seconds later a middle-aged faerie woman appeared in the doorway. Katya snatched the scissors out of Laurel's hand and gathered up the pile of card stock. "We need these all to be cut into rectangles this size," she said, handing over one of Laurel's freshly cut cards. "And this is of utmost importance, so it needs to take priority over whatever else you were doing."

"Of course," the woman said with a slight curtsy, as if she were speaking to a queen and not a young faerie half her age – maybe less. "Would you like me to do them here so you can have them as they are completed, or take them elsewhere and return them when the entire task is done?"

Katya looked over at Laurel and shrugged. "It's all right with me if she stays here; she has a point about getting them to us as soon as they're cut."

"That's fine," Laurel muttered, uncomfortable asking a grown woman to perform such a menial task.

"You can sit there," Katya said, pointing to Laurel's long window seat. "The light is good."

The woman simply nodded, took the card stock to the window, and immediately set about cutting them into crisp, straight rectangles.

Katya settled herself on the bed beside Laurel. "Now show me what you do with these note cards and I'll see how I can assist you."

"I can cut my own cards," Laurel whispered.

"Well, certainly, but there are far better uses of your time."

"I imagine there are far better uses of her time too," Laurel retorted, flicking her chin in the woman's direction.

Katya looked up and stared candidly. "Her? I shouldn't think so. She's just a Spring faerie."

Indignation built up in Laurel's chest. "What do you mean, just a Spring faerie? She's still a person, she has feelings."

Katya looked very confused. "I never said she didn't.

But this is her job."

"To cut my note cards?"

"To do whatever duties the Fall faeries have need of. Look at it this way," Katya continued, still in that bright, casual voice, "we probably saved her from sitting around just waiting for one of the other Falls to need something. Now come on, or we'll lose all the time she's saving us. Let me see which book you're on."

Laurel lay sprawled on her stomach, staring at her book. She was beyond reading; she'd been reading most of the morning and the words were starting to swim in front of her eyes, so staring was the best she could do. A light knock sounded from the doorway, where her intricately carved cherrywood door stood open. Laurel looked up at an elderly Spring faerie with kind, pink eyes and those perfectly symmetrical wrinkles she still wasn't quite used to.

"You have a visitor in the atrium," the faerie said, scarcely above a whisper. The Spring staff had been instructed to be very quiet around Laurel and avoid bothering her at all times.

The other students, too, apparently. Laurel never saw anyone but Katya, except at dinner, where she was mostly just stared at. But she was almost done with her last book – then it would be classroom time. She wasn't entirely sure if that was a good thing or not, but at least it was *different*.

"A visitor?" Laurel said. It took a few seconds before her study-weary brain put it together. Then it was all she could do not to shout with joy. *Tamani!*

Laurel walked down a few flights of stairs and took a slightly longer route so she could walk through a rounded, glass hallway lined with flowers in every colour of the rainbow. They were beautiful. In the beginning that was all Laurel saw in them – gorgeous colours stretching out in brilliant sheets all across the Academy grounds. But they were more than decoration; they were the tools of the Fall faeries. She knew them now, after almost a week of studying, and named them, instinctively, in her head. The blue delphinium and red ranunculus, yellow freesia and calla lilies, speckled anthurium, and her newest favourite – cymbidium orchids with their soft white petals and dark pink centres. She let her fingers brush the tropical orchids as she passed, reciting automatically its common uses in her head. *Cures poisoning from yellow flowers, temporarily blocks photosynthesis, phosphoresces when mixed correctly with sorrel.*

She had very little context for the lists of facts in her head, but thanks to her "note cards" – which she wryly admitted the Spring faerie had cut more neatly than she would have – they were memorised.

Leaving the flowery hall, Laurel hurried to the staircase, practically skipping down the steps. She spotted Tamani leaning against a wall near the front entrance and somehow managed not to shriek his name and run to him. Barely.

Instead of the loose shirts and breeches that she was so accustomed to, he was wearing a sleek tunic over black trousers. His hair was combed back carefully, and his face looked different without the tousled strands decorating it. As she raised her arms to hug him, a small halting motion of Tamani's hand stopped her. She stood, confused; then he smiled and bent slightly at the waist, his head inclined in the same gesture of deference the Spring staff insisted on using. "Pleasure to see you, Laurel." He gestured towards the door. "Shall we?"

She looked at him strangely for a moment, but when he flicked his head towards the exit again, she set her jaw and walked out the Academy doors. They headed down the front path that, instead of being straight like most neighbourhood walks at home, meandered through patches of flowers and greenery. And, unfortunately, other Fall students. She could feel their gazes following her, and even though most tried to hide their spying behind their books, some gawked openly.

It was a long, silent walk and Laurel kept sneaking glances back at Tamani, who persisted in walking two steps behind her. She could see a mischievous grin playing at the corners of his mouth, but he said nothing. Once they crossed through the gates he stopped her with a soft hand on her back and inclined his head towards a long line of tall bushes. She walked towards them and as soon as the Academy was blocked from her view by the pokey green stems, strong arms lifted her off her feet and spun her around.

"I have missed you so much," Tamani said, the grin she loved restored to his face.

Laurel wrapped her arms around him and held on for a long time. He was a reminder of her life outside the Academy, an anchor to her own world. The place she still called home. It was strange to realise that, over the course of a few short days, her most direct link to Avalon had now become her strongest tie to human life.

And, of course, he was himself. There was plenty to be said for that, too.

"Sorry about all that," he said. "The Academy is very particular about protocol between Spring and Fall faeries and I would hate for you to get in trouble. Well, I guess it's more likely I'd get in trouble, but regardless… let's avoid trouble."

"If we have to." Laurel grinned and reached both hands up into his hair, mussing it until it fell into its usually chunky strands. She grabbed his hands, exhilarated to be in friendly, familiar company again. "I'm so glad you came. I thought I'd go crazy if I had to spend another night studying."

Tamani sobered. "It's hard work, I'm sure, but it's important."

She looked down at her bare feet, speckled with dark soil. "It's not *that* important."

"It is. You have no idea how much we use all the things the Fall faeries make."

"But I can't really do anything at all! I haven't even started classroom work yet." She sighed and shook her head. "I just don't know how much I can learn in less than two months."

"Couldn't you come back… from time to time?"

"I guess so." Laurel looked up again. "If I'm invited."

"Oh, you'll be… *invited*." Tamani grinned as he said it, as though he found the word inherently amusing. "Trust me."

His eyes met hers, and Laurel felt hypnotised. After a nervous moment she turned away and started walking.

"So where are we going?" she asked, trying to cover her awkwardness.

"Going?"

"Jamison said you would take me sightseeing. I only get a few hours."

Tamani seemed completely unprepared for this conversation. "I'm not sure he meant—"

"I have been doing nothing but memorising plants for…" Laurel paused. "Six. Straight. Days. I want to see Avalon!"

A mischievous grin lit Tamani's face and he nodded. "Very well, then. Where would you like to go?"

"I – I wouldn't have any idea." Laurel turned to him. "What's the best place in Avalon?"

He took a breath, then hesitated. After another moment he said, "Do you want to do something with other fae or just the two of us?"

Laurel gazed down the hill. Part of her just wanted to be with Tamani, but she scarcely trusted herself to spend that long alone with him. "Can't we do some of both?"

Tamani grinned. "Sure. Why don't we—"

She placed one index finger against his lips. "No, don't tell me, let's just go."

In response, Tamani pointed down the hill and said, "Lead on."

A little shiver of excitement passed through her as the Academy grew smaller and smaller behind them. They passed the high stone walls that enclosed the gate and soon their path diverged into roads that wound through an occasional building – but these roads weren't paved. Instead, they were made of the same soft, black, nutrient-rich soil that covered the path from the gateway to the Academy. The soil cooled Laurel's bare feet and energised her steps. It was ten times better than any other walk she'd ever taken.

The farther they got from the Academy, the more crowded the streets became. They entered some kind of open-air fair with hundreds of faeries congregating in doorways, browsing in facade-fronted shops and milling about kiosks hung with sparkling wares. Everything was rainbow-hued and vivid and it took Laurel a few seconds to realise that the bright, multicoloured flashes she saw weaving through the crowds were the blossoms of the Summer faeries. One faerie passed close in front of her, carrying some kind of stringed instrument and sporting a stunning blossom that resembled a tropical flower. It was bright red streaked with a sunshiny yellow and had about ten broad petals that ended in sharp angles like the purpurea Laurel had studied only yesterday. But it was enormous! The lower petals floated just inches above the ground while the top petals arched over her head like an enormous crown.

Good thing I'm not a Summer faerie, Laurel thought, recalling the work she had put into concealing her own seasonal blossom less than a year ago. *That thing would never have fit under a shirt.*

Everywhere she looked she saw more of the vibrant, tropical-looking blossoms, in seemingly infinite variety. The Summer faeries were dressed differently too. They wore clothes of the same light, shimmery fabric that Laurel and all her classmates wore, only cut longer and more loosely, with ruffles and tassels and other adornments that fluttered in the air or trains that swept the ground behind them. *Showy*, Laurel decided. *Like their blossoms.*

She looked back to make sure she hadn't lost Tamani, but he was still there, two steps behind her left shoulder. "I wish you'd just lead the way," Laurel said, tired of craning her neck to see him.

"It's not my place."

Laurel stopped. "Your place?"

"Please don't make a scene," Tamani said softly, prodding her forward again with his fingertips. "It's just the way it is."

"Is this a Spring faerie thing?" Laurel said, her voice raised a little.

"Laurel, please," Tamani implored, his eyes darting from side to side. "We'll talk about it later."

She glared at him, but he refused to meet her eyes, so she surrendered for the moment and continued walking. She meandered through the kiosks for some time, delighting in the sparkling wind chimes and silky lengths of fabric displayed by shopkeepers who were, in some cases, dressed even more extravagantly than the crowd.

"What's this?" she asked, picking up a stunning string of sparkling diamonds – probably real ones – intertwined with tiny pearls and delicate glass flowers.

"It's for your hair," a tall, crimson-haired faerie offered helpfully. With fingers encased in stark white gloves that seemed far too formal to Laurel, he touched the end where a comb was cleverly hidden behind a cluster of glass blossoms. Naturally, because he was male, he had no blossom, but his clothing suggested that he, too, was a Summer. "May I?"

Laurel looked to Tamani and he smiled and nodded. She turned and the tall faerie fixed the bauble securely in her hair, then led her to a large mirror on the opposite side of the kiosk. Laurel smiled at her reflection. The silvery strand hung just to the side of where she parted her hair, down past her shoulders. It sparkled in the sun, bringing out the shine of the natural highlights in her blond hair. "It's beautiful," she said breathlessly.

"Would you like to wear it, or shall I wrap it in a box?"

"Oh, I couldn't—"

"You should," Tamani said quietly. "It looks lovely."

"But I..." She stepped around the tall shopkeeper and stood close to Tamani. "I have nothing to pay for it, and I'm certainly not going to let *you* pay for it."

Tamani laughed quietly. "You don't pay for goods here, Laurel. That's a very... human thing. Take it. He'll be complimented that you like his work."

Laurel glanced at the shopkeeper hovering just out of earshot. "Really?"

"Yes. Tell him it pleases you and that you'll wear it to the Academy; that's all the payment he wants."

It was all so unbelievable. Laurel felt nervous, momentarily unable to overcome her certainty that, any second now, a security faerie was going to pop out and arrest her. But Tamani wouldn't pull a trick like that on her... would he?

She took one more look in the mirror, then smiled at the tall faerie, hoping it didn't look too forced. "It's really, really beautiful," she said. "I'd like to wear it back to the Academy, if I may." The faerie beamed at her and made a slight bow. Laurel hesitantly began to walk away.

No one stopped her.

It was a few minutes before Laurel got over the feeling she'd just stolen something. She started paying attention to the other browsers and many of them also removed items from the displays and kiosks without giving anything in return but compliments and gratitude. After several minutes of observing other "shoppers", she forced herself to calm down.

"We should get something for you," she said, turning to Tamani.

"Oh, no. Not me. I don't shop here. My market square is down the hill a little farther."

"Then what's this?"

"This is Summer Square."

"Oh," Laurel said, panicking again. "But I'm a Fall. I shouldn't have gotten this."

Tamani laughed. "No, no, Winter and Fall faeries shop where they like. There are too few of them to have their own square."

"Oh." She thought for a minute. "So could I shop in your square too?"

"I guess you could, but I don't know why you'd want to."

"Why not?"

Tamani shrugged. "It's not pretty like the Summer

Square. I mean, the square's pretty; everything in Avalon is beautiful. But we don't need trinkets and decor. We need clothing, food, and the tools of our many trades. I get my weapons there as well as the elixirs and potions I need for my sentry kits – those things are sent down from the Academy. The Summer faeries need the flashy things; it's part of their trade. Those in the theatre, especially. But if you look closer, particularly in some of the inside shops, you'll find the more technical supplies. Paints and equipment for scenery, musical instruments, jewellery-making tools – that kind of thing." He grinned. "The kiosks have all the sparkles and such in them so they catch the sun and draw more shoppers."

They both laughed and Laurel reached up to touch the new hair comb. She wondered briefly what it would be worth back in California, and then dismissed the thought. It was nothing she'd ever sell, so it didn't matter.

The crowd was thinning as they walked farther from the marketplace. The broad earthen road was lined with houses now, and Laurel glanced from side to side in wonder. Each dwelling was made entirely of the same kind of sugar-glass that formed the picture window in Laurel's own room. The larger translucent orbs that opened out into the street were obviously living rooms; the slightly smaller pastel-tinged bubbles clustered on the sides and back Laurel suspected were bedrooms. Enormous curtains of pastel-coloured silk were tucked behind each dwelling, allowing the sun to shine more brightly into the remarkable buildings, but Laurel saw how they could be draped over the glass for privacy at night. Each house sparkled in the sun, and many were decorated with strings of crystals and prisms catching the light and making it dance, just like the prisms Laurel had in her room back home. The whole neighbourhood shimmered so brightly it was almost hard to look at, and Laurel realised that these were the "balloons" she'd seen from farther up the hill when she'd first arrived with Jamison. "They're so pretty," she mused.

"Indeed. I love to walk up through the Summer neighbourhoods."

The sparkling dwellings began to space out, and soon Laurel and Tamani were walking downhill again. The wide road cut through a meadow of clover with patches of flowers here and there; Laurel had only seen such meadows in movies. And even though she'd gotten used to the air in Avalon – always fragrant with the scent of fresh earth and blooming flowers – it was stronger out here, where the wind could freely carry each scent as it caressed her face. Laurel breathed in deeply, enjoying the invigorating breeze.

She paused when she realised Tamani wasn't beside her any more. She glanced back. He was crouched by the side of the path, wiping his hands on the cushiony clover. "What are you doing?" she asked.

Tamani sprang to his feet, looking sheepish. "I – um, forgot my gloves," he said quietly.

Laurel was confused for a second, then noticed that the clover looked a little sparkly. "You wear gloves to cover the pollen?" she guessed.

"It's polite," he said, clearing his throat.

Laurel thought back and realised that all the men in Summer Square had been wearing gloves. It made sense now. She hurried to change the subject to rescue Tamani from his obvious discomfort. "So what next?" she asked, her hand at her forehead, blocking the sun so she could see what lay farther down the road.

"I'm taking you to my favourite place in all of Avalon."

"Really?" Laurel said, excitement causing her to forget, momentarily, that she'd asked to be surprised. "Where?"

He smiled softly. "My home. I want you to meet my mother."

Chapter Four

A chill rippled up Laurel's back as nervousness and confusion battled for control. "Your mother?"

"Is... that all right?"

"You told me faeries didn't have mothers."

Tamani opened his mouth and then closed it again, his brow furrowing – the look he always got when he was caught in a half-truth. "I never actually said faeries don't have mothers," he said slowly. "I said things are different here. And they are."

"But you – I... I just assumed that since, you know, faeries come from seeds – you said you take care of yourselves!" she demanded, a little angry now.

"We do," Tamani said, trying to appease her. "I mean, mostly. Mothering is not quite the same here as it is in the human world."

"But you have a mother?"

He nodded, and she could tell he knew what was coming next.

"Do I have a mother? A faerie one, I mean?"

He was silent for a moment, and Laurel could see he didn't want to say it. Finally he shrugged, a tiny, almost invisible shrug, and shook his head.

Shock and disappointment surged through her. It didn't help that, despite the tension at home, she missed her mom acutely and was feeling more than a little homesick. Tears threatened, but Laurel refused to let them come. She spun on her heel and continued walking down the hill, glad there wasn't anyone close by. "Why not?" she asked peevishly.

"You just don't."

"But you do. Why do you have one?" She knew she sounded childish and petulant, but she didn't care.

"Because I'm not a Fall or Winter faerie."

Laurel stopped and turned back to Tamani. "So? Are we born differently?"

Tamani shook his head.

"The seed I was born in, it was made by two faeries, right?"

Tamani hesitated, then nodded.

"Then where are they? Maybe I could—"

"I don't know," Tamani said, cutting her off. "No one knows. The records of it are destroyed," he finished quietly.

"Why?"

"Fall and Winter faeries don't stay with their parents. They are children of Avalon; children of the Crown. It's not like in the human world," he added. "Relationships are not the same."

"So the relationship you have with your mother isn't like the relationship I have with mine back home?" Laurel asked. She knew referring to someplace besides Avalon as *home* would bother Tamani, but she was too angry to feel bad about it.

"That's not what I meant. When you make a seed, it's just a seed. It is very, very precious because it is the potential for new life, but the relationship does not begin with the seed. It begins when the sprout blooms and the seedling goes home to live with its parents – but only Spring and Summer faeries live with their parents. Your… seed makers—"

"Parents," Laurel interrupted.

"Fine. Your parents might have been disappointed when they found out you wouldn't be their seedling, that you would never come home with them, but they would mostly celebrate their contribution to society. As far as they were concerned, you weren't a person yet. They wouldn't have missed you, because they didn't know you."

"Is that supposed to make me feel better?"

"Yes, it is." His hand came to her shoulder, pulling her to a stop before she could turn on to the broad central road. "Because I know how unselfish you are. Would you rather you were able to experience the reunion with a long-lost set of parents who had been suffering for years missing and loving you, or would you rather they weren't hurting while you were raised by human parents who adore you?"

Laurel swallowed. "I hadn't thought of it that way."

Tamani smiled softly and lifted a hand to her face, tucking a strand of hair behind her ear and letting his thumb rest on her cheek. "Trust me, it's no picnic missing you. I wouldn't wish it on anyone."

Without meaning to, Laurel leaned into Tamani's hand. He shifted forward until his forehead rested on hers, hands cupping the sides of her face, then trailing slowly down her neck. Only when the tip of his nose brushed hers – ever so softly – did she realise he was about to kiss her. And that she wasn't entirely sure she wanted to stop him.

"Tam," she whispered. His lips were just a breath away from hers.

His fingers tightened ever so softly against her neck, but he stopped and pulled back. "Sorry," he said. He moved his face, letting his lips fall instead on her forehead before pulling away and pointing back down the wide road that cut through the meadow. "Let's keep going. I should probably get you back to the Academy in another hour or so."

Laurel nodded, not sure which emotion was strongest. Relief. Disappointment. Loneliness. Regret.

"How... how did my parents know I would be a Fall faerie?" Laurel asked, trying to find a more neutral subject.

"Your sprout opened in the Fall," Tamani said simply. "All faeries emerge from their sprout in the season of their powers."

"Sprout?"

"The flower you were born from."

"Oh."

Laurel had nothing else to ask without bringing the subject back to faerie parentage, so she was silent, trying to absorb this new development – and Tamani followed her lead. They walked a little farther until the pedestrian traffic thickened and more houses began to dot the road. These were different from the ones she'd seen around the Summer Square. They had the same climbing vines that decorated much of the Academy – the ones with flowers that opened when the moon came up. But rather than the transparent walls she was used to, these buildings were made of wood and bark – sturdy lean-tos, small houses, a few cottages with loosely thatched roofs. They were charming and quaint and every other fairy-tale word she'd ever heard used to describe small homes. But a sense of difference permeated the air.

"Why aren't these houses transparent?" Laurel asked.

"These are Spring faerie homes," Tamani replied, still hovering at her left shoulder.

"And… ?"

"And what?"

"Why does that matter?"

"Summer faeries need to photosynthesize enormous amounts of sunlight in order to create their illusions and the light needed for fireworks. They need to be exposed to every hour of sunlight possible. Plus," he added after a brief pause, "these houses are easier to build and keep up. There are a lot of us, after all."

"How many Spring faeries are there?"

Tamani shrugged. "I don't know for sure. Somewhere around eighty per cent of the population."

"Eighty? Really? How many Summer faeries?"

"Oh, I'd guess fifteen per cent. Probably a smidge more."

"Oh." She didn't ask about Fall faeries. She could do the math. Tamani had told her that Winter faeries were the rarest of all, with maybe one born in a generation, but Fall faeries were apparently rare enough. Laurel supposed that subconsciously she'd also realised there were fewer Fall faeries, but she hadn't understood just how limited their numbers were. No wonder they didn't have their own square.

The housing was growing dense, and other faeries were teeming around them now. Some were gloved and carried gardening implements, several quite alien to Laurel despite her mother's passion for plant life. Others busied themselves outside their homes washing clothing too delicate to be their own. Laurel noticed several carts laden with food, from raw fruits and vegetables to fully prepared meals wrapped in grape leaves or the petals of some enormous flower that smelled vaguely like gardenias.

One Spring faerie who hurried by was carrying a staff like a shepherd's crook, with a small pot dangling from the curved top. At least a dozen vials of liquid were strapped across his chest. Laurel cast a questioning glance over her shoulder, but Tamani just pointed one finger forward with a smile.

Laurel turned and realised that the low murmur of the crowd was rising in pitch and timbre. But only when a cloud of buzzing insects materialised, seemingly from nowhere, did Laurel understand why. She bit off a shriek as she found herself enveloped in a cloud of extremely active honeybees.

As quickly as they had come, they were gone. Laurel turned to watch the swarm disappear into the crowd, following the Spring faerie with the shepherd's crook. Laurel recalled from her reading several ways animals and insects "and other lower life-forms" could be influenced and even controlled by scent. She momentarily pondered the usefulness of tame bees to a society of plants, but her musing was derailed by Tamani's laughter.

"Sorry," he said with a chuckle. A smile still ticked at the side of his mouth. "But you should have seen your face."

Laurel's instinct was to be mad, but she suspected her face *had* looked pretty funny. "Am I going the right way?" she asked, as though nothing out of the ordinary had just occurred.

"Yes, I'll let you know when it's time to turn."

"We're in Spring now, right? Why does it matter if you walk behind me? It makes me feel lost."

"I apologise," Tamani said, his voice tense. "But this is the way things are around here. You walk behind a faerie who is more than one rank above you."

She paused and Tamani almost bumped into her. "That is the stupidest thing I've ever heard." She turned to Tamani. "And I won't do it."

Tamani sighed. "Look, you're privileged enough to have standards like that; I'm not." He glanced at the crowd flowing around them and finally said, quietly, "If I don't do it, it's not you who gets in trouble, it's me."

Laurel didn't want to let it go, but she didn't want Tamani to be punished for her ideals, either. With one more glance at his downcast eyes, Laurel turned and continued walking. She was increasingly aware of how much she stood out; much more so than in Summer Square. Aside from their various trade implements, everyone around her looked... well... like Tamani. They were dressed in simple, canvas-like material, mostly cut into breeches or calf-length skirts. But as with all faeries, they were attractive and neat. Rather than looking like a stereotypical working class – with worn faces or shabby clothes – they looked more like actors *pretending* to be working class.

Much less charming was the way everyone who caught her eye stopped their conversation, smiled, and did the same slight-bend-at-the-waist thing Tamani had done when he'd met her at the Academy. As she and Tamani passed, their chatter would begin again. Several greeted Tamani and tried to say something. He waved them away, but one word in particular kept floating to Laurel's ears.

"What's a Mixer?" she asked once there was a break in the crowd.

Tamani hesitated. "It's a little weird to explain."

"Oh, well, never mind then, because explaining weird things to me has definitely never been part of this relationship."

Her sarcasm brought a sheepish smile to Tamani's face. "It's kind of a Spring faerie thing," he said elusively.

"Oh, come on," she said. Then added teasingly, "Tell me or I'll walk *beside* you."

When he didn't respond, she slowed down and then quickly spun away from his hand and repositioned herself right by his side.

"Fine," he said in a whisper, pushing her gently back up in front of him. "A Mixer is a Fall faerie. It's not a bad name or anything," he continued in a rush. "It's just a... nickname. But it's something we would never call a Fall to their face."

"Mixer?" Laurel said experimentally, liking the feel of it on her tongue. "Because we make things," she said, laughing. "It's fitting."

Tamani shrugged.

"What's a Summer?"

Now Tamani cringed a bit. "A Sparkler."

Laurel laughed, and several of the cheerily clad Springs glanced her way before returning to their work with a little too much of an air of purpose. "What about Winters?"

Tamani shook his head. "Oh, we would never take Winter faeries so lightly. Never," he added emphatically.

"What do you call yourselves?" she asked.

"Ticers," Tamani said. "Everyone knows that."

"Maybe everyone in *Ticer-ville*," Laurel said. "But I didn't."

Tamani snorted when she said *Ticer-ville*. "Well, now you do."

"What does it mean?" Laurel asked.

"Ticer, like en-*tice*-ment. It's what we all do. Well, what we *can* do, anyway. Mostly only sentries ever use it."

"Oh," Laurel said with a grin. "Ticer. Got it. Why do only sentries use it?"

"Um," he began uncertainly, "remember last year when I tried to use it on you?"

"Oh, that's right! I'd almost forgotten." She turned to

him in mock anger. "I was mad at you!"

Tamani chuckled and shrugged. "Point is, it didn't work very well because you're a faerie. So only sentries – and specifically sentries who work outside Avalon – ever really have a chance to use it on non faerie creatures."

"Makes sense." Her curiosity sated, Laurel began walking again. Soft fingers touched her waist, guiding her through the still-heavy crowds.

"To the right here," Tamani said. "We're almost there."

Laurel was glad to find herself turning down a much less crowded side street. She felt conspicuous and self-conscious and wished she had asked the tall faerie at the kiosk to put the hair jewels in a box. No one else here was wearing anything even remotely similar. "Are we there yet?"

"That house up there," Tamani said, gesturing. "The one with the big flower boxes up front."

They approached a small but charming house made from a hollowed-out tree, though the tree wasn't like anything Laurel had ever seen before. Instead of a thick trunk growing straight up, it had a wide base and grew out in a round shape, like an enormous wooden pumpkin. The trunk narrowed again at the top and continued to grow up, sprouting branches and leaves that shaded the house. "How does it grow like that?"

"Magic. This house was a gift to my mother from the Queen. Winter faeries can ask the trees to grow any way they please."

"Why did your mother get a gift from the Queen?"

"As a thank-you for years of distinguished service as a Gardener."

"A gardener? Aren't there a ton of gardeners?"

"Oh, no. It's a very specialised field. One of the most prestigious positions a Spring faerie can aspire to."

"Really?" Laurel said sceptically. She'd seen dozens of gardeners just around the Academy.

Tamani looked at her strangely for a moment before understanding blossomed across his face. "Not like human gardeners. We would call those Tenders here, and yes, there are a lot of them. I suppose you might call my mother a... a midwife."

"A midwife?"

If Tamani heard the question, he made no sign. He knocked softly on the ash door of the strange tree house. Then, without waiting for a response, he opened it. "I'm home."

A squeal sounded from inside the house and a flutter of colourful skirts wrapped itself around Tamani's legs. "Oh, my goodness, what is this?" He detangled the young faerie and lifted her over his head. "What is this thing? I think it's a Rowen flower!" The little girl squealed as Tamani tucked her against his chest.

The girl looked like she was maybe a year old, scarcely more than an infant. But she walked steadily and her eyes betrayed intelligence. Intelligence and, Laurel felt certain without knowing why, mischief.

"Have you been a good girl today?" Tamani asked.

"Of course," the young faerie said, far more articulately than Laurel would have thought possible for a child so small. "I'm *always* a good girl."

"Excellent." He turned his gaze towards the inside of the house. "Mother?" he called.

"Tam! What a surprise. I didn't know you were coming today." Laurel looked up and felt suddenly shy as an older female faerie walked into the room. The woman was beautiful, with a lightly lined face, pale green eyes just like Laurel's, and a broad smile that was beaming at Tamani. She didn't seem to have noticed Laurel yet, half hidden behind him in the doorway.

"I didn't know myself until this morning."

"No matter," the woman said, taking Tamani's face in both hands and kissing his cheeks.

"I brought company," Tamani said, his voice suddenly quiet.

The woman turned to Laurel and, for a second,

concern masked her face. Then recognition dawned and she smiled. "Laurel. Look at you; you've hardly changed a bit."

Laurel smiled back, but her face fell when Tamani's mother inclined her head and bent at the waist.

Tamani must have felt Laurel stiffen, because he squeezed his mother's hand and said, "Laurel's had enough formality for one day. She's just herself in this house."

"All the better," Tamani's mother said with a smile. Then she stepped forward and took Laurel's face, just like she had Tamani's moments before, and kissed both cheeks. "Welcome."

Tears sprang to Laurel's eyes. It was the warmest greeting she'd had from anyone except Tamani since arriving in Avalon. It made her miss her own mother acutely. "Thank you," she said softly.

"Come in, come in; no need to stand in the doorway. We have windows enough for that," Tamani's mother said, shooing them in. "And since we're doing away with the formality, you can just call me Rhoslyn."

Chapter Five

The inside of the house was similar to the dormitory Laurel lived in, except that everything looked simpler. Buttercups specially treated to glow in the evenings – *with ash bark and essence of lavender,* Laurel recited automatically in her head – hung from the rafters and swung gently back and forth with the slight breeze coming in from the six open windows around the room. Instead of silk, the curtains were made from a material that looked more like cotton, and the coverings on the chairs throughout the room were the same. The floors were a soft wood rather than plush carpeting, and Laurel carefully dusted off her feet on the thick mat before stepping into the house. Several watercolour paintings hung from the walls in bevelled frames.

"These are beautiful," Laurel said, leaning forward to get a closer look at one that featured a flowerbed full of very tall stems with a single bud at the top of each, ready to bloom.

"Thank you," Rhoslyn said. "I've taken up painting since retiring. I enjoy it."

Laurel turned to another painting, this one featuring Tamani. She smiled at the way Rhoslyn had so perfectly caught his brooding features. His eyes were serious in the painting, and he was looking at something just beyond the frame. "You're very good," Laurel said.

"Nonsense. I'm just entertaining myself with some cast-off Summer supplies. Still, you can never go wrong when you're painting a subject as handsome as our Tamani," she said, wrapping an arm around his waist.

Laurel looked at them – Rhoslyn, even smaller than Laurel, gazing proudly at Tamani, Tamani balancing the little faerie on his hip as she clung to his chest. Laurel momentarily felt disappointed realising he had a life that didn't include her; but she chided herself immediately. Most of her own life did not include him, so it was selfish to wish for more from him than she was willing or able to give herself. She smiled at Tamani and pushed away her gloomy thoughts.

"Is this your sister?" Laurel asked, pointing to the faerie child.

"No," Tamani said, and Rhoslyn laughed.

"At my age?" she said with a smile. "Earth and sky, no. Tam is my youngest and I was a bit old even for him."

"This is Rowen," Tamani said, poking the little girl's ribs. "Her *mother* is my sister."

"Oh. Your niece," Laurel said.

Tamani shrugged. "We don't really use terms here for anything other than *mother*, *father*, *brother*, and *sister*. Beyond that, we all belong to each other, and we help out with everyone's children." He tickled the little faerie, and she squealed in delight. "Rowen here may get extra attention from us because she is more closely connected than other seedlings, but we don't stake claims beyond that. We're all family."

"Oh." It was a concept Laurel both liked and disliked. It would be fun to have a whole society of people who considered themselves part of your family. But she would miss the ties she had to her admittedly sparse extended family.

Laurel blinked in surprise at a small creature that looked like a purple squirrel with pink butterfly wings perched on Rowen's shoulder. Laurel was sure it hadn't been there a few moments ago. As she watched, Rowen whispered to the thing, then laughed quietly, as if sharing a friendly joke.

"Tamani?" Laurel whispered, not taking her eyes from the strange thing.

"What?" Tamani responded, following her gaze.

"What is that thing?"

"That's her familiar," Tamani responded, suppressing a grin. "At least for the moment. She changes it regularly."

"Is there any need to tell you I'm totally confused?"

Tamani found a stool and sat, setting Rowen back on the floor. He stretched his legs out in front of him. "Think of it as a not-so-imaginary imaginary friend."

"It's imaginary?"

"It's an illusion." He grinned as Laurel continued to look flustered. "Rowen," Tamani said, his voice warm, "is a Summer faerie."

Rowen smiled shyly.

Rhoslyn beamed. "We're very proud of her."

"Creating an illusionary playmate is one of the first manifestations of a Summer faerie's magic. Rowen's been making hers since about two weeks out of her sprout. It's like having a special blanket or pet plaything but way more fun. For one thing, my favourite toys never moved like that."

Laurel eyed the purple squirrel-thing warily. "So it's not real?"

"Only slightly more real than any other faerie's imaginary friend."

"That's amazing."

Tamani rolled his eyes. "Amazing, nothing. You should see the heroic rescuers she conjures up to save her from the monster under the bed." He paused. "Which is also her creation."

"Where are her parents?"

"They're up in Summer this afternoon," Rhoslyn said. "Rowen is almost of the age to begin training, and they're making arrangements with her director."

"So young?"

"She's almost three," Tamani replied.

"Really?" Laurel said, studying the girl as she played on the floor. "She looks so much younger," she said quietly. She paused. "And acts much older. I was going to ask you about that."

Rowen stared up at Laurel. "I'm just like all the other fae my age. Aren't I?" She directed her question to Tamani.

"You're perfect, Rowen." He scooped her on to his lap, and the pink-and-purple thing settled on to the top of his head.

Laurel forced herself to look away, although she did wonder if it was rude to stare, if the thing you were staring at wasn't really there. "Let me tell you something about Laurel," Tamani said to Rowen. "She's very special. She lives in the human world."

"Just like you," Rowen said matter-of-factly.

"Not exactly like me," Tamani said, laughing. "Laurel lives *with* the humans."

Rowen's eyes widened. "Really?"

"Yes. In fact, she didn't even know she was a faerie until last year, when she blossomed."

"What did you think you were?" Rowen asked.

"I thought I was human, like my parents."

"That's silly," Rowen said dismissively. "How could a faerie be a human? Humans are strange. And scary," she added after a short pause. Then she whispered conspiratorially, "They're *animals*."

"They're not so scary, Rowen," Tamani said. "And they look just like us. If you didn't know anything about faeries, you might think you were a human too."

"Oh, I could never be a human," Rowen responded soberly.

"Well, you'll never have to be," Tamani said. "You're going to be the most beautiful Summer faerie in Avalon."

Rowen smiled and lowered her eyelids demurely and

Laurel had no doubt Tamani was right. With her soft, curly brown hair and long lashes, she was as pretty as any baby Laurel had ever seen. Then she opened her rosebud mouth wide into a yawn.

"Nap time, Rowen," Rhoslyn said.

Rowen's face fell and she started to pout. "But I want to play with Laurel."

"Laurel will be back another time," Rhoslyn said, her eyes darting to Laurel's as if to test the validity of that promise. Laurel nodded quickly, not certain if it was the truth. "You can sleep in Tam's bed," Rhoslyn added when Rowen still hung back. "I hope you don't mind," she said to Tamani, who shook his head.

The little faerie's face brightened considerably and Rhoslyn herded her down the narrow hall, leaving Tamani and Laurel alone.

"Is she really only three?" Laurel asked.

"Aye. And very normal for a faerie her age," Tamani said, lounging in the broad armchair. It was fascinating for Laurel to watch him. She had never seen him quite so at ease.

"You told me that faeries age differently, but I..." Her voice trailed off.

"You didn't believe me?" Tamani said with a grin.

"I believed you. Just, seeing it is something else." She

looked over at him. "Are faeries ever babies?"

"Not in the sense that you mean."

"And I was older than Rowen when I went to live with my parents?"

Tamani nodded, a small smile flirting with the corners of his mouth. "You were seven. Just barely."

"And you and I – we went to school together?"

He chuckled. "What good would Fall faerie classes have done me?"

"So how did I know you?"

"I spent a lot of time at the Academy with my mother."

As if sensing she was being spoken of, Rhoslyn walked back into the room with cups of warm heliconia nectar. Laurel had tasted it once at the Academy, where she was informed that the sweet beverage was a favourite in Avalon and often hard to come by. She felt complimented to be served it now.

"What is a Gardener?" Laurel asked, addressing Rhoslyn now. "Tamani said it was like a midwife."

Rhoslyn clicked her tongue disparagingly. "Tamani and his human words. Can't say I know what a *midwife* is, but a Gardener is a Tender who nurtures germinating sprouts."

"Oh." But Laurel was still confused. "Don't the parents take care of them themselves?"

Rhoslyn shook her head. "Not enough time. Sprouts need constant and very specialised tending. We all have daily tasks to do, and if every mother took off a year or longer to tend her sprout, too many jobs would go undone. Besides, a couple might decide to make a seed just to get out of a year of work, and new life is far too important to be undertaken for so frivolous a reason."

Laurel wondered what Rhoslyn would have to say about the many frivolous reasons humans found for having babies, but she remained silent.

"Sprouts are nurtured in a special garden at the Academy," Rhoslyn continued, "like all the other important plants and flowers. Spring and Summer seedlings learn to work by watching others, often their own parents, so Tamani spent a lot of time at the Academy with me."

"And I was there?"

"Of course. From the time your sprout opened, just like all the other Fall faeries."

Laurel looked up at Tamani and he nodded. "From the very first day. Like I said. They don't know you."

Laurel nodded forlornly.

"Laurel's having a little difficulty with her lack of fae parents," Tamani explained quietly.

"Oh, don't fret," Rhoslyn chided. "The separation is an

important part of your upbringing. Parents would just get in the way."

"What? How?" Laurel asked, a little disturbed by the casual tone that Rhoslyn – a mother herself – was using to dismiss Laurel's unknown parents.

"Chances are good your parents were Spring faeries; they would have had no idea how to teach a young Fall seedling. A Fall must be free from these kinds of random attachments with lower faeries," she said calmly, as if she were not speaking of herself. "They must learn to cultivate their minds to do the work they're expected to perform. Fall faeries are very important to our society. After even this short time at the Academy, surely you must see that."

Laurel's mind latched on to the phrase *random attachments*. Parents were far more than that. Or at least they should be.

Despite the cosiness of Tamani's home, Laurel found herself wanting to flee the conversation. "Tamani," she said abruptly, "we've walked so far; I'm worried that we'll be late getting back to the Academy."

"Oh, don't concern yourself," Tamani said. "We've been walking along a big circle, just catching the edges of the settled districts. We're not far from the Queen's woods now, and that borders the grounds of the Academy. Still," he continued, addressing his mother now, "we should be going. I promised the Academy staff this would be a short visit." Tamani looked at Laurel with concern in his eyes, but she looked away.

"Of course," Rhoslyn said warmly, completely unaware of the tension she had created. "Come back anytime, Laurel. It was lovely to see you again."

Laurel smiled numbly. She felt Tamani's fingers twine through hers, tugging her towards the door.

"Will you be back, Tam?" Rhoslyn asked just before they crossed the threshold.

"Yes. I have to return to the gate at sunrise, but I'll stay tonight."

"Good. Rowen should be gone by the time you come back. I'll make sure your bed is ready."

"Thank you."

Laurel said goodbye and turned, leading the way back to the main road they had walked down only a short hour before. When Tamani released Laurel's hand and resumed his place a few steps behind her, she grumbled incoherently and crossed her arms over her chest.

"Please don't be this way," Tamani said quietly.

"I can't help it," Laurel said. "The way she talked, she—"

"I know it's not what you're used to, Laurel, but that's how it is here. I'm sure none of your classmates give it a second thought."

"They don't know any better. You do."

"Why? Because I know how humans do it? You're assuming that your way is better."

"It *is* better!" Laurel said, whirling around to face him.

"Maybe for humans," Tamani countered in a strong, quiet voice. "But humans are not faeries. Faeries have different needs."

"So you are saying you like this? Taking faeries away from their parents?"

"I'm not saying either is better. I haven't lived around humans nearly enough to judge. But consider this," he said, placing one hand on her shoulder, his touch softening the edge of his words. "What if we lived here in Avalon like you do in the human world? Every time some Springs get a Fall seedling, it gets to live with them. They get to raise her. Except that she leaves them to go and study at the Academy for twelve hours a day. They never see her. They don't understand anything she's doing. On top of that, they don't have a garden at their house – a garden she needs to do her classwork – so now she's gone for fourteen, sixteen hours a day. They miss her; she misses them. They never see one another. Eventually they *are* like strangers, except that, unlike now, the parents know what they are missing out on. And it hurts, Laurel. It hurts them, and it hurts her. Tell me how that's better."

Laurel stood in shock as the logic sank in. Could he be right? She hated even considering it. And yet, it had a certain brutal efficiency she couldn't deny.

"I'm not saying it's better," Tamani said, his voice gentle. "I'm not even saying you have to understand, but don't think us devoid of emotion because we separate uppers from lowers. We have our reasons."

Laurel nodded slowly. "What about fathers?" she asked, her tone quiet now, the anger gone. "Do you have a father?"

Tamani fixed his gaze firmly on the ground. "I did," he said, his voice low and slightly choked.

Guilt rushed over her. "I'm so sorry. I don't mean to… I'm sorry." She touched his shoulder, wishing there was something more she could do.

Tamani's jaw was clenched, but he forced a smile, anyway. "It's all right. I just miss him. It's only been about a month."

A month. Right when he would have been expecting her to come visit him at the land. *But I didn't come.* Her chest felt empty. "I… I didn't know." She paused.

He smiled. "It's fine, really. We all knew it was coming."

"Really? What did he die of?"

"He didn't die, really. It's kind of the opposite of dying."

"What does that mean?"

Tamani took a deep breath and let it out slowly. When he looked up at Laurel again, he was his old self – his mourning hidden away. "I'll show you sometime. It's something you have to see to understand."

"But can't we – ?"

"We don't have time today," Tamani said, cutting her off with a tone that had just a hint of tightness beneath it. "Come on. I'd better get you back so they'll let me take you again next time."

"Next week?" Laurel said hopefully.

Tamani shook his head. "Even if I had that much Avalon leave, they won't let you away from your studies. In a few weeks."

Laurel found the concept of "Avalon leave" strangely disconcerting – but not as disconcerting as being cooped up in the Academy indefinitely. *A few weeks?* He may as well have said forever. She could only hope that her next phase of education would pass the time more quickly than sitting in her room with a stack of textbooks.

Chapter Six

Laurel studied her appearance in the mirror the next morning, wondering just what, exactly, an acolyte-level student was supposed to look like. After the fiasco of her first dinner in Avalon, she had taken pains to dress appropriately, but asking anyone what to wear never got her more than a smiling encouragement to wear "whatever you find most comfortable". She considered her hair – pulled up in a ponytail – then untied the ribbon, letting it fall back down around her shoulders. As she was sweeping it up again, a knock sounded at her door. She opened it and peered out at Katya's smiling face.

"I thought I'd come show you where to go, for your first official day of classes," Katya said brightly.

"That would be great," Laurel said, smiling in relief. She glanced at Katya's outfit – a long, flowing skirt and a sleeveless, scoop-necked top. Laurel was wearing a calf-length sundress made out of a light material that swung in the breeze and rustled about her legs when she walked. She decided her outfit was similar enough to Katya's that she wouldn't look completely out of place.

"Are you ready, then?" Katya asked.

"Yeah," Laurel said. "Just let me grab my bag." She shouldered her backpack, which got a sidelong glance from Katya. With its thick, black zippers and nylon weave – not to mention the Transformers patch David had ironed on to it a few months back as a joke – it contrasted sharply with Katya's canvas shoulder bag. But Laurel had nothing else to carry her note cards in; besides, it was comforting to carry her old, familiar backpack.

They headed out the door and, after a few turns, started down a long hallway lined with sugar-glass windows that flashed in the sunrise and projected the girls' reflections on the opposite windows. Laurel studied their reflections as they walked, and for a moment lost track of which was her own. Katya was about Laurel's height and also had blond hair, though hers was short and curled at cute angles all around her head. Most of the other faeries at the Academy coloured their hair and eyes by manipulating their diets, so red- and green- and blue-haired faeries far outnumbered plain blondes and brunettes. It was an interesting approach to fashion that, under other circumstances, Laurel thought she might enjoy. As it was, she had her hands full with the nuances of the unofficial dress code.

They reached a set of double doors from which emanated the scent of rich, damp earth. "We'll be here for today," Katya said. "We meet in different places, depending on our projects. But class is in here about half the time." She pulled open the door, and a wave of chatter drifted out.

Behind the door was a room unlike any classroom Laurel had ever seen. She would ordinarily have called it a greenhouse. Planter boxes full of various greenery lined the perimeter of the huge room, under tall windows that stretched from ceiling to floor; skylights were mounted into the sharply pitched roof, and the whole room was tropically warm and humid. Laurel was immediately grateful for the light material of her sundress, and understood why her wardrobe contained so many like it.

There were no desks, though there was a long table running down the middle of the room full of lab equipment. Laurel could imagine David geeking out over it: beakers and vials, droppers and slides, even several instruments resembling microscopes, and rows and rows of bottles filled with colourful liquids.

But not a desk to be seen. Laurel was a little surprised to realise that this was a relief. Reminded her of her homeschooling days.

The faeries themselves sent a thrill of nervousness down Laurel's back. The buzz of conversation, slightly muffled by the abundant greenery, filled the room; perhaps a hundred faeries were milling about, clustered together in front of planter boxes or standing in circles and chatting. According to Aurora, the acolytes Laurel was here to study with could be anywhere from fifteen years old to forty, depending on their talent and dedication, so how much she had in common with her classmates was anyone's guess. She didn't recognise hardly anyone in the room; just a face here and there from the dinners. This put her at a significant disadvantage because she was sure most of them would remember her from before – would remember her as someone she herself did not.

As Laurel stood with her feet frozen to the damp stone floor, Katya waved at a group of female faeries standing around what looked like a large pomegranate bush. "It will be a few minutes before the professors arrive," she said, "and I want to check on my pear tree before they get here. Do you mind?"

Laurel shook her head. *Mind? I wouldn't know what else to do.*

Katya walked over to a planter box with a small, leafy tree in it and pulled a composition book out of her shoulder bag.

Pear, Laurel thought automatically. *For healing; neutralises most poisons. The juice from the blossoms protects against dehydration.* "What are you doing with this?" she asked.

"Trying to make it grow faster," Katya said, squinting at several marks on the trunk of the small sapling. "It's a fairly rudimentary potion, but I just can't quite get the knack of it." She picked up a vial of dark green liquid and held it up to the sun. "If you need a potion to cure ailments, I'm your Mixer." Laurel blinked at Katya's casual use of the word; after all, Tamani had suggested it was a Spring faerie word, and even implied it wasn't entirely polite. Katya apparently thought otherwise. "But simply enhancing already functional aspects grows knots in my mind," Katya finished, not noticing Laurel's reaction.

Laurel let her gaze wander around the room. Some of the faeries looked up to meet her eyes, some glanced away, others smiled, and a few just stared outright until it was Laurel who finally had to look away. But when she met the gaze of a tall, purple-eyed faerie with a straight, dark brown fringe, Laurel was surprised to find herself at the sharp end of a pointed glare. The tall faerie tossed her long hair over her shoulder and, rather than simply looking away, turned all the way around and presented Laurel with her back.

"Hey, Katya," Laurel whispered. "Who's that?"

"Who?" Katya asked, a little distracted.

"Across the room. Long dark hair. Purple roots and eyes."

Katya glanced over quickly. "Oh, that's Mara. Did she give you a look? Just ignore her. She has issues with you."

"With me?" Laurel almost squeaked. "She doesn't even know me!"

Katya bit at her bottom lip, hesitant. "Listen," she said quietly, "no one really likes to talk about how much you don't remember. We all make the memory potions," she added quickly, before Laurel could interrupt. "We learn how, as initiates. I made my first successful batch when I was ten. But they're supposed to be for humans, trolls – you know, animals. They don't work the same in faeries."

"Like being immune to enticement?" Laurel asked.

"Not exactly. If faeries were immune to Fall magic, we wouldn't be able to use beneficial potions. But potions made for animals don't function the same in plants, and who in their right mind would specifically brew a potion to rob memories from another fae? I mean, Fall faeries did study faerie poisons in the past – long before I sprouted – but there was a faerie who... she took it too far," Katya said, her voice almost a whisper. "So it's strongly discouraged now. You have to have special permission to even read the books about it. You're a special case, because they didn't want you to be able to reveal anything to the humans, even by accident. But still, having an amnesiac faerie around – to be frank, a victim of magic we're not even allowed to study any more – you're kind of a walking taboo. No offence." She flicked her head towards Mara. "Mara hates it the worst. A few years ago she applied to study faerie poisons and was refused, even though she's the best in the class and already an expert with animal poisons."

"And she hates me because of that?" Laurel asked, confused.

"She hates that you are evidence of a potion she doesn't know how to make. But on top of that, she knows you, or did. Almost all of us in here did, to one extent or another."

"Oh," Laurel said softly.

"Before you ask, I didn't really know you before you

were selected as the scion, and even then it was only from a distance. But Mara," she said, flicking her head towards the tall, statuesque faerie, "was pretty good friends with you."

"Really?" Laurel said, feeling both stupid that she had to find out from someone else who her friends were and mystified that having been friends with someone in the past could justify such a glare.

"Yes, but Mara was in the running to be the scion too, and she was really upset when you got the spot instead of her. She saw it as a failure instead of what it really was – that you fit the parameters better than she did. Being blond apparently was the clincher," Katya said with a wave of her hand. "'Humans like blond babies,' they said."

Laurel choked a little at that, coughing to clear her throat and drawing quite a bit of attention from the other faeries. Even Mara turned her head to glare at Laurel once more.

"I suspect she's been out to prove herself ever since," Katya said. "She's really talented; rose to acolyte way earlier than most of us. She's just about ready to become a journeyman, and as far as I'm concerned, the sooner the better." Katya turned back to her tree. "She can go study with *them*," she muttered.

Laurel angled her body that way too but kept peering at Mara out of the corner of her eye. The slender, languid faerie lounged against the counter with the grace and beauty of a ballerina, but her eyes took in the whole room, weighed it in the balance, and seemed to find it wanting. Could they have ever really been friends?

An entourage of middle-aged-looking faeries strode into the room, the one in the lead clapping her hands for the students' attention. "Gather, please," she said in a surprisingly quiet voice. But the sound carried throughout the room, which had gone completely silent. Every faerie had stopped talking and turned to the instructors as they entered.

Well, Laurel thought, *that's way different from at home.*

The faeries walked in from all sides of the room to gather in a large circle around the twenty or so teachers. The faerie who had called everyone together took the lead. "Anyone starting a new project today?"

A few hands went up. As soon as they did, the other faeries shuffled and made room for them to come to the front. One at a time each faerie – or sometimes a small group – described the project they were starting, its purpose, how they planned to go about doing it, how long they thought it would take, and other details. They fielded a few questions from the staff and even some from the other students.

The projects all sounded very complex, and the faeries kept using phrases Laurel didn't understand; phrases like *monastuolo receptors* and *eukaryotic resistance matrices* and *capryilic hleocræft vectors*. After a few minutes of this her attention began to wander. She glanced around the circle as the faeries made their presentations. The other faeries were standing quietly, listening. No one fidgeted; hardly anyone whispered, and even when they did, it seemed to be about the project being described. It was almost half an hour before all the new projects were accounted for, and everyone remained quiet and attentive.

It was a little creepy.

"Did anyone complete a project yesterday?" the instructor asked, once everyone had reported. A few more hands went up, and again the crowd shuffled to bring those students to the front.

As the faeries reported on their finished projects, Laurel glanced round the classroom with fresh eyes. The plants that grew here were as varied as those growing outside, but they seemed more haphazard in their diversity. Many were surrounded by sheaves of paper, scientific equipment, or fabrics strategically draped to filter the sunlight. This wasn't a greenhouse, really; it was a laboratory.

"When I observed your project last week, it didn't seem to be going well." One of the professors, a male faerie with a deep, rich voice, was questioning a small brunette faerie who looked quite young.

"It wasn't," the faerie said simply, without any kind of shame or self-consciousness. "In the end, the project was a complete failure."

Laurel cringed, waiting for the derisive whispers and giggles.

But they didn't come.

She glanced around. The other faeries were paying very close attention. In fact, several were nodding as the faerie described various aspects of her failure. No one seemed discouraged in the least. Another big – and rather refreshing – difference from home.

"So what do you have planned now?" the same teacher questioned.

The young faerie didn't miss a beat. "I have more studying to do to determine why the serum didn't work, but once that is complete, I would like to start again. I'm determined to find a way to restore the use of the viridefaeco potion to Avalon."

The instructor thought about this for a moment. "I'll

approve that," he finally said. "One more round. Then you will need to return to your regular studies."

The young faerie nodded and said thank you before returning to the circle.

"Anyone else?" the head instructor asked. The faeries looked around for raised hands, but there were none. "Before you disperse," the instructor said, "I think you are all aware that Laurel has returned to us, even if only for a short while."

Eyes turned to Laurel. She got a few smiles but mostly curious stares.

"She will be with us for the next several weeks. Please allow her to observe you freely. Answer her questions. There is no need for her to decant anything, particularly if it is a delicate undertaking, but please take the time to explain to her what you are doing, how, and why. Dismissed." She clapped her hands once more, and the faeries dispersed.

"What now?" Laurel whispered to Katya. The buzz of conversation had returned to the room, but whispering still felt appropriate to Laurel after the silence of the last hour.

"We go work," Katya said simply. "I have two long-term projects I'm working on right now, and then repetition work."

"Repetition work?"

"Making simple potions and serums for the other faeries in Avalon. We learn how to make them when we're quite young, but they only trust the higher level students to prepare the products that are actually distributed among the populace. We have monthly quotas and I've been so focused on my pear tree that I'm a little behind."

"You all just… work? On whatever you want?"

"Well, advanced projects need to be approved by the faculty. They'll wander through here and check up on us periodically. But yes, we decide on our own projects."

The whole process reminded Laurel of the years she'd spent being homeschooled by her mother, building a curriculum around her personal interests and learning everything at her own pace. She smiled at the memory, even though she had long since stopped begging her mom to return to homeschooling – thanks in no small part to David and her friend Chelsea.

But here Laurel didn't have a project of her own, and wandering the room didn't seem like it would help her actually learn anything. Even after two weeks of memorising plant uses, she simply didn't know enough to ask meaningful questions of the students. So she was relieved when she saw a familiar face enter the room –

an emotion she had doubted she would ever feel upon seeing the stern face of Yeardley, the fundamentals instructor.

"Is she ready?" Yeardley asked, addressing Katya instead of her.

Katya smiled and prodded Laurel forward. "She's all yours."

Laurel followed Yeardley to a station at the table lined with equipment. Without so much as a greeting, he began to quiz her on the second batch of books she had been reading the past week. She didn't feel complete confidence in any of her answers, but Yeardley seemed pleased enough with her progress. He reached into his own shoulder bag and pulled out... more books.

Disappointment washed over her. "I thought I was done reading," Laurel said before she could stop herself.

"You are never *done*," Yeardley said, as if it were a bad word. "Each caste has its essential nature. The essence of Spring magic is social; it trades on empathy. Summer faeries must hone their sense of aesthetics; without art, their magic is thin indeed. The essence of our magic is intellect; knowledge gleaned through careful study is the reservoir from which our intuition draws its power."

That didn't sound like magic to Laurel. Mostly it sounded like a lot of hard work.

"That said, these are my books, not yours."

Laurel managed to stifle a sigh of relief.

"Laurel."

She looked up at the tone of his voice. It wasn't stern, the way it had been a moment earlier. It was tense – worried, even – but there was a softness to it that hadn't been there before.

"Normally at this point I would begin teaching you rudimentary potions. Lotions, cleansing serums, nutritional tonics – that sort of thing. The things we teach novices. But you're going to have to come back at a less important time and learn those or catch up on your own. I'm going to teach you defensive herbology. Jamison insisted, and I'm in full agreement with his decision."

Laurel nodded, feeling a rush run through her. Not just from excitement at starting actual lessons, but because of the reason for the acceleration: the threat of the trolls. This was what she'd been waiting for.

"Most of what I teach you will be beyond your abilities to replicate, likely for quite some time, but it will be a start. I expect you to work hard, for your own sake more than mine."

"Of course," Laurel replied earnestly.

"I've had you reading about a variety of plants and their uses. What you may not yet realise is that making potions, serum, elixirs, and the like is not simply about mixing essences together in the right amounts. There is always a general guideline – a recipe, if you will – but the process as well as the result will differ from one Fall faerie to the next. What we teach in the Academy is not about recipes, but following your intuition – trusting the ability that is your birthright, and using your knowledge of nature to enhance the lives of everyone in Avalon. Because the most essential ingredient in any mixture is *you* – the Fall faerie. No one else can do what you do, not even if they follow your rituals with unerring precision." He reached into his bag and pulled out a small pot with a little green plant growing in it, its buds tightly closed.

"You must learn to feel the very core of the nature you work with," he continued, touching the plant gently, "and to form a connection with it, so close, so intimate, that you know not only how to bend its components to your will" – he searched through a row of bottles and picked one up, opening it and dabbing a drop of its contents on his finger—"but to unlock its potential and allow it to thrive as no one else can." He carefully touched each of the closed blossoms with his wet finger and as he pulled his hand away, the tiny buds opened to reveal bright purple flowers.

He looked up into Laurel's wide eyes. "Shall we begin?"

Chapter Seven

Laurel knelt on the bench in front of her window with her nose pressed against the glass, squinting at the path that led to the front gates of the Academy. Tamani said he'd arrive at eleven o'clock, but she couldn't help but hope he would come early.

Disappointed, she wandered back to her work – today, a monastuolo serum that was clearly going horribly wrong. But Yeardley insisted that seeing her failures through to the end, even when she knew they were doomed, would teach her better what *not* to do. It seemed like a waste of time to Laurel, but she had learned not to second-guess Yeardley. Despite his gruff exterior, the past month had shown her another side of him. He was obsessed with herbology and nothing delighted him more than a devoted student. And he was always, *always* right. Still, Laurel remained sceptical of this particular rule.

She was about to sit down and toss in the next component when someone knocked on her door. *Finally!* Taking a moment to check her hair and clothes in the mirror, Laurel took a deep breath and opened her door to Celia, the familiar Spring faerie who had not only cut her note cards but done hundreds of little favours for her over the last few weeks.

"There's someone here for you down in the atrium," she said, inclining her head. No matter how many times Laurel asked them not to, the Spring faeries *always* found a way to bow to her.

Laurel thanked her for the message and slipped out of the door. Every step she took made her feel a bit lighter. It wasn't that she disliked her lessons – on the contrary, now that she understood them better, they were fascinating. But she had been right about one thing from the start: It was a lot of work. She studied with Yeardley for a full eight hours each day, observed the Fall faeries for several hours, and each night she had more reading to do as well as practising potions, powders, and serums. She was occupied from sunrise to sunset, with only a short break for dinner right at the end of the day. Katya assured her it wasn't like that for all Falls; that they worked and studied "only" about twelve hours a day. Even that seemed way excessive to Laurel.

But at least *they* got time off. Laurel didn't.

"I will admit that the amount of work expected of you is a just a little excessive," Katya said one day – a huge concession from the studious, loyal Fall. She was rather like David in that way. But when Laurel had tried to compliment her by saying so, Katya had been mortally offended at being compared to a human.

So when Tamani's note arrived three days ago requesting Laurel's company for an afternoon, she had been ecstatic. Just a small break, but it was a welcome chance to rejuvenate herself and prepare for one last gruelling week of study before she went back to her parents.

Laurel was distracted enough that she almost missed Mara and Katya standing at the railing of a landing that overlooked the atrium.

"He's here again," Mara said, disdain dripping from her perfect ruby lips. "Can't you make him wait outside?"

Laurel raised one eyebrow. "If I had it my way, he'd meet me in my bedroom."

Mara's eyes widened and she glared at Laurel, but Laurel had grown only too accustomed to vaguely menacing looks from this statuesque beauty. Things had not gotten better since that first surprising glare in the lab. Laurel generally just avoided looking at Mara at all. And even the one time Laurel had asked her a question about her project – fittingly, research on a cactus – Mara had simply turned her back and pretended not to hear.

With her head held high, Laurel walked on without another word.

Katya fell into step with her. "Don't bother with her," she said, her tone warm. "Personally, I think it's rather brave of you."

Laurel glanced at Katya. "What do you mean, brave?"

"I don't know many Spring faeries outside of our staff." Katya shrugged. "Especially soldiers."

"Sentries," Laurel corrected automatically, not really sure why.

"Still. They just seem so… coarse." She paused and peeked over the railing into the atrium, where Tamani would be waiting. "And there are so *many* of them."

Laurel rolled her eyes.

"Of course, the two of you have known each other for a long time, so I suppose it's different."

Laurel nodded, although it was only a partial truth. As far as she could remember, she had known Tamani for less than a year. But a year was a lot longer than she could remember knowing any of the Fall faeries she now saw every day. "Well, I'll see you later," Laurel said brightly, the weariness of the last several weeks nothing more than a wispy memory.

"How long will you be?" Katya asked with wide eyes.

As long as I can, she thought. But to Katya she said, "I don't know. But if I don't see you tonight, I'll see you tomorrow."

Katya didn't look convinced. "I really don't think you should go alone. Perhaps Caelin could accompany you."

Laurel suppressed the urge to roll her eyes again. By some fluke, Caelin was the only male Fall near Laurel's age. And even with his puny stature and squeaky voice, he insisted on playing the role of protector for all his "ladies", as he had dubbed them. The last thing she needed was him hanging around trying to prove he was better than every other male they encountered. Which was *exactly* what Caelin would do.

She didn't even want to think about how Tamani would react.

A small smile crossed her face. Then again, maybe it would be interesting. Caelin didn't look like he'd last ten seconds in Tamani's presence. She would enjoy seeing him put in his place. But not as much as she would enjoy time alone with Tamani. "Trust me, Katya, I don't need a chaperone."

"If you say so." Katya smiled. "Have a good time," she said, her tone both earnest and doubtful.

"So where are we going?" Laurel asked after she and Tamani completed the charade of walking silently and formally through the Academy grounds and out of the gates.

"Can't you tell?" Tamani asked with a grin, gesturing to the large wicker basket swinging from his left hand.

"I said where are we going, not what are we doing." But there was no annoyance in her tone. It felt so good to leave the Academy behind, to feel the fresh wind on her face, the soft soil under her feet, and to see Tamani out of the corner of her eye, following behind her. She wanted to spread her arms and spin and laugh but managed to hold herself in check.

"You'll see," he said, his fingers at her back, guiding her down a fork in the path that led away from the houses they'd strolled through last time. "I want to show you something."

As they walked, the path narrowed and steepened; after a few minutes they crested the tall hill and for a moment Laurel thought something was wrong with her eyes. Shading the hilltop's considerable expanse was an enormous tree with broad branches that spread wide. It vaguely resembled an oak tree, with lacy, elongated leaves, but rather than having a tall, statuesque trunk, it was enormously stout, knobby, and misshapen. Laurel suspected it would dwarf even the mightiest of the redwoods growing in the national forest that bordered her land outside of Orick.

Aside from its immensity, it didn't appear too out of the ordinary, but when Laurel stepped under the shade of its branches she gasped as she felt... something... something she couldn't identify or explain. It was almost as though the air had grown thicker, swirling around her body like water. *Living* water that crept into the air she breathed and filled her, inside and out.

"What is this?" she gasped as soon as she found her voice. She hadn't even realised that Tamani had closed the distance between them and placed a steadying hand at her waist.

"It's called the World Tree. It... it's made out of faeries."

"How..." Laurel wasn't even sure how to finish the question.

Tamani's brow furrowed. "I guess it's... well, it's a long story." He led her closer to the trunk. "Ages and ages ago – before there were humans, even – faeries sprang from the forests of Avalon. According to legend, we didn't yet speak. But there was one faerie, the very first Winter faerie, who had greater power than any faerie before or since. And with that power came tremendous wisdom. When he felt that his time was growing close, he sought to pass on the wisdom he had gained. So instead of waiting until he wilted, he came to this hilltop and prayed to Gaia, the mother of all Nature, and told her that he would give up his life if she would preserve his consciousness in the form of a tree."

"So... he... is this tree?" Laurel asked, stepping close to the knobby trunk.

Tamani nodded. "He is the original tree. And other faeries could come up here with questions or problems. And if they listened very carefully, when the wind blew, they would hear the rustling of the leaves and he would share his wisdom. Years went by and soon the birds taught the faeries to speak and—"

"Birds?"

"Yes. Birds were the first creatures faeries heard singing and vocalising and we learned to use our voices from them."

"What happened then?"

"Unfortunately, when faeries started talking and singing they eventually forgot how to listen to the rustling leaves. The World Tree was just another tree for a very long time. Then Efreisone became King. Efreisone was also a scholar and he found legends about the World Tree scattered through his ancient texts. Once he pieced together the whole story, he wanted nothing more than to revive the World Tree and harness its wisdom. He spent hours and hours in the shade of this tree, caring for it and bringing it back from its dormancy. And in those hours he discovered that he was beginning to hear the words the tree was saying. From it he learned the stories of the ages, and every evening when he returned home he would write them down and share them with his subjects. And when he felt that his time was growing short, he decided to join the tree."

"What do you mean, join the tree?"

Tamani hesitated. "He… he grafted himself into the tree. Grew into the tree and became part of it."

Laurel tried to visualise it. It was both grotesque and fascinating. "Why would he do that?"

"Faeries who become part of the World Tree release their consciousness into it. The wisdom of thousands of faeries lives in that tree. Thousands of thousands." He paused. "They are called the Silent Ones."

Realisation blossomed on Laurel's face and she gasped quietly. "Your father did that. He's part of this tree."

Tamani nodded.

Laurel stepped away from the tree, feeling suddenly intrusive. But after a moment, she reached out and touched the trunk with tentative fingers. Yeardley had taught her to feel the essence of any plant with careful fingertips – one of the few lessons she had picked up both easily and quickly. She closed her eyes and felt for it now, her hands pressed against the bark.

It was like no other plant she had ever felt. The life didn't hum gently under her hands, it roared like a mighty river; crashed like a tsunami. She sucked in a quick breath as something like a song flowed into her hand, up her arm, and seemed to fill her from head to foot. She turned to Tamani with wide eyes. "So he lives forever."

"Yes. But inaccessible to us, so it's as if he has died. I – I miss him."

Laurel pulled her hand away from the tree and slipped it into Tamani's. "How often do faeries do that?"

"Not often. It requires sacrifice. You have to join the tree while you still have the strength to go through the process. My father was only a hundred and sixty – he had a good thirty or forty years ahead of him – but he felt himself start to weaken and knew he had to act soon." He laughed morbidly. "It's the only time I ever heard my parents argue."

He paused and his tone became sombre again. "If you join the tree, you must go alone, so I don't know which part of the tree he chose. But sometimes I swear I can see the features of his face on that branch three limbs up," he said, pointing. He shrugged. "Wishful thinking, probably."

"Maybe not," Laurel said, desperate to provide some words of comfort. After a heavy silence she asked, "How long does it take?" In her mind she saw an elderly faerie being overtaken by the large tree, his life slowly choked from him.

"Oh, it's quick," Tamani said, washing away the gruesome picture from Laurel's mind. "Don't forget that both the faerie who became the tree and the first one to join were Winter faeries. The tree retains some of that immense power. My—" He hesitated. "My father told me that you select your spot on the tree and submit yourself to it and when your mind is clear and your intentions burn true, the tree sweeps you up and you are changed instantly." She saw his eyes wander back up to the spot where he thought he could see his father's features.

Laurel edged a little closer. "You said the tree communicates. Can't you talk to him?"

Tamani shook his head. "Not to him specifically. You

talk to the tree as a whole, and it speaks back in one voice."

Laurel looked up at the towering branches. "Could I talk to the tree?"

"Not today. It takes time. You have to come and tell the tree your question, or concern, then you sit, in silence, and listen until your cells remember how to understand the language."

"How long does it take?"

"Hours. Days. It's hard to predict. And it depends on how carefully you listen. Also how open you are to the answer."

She hesitated for a long time before asking, "Have you done it?"

He turned to her, his eyes unguarded as she'd seen them only a few times before. "I have."

"Did you get your answer?"

He nodded.

"How long did it take?"

He hesitated. "Four days." Then a grin. "I'm stubborn. I wasn't open to receiving the right answer. I was determined to get the answer I wanted."

She tried to imagine Tamani sitting silently beneath the tree for four days. "What did the tree say?" she whispered.

"Maybe I'll tell you someday."

Laurel's mouth went dry as his eyes just looked at her and the living air swirled around her. Then Tamani smiled and gestured to a patch of thick grass several yards outside the shady canopy of the World Tree.

"Can't we eat here?" she asked, reluctant to leave the trunk of the tree.

Tamani shook his head. "It's not polite," he said. "We leave the tree available for answer seekers as much as possible. It's a very private thing," he added.

Although Laurel could understand that, she was still a little sad to step out of the shadows and into the sun. Tamani set out a sparse picnic – there simply wasn't much need to eat in the nourishing Avalon sunlight – and they both settled down in the grass, Laurel flopping on to her stomach and enjoying, for this brief interlude, just doing nothing.

"So how are your studies?" Tamani asked.

Laurel considered the question. "Amazing," she finally answered. "I never knew how many things you could do with plants." She rolled over to face him, her head propped up on her elbow. "And my mom's a naturopath, so believe me, that's saying something."

"Have you learned a lot?"

"Kind of." She furrowed her eyebrows. "I mean,

technically I have *learned* a ton. More than I ever thought I could absorb in just a few weeks. But I can't actually *do* anything." She sighed as she slumped back down. "None of my potions work. Some of them get closer than others, but not a single one has really been right yet."

"None of them?" Tamani asked, an undercurrent of worry in his voice.

"Yeardley says it's normal. He says it can take years to get your first potion just right. I don't have that kind of time; not here in Avalon, or before I need to protect my family. But he says I'm doing well." She turned to look at Tamani again. "He says that even though I can't remember, it's obvious to him that I am relearning. That I'm catching on unnaturally fast. I hope he's right," she grumbled. "What about you? Your life has got to be more interesting than mine at the moment."

"Actually, no, it's really not. It's been very quiet at the gate. Too quiet." He was sitting with his knees pulled up to his chest with his arms wrapped around them, looking at the World Tree. "I've been doing a lot of scouting lately."

"What do you mean, *scouting*?"

He glanced over at her for a second before his eyes returned to the tree. "Leaving the gate. Venturing out to get a better lay of the land." He shook his head. "We haven't seen a single troll in weeks. And somehow, I don't think it's because they've suddenly given up on Avalon," he said with a tense laugh. He sobered. "I'm looking for the reason why, but there's only so much I can do. I'm not human – I don't know how to blend in to the human world. So I can't get all the information I want. I'm – I'm missing something," he said firmly. "I know it. I can feel it." He shrugged. "But I don't know what it is or where to find it."

Laurel glanced at the tree. "Why don't you ask them?" she asked, pointing.

He shook his head. "It doesn't work that way. The tree's not omniscient, nor is it a fortune-teller. It's the combined wisdom of thousands of years, but it's never been outside of Avalon." He shook his head. "Even the Silent Ones can't help me with this. I have to do it myself."

They lay there for several minutes, sprawled back, enjoying the warm sunshine. "Tam?" Laurel said hesitantly.

"Hmm?" Tamani's eyes were closed and he looked almost asleep.

"Do…" Laurel hesitated. "Do you get tired of being a Spring faerie?"

His eyes popped open wide for a second before he closed them again. "How so?"

She was quiet, trying to think of a way to ask without insulting him. "No one thinks Spring faeries are as good as anyone else. You have to bow, and serve, and walk behind me. It's not fair."

Tamani was quiet for a while, his tongue running along his bottom lip as he thought. Finally he said, "Do you get tired of people thinking you're a human?"

Laurel shook her head.

"Why not?"

She shrugged. "I look like a human; it makes sense."

"No, that's the logical reasoning for *why* people think you are a human. I want to know why it doesn't bother you."

"Because everyone has always thought I was a human. I'm used to it," she said, the words out of her mouth before she realised she had walked right into his trap.

He grinned. "See? It's the same thing. I've always been a Spring faerie; I've always acted like a Spring faerie. May as well ask me if I'm tired of being alive. This is my life."

"But don't you, on some level, realise it's wrong?"

"Why is it wrong?"

"Because you're a person, just like everyone else here.

Why should what kind of faerie you are define your social status?"

"I think the way human social status is defined is just as outrageous. More, maybe."

"How so?"

"Doctors, lawyers – why are they so respected?"

"Because they're educated. And doctors save people's lives."

"So you pay them more, and they have a higher place in society, right?"

Laurel nodded.

"How is this any different? Fall faeries are more educated; they save lives too. Winter faeries do even more: They keep Avalon safe from outsiders, protect our gateways, keep us from being discovered by humans. Why shouldn't they be more revered?"

"But it's just happenstance. No one chooses to be a Spring faerie."

"Maybe not, but you choose to work as hard as you do. All the Falls do. It's not like you just sit around and mix up an occasional potion. You've told me how much you study. Every Fall studies hard. Even if they don't choose to be a Fall faerie, they choose to work and hone their skills to help *me*. If that's not worth my respect, I don't know what is."

It did make sense, sort of. But it still rubbed Laurel the wrong way. "It's not just that Fall and Winter faeries are revered," she said, "it's that Spring faeries are looked down on. There are so many of you," she said, her conscience pricking a little when she remembered that Katya had said the same thing only a short time before – though not in quite the same tone of voice. "The Winter faeries may protect Avalon, but it's the Spring faeries who make it function. You guys do almost all the jobs. I mean, Summers do the entertaining and such, but who makes the food, who builds the roads and houses, who sews and washes all my clothes?" she asked, her voice starting to rise. "You do. Spring faeries do! You're not nothing; you're *everything.*"

Something in Tamani's eyes told her she'd hit a soft spot. His jaw was tight and he took a few moments to think before answering. "Maybe you're right," he said softly, "but that's just the way it is. It's the way it's always been. The Spring faeries serve Avalon. We're happy to serve," he added, a touch of pride colouring his tone. "*I'm* happy to serve," he added. "It's not like we're slaves. I'm a completely free faerie. Once my duties are done, I can do what I want and go where I please."

"Are you free?" Laurel asked.

"I am."

"How free?"

"As free as I want to be," he replied a little hotly.

"Are you free to walk beside me?"

He was silent.

"Are you free to be anything more than a friend to me? *If*," and she stressed the *if* heavily, "I ever decided to live in Avalon and wanted to be with you, would you be free enough to do that?"

He looked away, and Laurel could tell he'd been avoiding a conversation like this.

"Well?" she insisted.

"If you wanted it," he finally said.

"If *I* wanted it?"

He nodded. "I'm not allowed to ask. You would have to ask me."

Her breath caught in her chest, and Tamani looked at her.

"Why do you think David bothers me so much?"

Laurel looked down at her lap.

"I can't just storm in and proclaim my intentions. I can't 'steal' you away. I just have to wait and hope that, someday, you'll ask."

"And if I don't?" Laurel said, her voice barely above a whisper.

"Then I guess I'll be waiting forever."

Chapter Eight

Laurel stood in her room, looking over the wild assortment of things splayed across her bed. She had come to appreciate her faerie-made clothing for more than just its beauty; it was like nothing you could find in the human world. Most of it was made out of a silky gossamer-like fabric that – although Laurel couldn't be certain they weren't teasing her – several of the other faeries said was made from spider silk. Whatever it was made from, it allowed for full-body photosynthesis, so Laurel didn't feel the need to always wear tank tops and shorts like she did at home.

And then there was the dress she'd found in one of the Summer kiosks during a short walk she'd taken to clear her head after an especially gruelling day. It was beautiful and just her size; a dark blue gown, cut low in the back to accommodate a blossom, with a skirt that was fitted to the knees then flared out, mermaid style. An overskirt of soft, sheer ruffles wound around the dress and floated on the lightest breeze. She had felt a little guilty taking it – after all, she had no occasion to wear it to – but it was just too perfect to leave behind.

She also had lots of long, sweeping skirts, peasant-cut shirts that reminded her of Tamani's, and a few short skirts and dresses that made her feel like a storybook faerie. Just for fun.

But only a fraction of it would fit into her backpack.

And she wasn't leaving without her kit.

Of all the things they'd given her, that was the most precious. About the size of a shoe box, her kit – presented to her by Yeardley that morning – contained dozens of essences. Specifically, it held several troll-deterring potions made by Fall faeries with far greater skill than Laurel. It also held many of the extracts she could use to further protect her home and family. Assuming she improved with practice, at any rate. It was worlds better than nothing.

But the kit half filled her backpack.

As she stood pondering the bed full of clothes, Katya stepped into her doorway and tossed something on to the bed. "You look like you could use this," she said with a laugh.

Laurel picked up a pink bag that looked like soft tissue paper. She had a sneaking suspicion it was much stronger than it appeared. "Thanks," she said. "I was just going to ring for Celia to see if she could find something."

Katya looked at the pile of clothes on the bed, then dubiously at Laurel's backpack. "You weren't really going to try to get all that in there, were you?"

"No," Laurel said with a grin.

"Good," Katya said with a tinkling laugh. "I think that would take Winter-level magic."

Laurel laughed at the joke that only another faerie would get. She loosened the drawstring at the top of the bag and caught sight of a *K* embroidered on one side in beautiful calligraphy. "I can't take this. It's monogrammed."

Katya looked over. "Oh? Honestly, I hadn't noticed. I've got loads of them."

"Really?"

"Sure. They used to come back like that whenever I sent out my laundry. I guess they're using someone different now."

Laurel started pushing clothes into the pink bag. She would still have to leave some things behind, but it was an improvement.

For several seconds Katya watched silently, then – almost timidly – asked, "Do you really have to leave?"

Laurel looked up in surprise. With a few notable exceptions, the other faeries had been nice to her – and very chatty – but Laurel would not have called any of them friends. Obviously Katya felt otherwise. "I'll be back," Laurel said.

"I know." Katya forced a smile then asked, "But do you really *have* to go back? I've only heard bits and pieces, but word is that your assignment has been completed. You have gained title to the land that holds the gate. Can't you come back now?"

Laurel looked down at the clothes she was folding, avoiding Katya's eyes. "It's more complicated than that. I have family, friends. I can't leave them alone."

"You could go visit," Katya suggested brightly, but Laurel sensed solemnity in her intent.

"It's more than just wanting to see them," Laurel said seriously. "I have to protect them. They're in danger because of me and I have a duty to them."

"A duty to humans?"

Laurel clenched her jaw. It wasn't really Katya's fault. She didn't know any better. She'd never even seen a human before. An idea struck her, and rather than responding, Laurel dug into a small pocket in her backpack and pulled out a small photo. It was a picture of her and David at a dance earlier that spring. David stood behind her, his arms wrapped around her. The photographer had caught Laurel just as she had turned to look at David, her profile a laughing silhouette, David looking down at her with longing in his eyes. It was one of her very favourite pictures. She handed it to Katya.

A smile streaked across Katya's face. "You're entwined already?" she squealed. "You didn't tell me," she said, her eyes wide in rapt fascination. She glanced around the room and lowered her voice. "Is he Unseelie? I've heard of them. They live just outside the gates and—"

"No," Laurel said, cutting her off. "That's David. The human I told you about."

Katya's face fell with disbelief. "A human?" she said, aghast. She looked back down at the photo, a wrinkle of distaste forming between her eyebrows. "But... he's *touching* you."

"Yes, he is," Laurel said hotly, snatching the picture back. "He's my boyfriend. He touches me and kisses me and—" She forced herself to stop talking for a few seconds. "He loves me," she said boldly but calmly.

Katya stared at her for several seconds before her face softened. "I just worry for you out there," she said, her eyes still flitting to the shocking picture. "Humans have never been kind to faeries."

"What do you mean?"

The look on Katya's face was one of genuine concern. She shrugged. "It's been a long time since Avalon involved itself in human affairs. I know it's necessary, sometimes. But it seems like relationships between humans and faeries always end badly."

Laurel's head jerked back. "Really?"

"Sure. Sanzang, Scheherazade, Guinevere. And then there was that disgraceful incident with Eve."

Katya didn't notice the photo flutter, forgotten, out of Laurel's frozen hands.

"And there are others. Every time Avalon reaches into the human world, something goes wrong. That's all I'm saying."

"My family loves me; David, too. They would never do anything to hurt me."

"Just be careful," Katya said.

Laurel packed silently for a few minutes, wrapping her hair jewels in one of her long skirts. After she scoured the room, looking for anything else she'd missed, she looked over at Katya, one eyebrow raised. "Eve? Seriously?"

"Of course. Why? What do the humans say about her?"

Laurel was waiting on a brocaded chaise when the doors of the Academy opened for Jamison and his ever-present guards. That was one reason not to wish to be a Winter faerie. Laurel certainly wouldn't want to be followed around everywhere she went. Being followed around *half* the time was more than enough.

"Laurel, my dear," Jamison said, his hands outstretched. He clasped her hands in his and smiled at her like a doting grandfather before settling down beside her on the chaise. "Yeardley tells me you were an excellent student."

Laurel smiled at the praise from the stern professor.

"He was pleased to inform me that you have great talent," Jamison continued. "*Phenomenal* was, I believe, the word he used. Though I wasn't surprised in the least," he said, turning a warm smile to her. "I sensed your incredible potential when I met you last year."

"Oh, no," Laurel said, surprised. "I'm not like that. I'm so far behind already, I'll never—"

"Oh, I think you will. You've even more potential than we suspected when you were just a seedling. With time and practice, I am sure your abilities will blossom spectacularly. You might even be as great as… well, never mind that. You just nurture your own considerable abilities. They are strong." He patted her hand. "I happen to be an excellent judge of these things."

"Are you?" Laurel said quietly, a little surprised at her own boldness. But being so woefully far behind the other faeries her age had been beyond discouraging; she longed to hear such confident proclamations.

The smile disappeared, replaced by a grave expression. "I am indeed. And you will need the skills you've learned. I suspect you will need them sooner, rather than later." He turned to Laurel, his face very serious. "I'm glad you came," he said earnestly. "The work we have for you is far more important than we ever expected. Your lessons this summer have been rigorous and taxing, but you must persevere. Practise the skills you have learned, master them. We may yet have need of you in the human world."

Laurel looked up at him. "But haven't you always intended for me to return to Avalon and resume my studies?"

"Originally, yes," Jamison said. "But things have changed. We must ask more of you. Tell me, Laurel, what do you know of erosion?"

Laurel couldn't imagine what this had to do with anything, but she answered anyway. "Like when water or wind wears away the ground?"

"That's right. Given enough time, wind and rain will carry the tallest mountain into the sea. But," he said, raising a finger, "a hillside covered in grass will resist erosion, and a riverbank may be held in place by bushes and trees. They spread their roots," he said, extending his hands with his story, "and grab hold. And though the river will pull at the soil, if the roots are strong enough, they will prevail. If they cannot, they will eventually be carried away too.

"For nearly two thousand years, we have guarded our homeland from exploitation by trolls and humans alike. Where erosion threatens our defences, we plant seeds – like yourself. When we placed you with your parents, you were only expected to do as most faeries do – to grow where you were planted. Your entire task was to live and grow and inherit the land, along with an unimpeachably human identity, which is helpful in concealing our transactions from the trolls. We didn't intend to bring you back to the Academy until you reached adulthood in the human world.

"But now your role will be more active." He placed one hand on her arm, and Laurel was filled with sudden trepidation. "Laurel, someone is moving against us, against our land and our people, and time is not on our side. We need you to stretch your roots, Laurel. We need you to fight the raging river, whatever it may prove to be. If you cannot—"

Abruptly he looked away, peering out the picture window at the countryside of Avalon spread out below them. It was a moment before he spoke again. "If you cannot, I fear that all of this will crumble into nothing."

"You're talking about the trolls," Laurel said when she found her voice. "You're talking about Barnes." She hadn't spoken his name aloud in months – there had been no sign of him since December – but he was never far from her thoughts. Ever since last fall she'd been jumping at shadows and peeking around corners.

"I would be a fool to believe that he acted alone," Jamison said. He turned back to Laurel, meeting her gaze with his pale blue eyes that matched the barely distinguishable roots in his silvery hair. "And so would you."

"Who would align with him? And why?" Laurel asked.

"We don't know," Jamison replied. "What we do know is that Barnes himself is alive and out there somewhere."

"But he can't use me any more. He can't make me sell him the land," Laurel protested.

Jamison smiled sadly. "If only it were that simple. There are still many things he can use you for. Even though he knows where the land is, he doesn't know where the gate is. He could try to use you to discover that."

"Why does he need to know? Can't he just come in with his hordes and raze the whole forest?"

"He could try, but don't underestimate the skills of our sentries, or the strength of the gate and the magic of the Winter faeries. The gate can be destroyed, but it would require a tremendous amount of concentrated force. If he cannot find exactly where the gate is, he cannot destroy it."

"I would never tell," Laurel said fervently.

"I know that. And deep down, I suspect that *he* knows that. But that will not stop him from seeking revenge on you, anyway. There are no other creatures in whom the concept of revenge is rooted so deeply as trolls. They feel the desire for vengeance more acutely than almost any other emotion. For that reason alone, he will come for you."

"Then why hasn't he?" Laurel asked. "He's had plenty of opportunities. It's been more than six months." She shrugged. "Maybe he really is dead."

But Jamison shook his head. "Have you ever observed a Venus flytrap?" he asked.

Laurel snickered inwardly, remembering her conversation with David about flytraps last year. "Yeah,"

Laurel said. "My mom had one when I was little."

"Have you ever wondered how the flytrap is able to catch the flies?" Jamison asked. "The fly is faster, can see danger approaching, has the ability to flee with the greatest of ease. Logically, every flytrap should starve to death. Why don't they?"

Laurel shrugged.

"Because they are patient," Jamison said. "They are so still and seem harmless. They do nothing until the fly has wandered, complacently, into the heart of the trap. Only when capture is virtually inevitable does the flytrap move. Trolls are patient too, Laurel. Barnes will wait; he will wait until you relax and stop being careful. Then, and only then, will he strike."

Laurel felt her throat tighten. "What can I do to stop him?" she asked.

"Practice what Yeardley has taught you," Jamison replied. "That will be your greatest defence. Be especially careful when the sun is down—"

"Barnes can go out during the day," Laurel interrupted. "We already know that."

"It is not foolproof," Jamison said, his voice betraying no annoyance at her interruption, "but it is still a fact that Barnes – any troll – will be at his weakest during the day, and *you* will be weakest when the sun has gone down.

Being careful after sundown will not stop them, but it will at least cost them their advantage." He sat a little straighter. "And it will give your guardians theirs."

"My guardians?"

"After the incident last fall, we placed sentries in the woods near your new home. Shar did not want me to tell you – he feared it would only make you skittish – but I feel you have a right to know."

"I'm being spied on again?" Laurel said, the old grudge rising up within her.

"No," Jamison said firmly. "You are simply being guarded. There will be no faeries peeking into your windows or infringing upon your private moments. But your *house* is being watched and protected. It has also been warded against trolls; as long as you are in it, only the strongest of trolls can reach you. But be aware that the woods behind your house are home to more than just trees. The sentries are there to keep you from harm."

Laurel nodded, her jaw tight. It still bothered her that she had been closely watched – and occasionally made to forget – by sentries for most of her life in the human world. Even this slightly less intrusive reinstatement of her personal guard felt instantly confining. But how could she argue? She had seen Barnes's rage firsthand, watched him shoot Tamani, then drop twelve feet from a window and run off after Laurel shot him. He was a force to be reckoned with and even though Yeardley had faith in her fledgling skills, Laurel didn't. She needed help, and there was no way to deny it.

Jamison was right, as usual. He exuded wisdom – even the wisest instructors at the Academy were pale, flickering candles next to the nourishing solar illumination of Jamison's insights. It seemed silly that he was here, comforting her in the face of fear and self-doubt, when Avalon could be benefiting more directly from his guidance.

"Why—" But Laurel cut off her own question. She'd often wondered why, with so few Winter faeries to choose from, Jamison had not been selected as the ruler of Avalon. But it was none of her business.

"Go on."

Laurel shook her head. "It's nothing."

"You want to know…" Jamison studied her face, then smiled. He looked a little surprised but not at all displeased. "You want to know why I'm not King?"

Laurel drew in a breath quickly. "How did you – ?"

"Some things in life are nothing more than chance, and this is one of them. The late Queen was a few years older than me but young enough to become the Queen at the time of succession. And by the time she passed to the earth" – he laughed—"well, I was no longer a sapling, to be bent and shaped into the role. Perhaps if there had been no other Winter faeries to take the crown... but thankfully, we have not been so desperate in many generations."

"Oh." Laurel didn't know what else to say. *I'm sorry* seemed somehow inappropriate.

"It doesn't bother me," Jamison said, again seeming to read her thoughts. "I spent more than a hundred years as an adviser to one of the greatest Queens in Avalon's considerable history." The sparkle returned to his eye. "Or, at least, that is how I feel." He sighed wearily. "This new Queen... well, with the growth that only time and experience can bring to fruition, perhaps her judgement will improve."

His criticism of the Queen, though gentle, shocked Laurel. As far as she could tell, no one ever said anything untowards about her. But it made sense that another Winter faerie would have more freedom to speak his mind. She couldn't help but wonder what, specifically, he thought the Queen was misjudging.

The thoughtful look on Jamison's face made Laurel think of Tamani's father. "Will you become a... a Silent One, Jamison?"

He looked down at her and laughed very softly.

"Now who told you about them?"

She ducked her head in slight embarrassment and said nothing. When she looked up, Jamison was not looking at her but out the eastern window, where the World Tree's gnarled branches and vast canopy could just be seen over the tops of the other, more ordinary trees, if you knew what you were looking for.

"It was Tamani, was it not?"

Laurel nodded.

"He's brooded too much since his father undertook the joining. I hope you can help him find his happiness again."

Again Laurel felt guilty and hoped Jamison didn't know how long she had stayed away when Tamani had been expecting her.

"I'd have dearly loved to follow in Tam's father's footsteps," Jamison said. "But the time has passed for me. I wouldn't have the stamina any more." He looked back down at her, his smile crowding the sadness from his face – though not entirely. "I'm needed here. Sometimes one must put aside one's own desires in order to serve the greater good. I fear Avalon is – as it has been so often in the past – balanced on a knife's edge. I—" He glanced over at the guards, but they were studiously looking away. Nonetheless, he lowered his voice. "I have been to the tree, and I have listened to the wind."

Laurel held her breath, her eyes locked with Jamison's.

"There is a task for me still. Something no one but I can... or will... do. And so I am content to stay."

Before she could question him further, Jamison stood and offered Laurel his arm. "Shall we proceed?"

They followed the familiar path out of the Academy, down to the walled square that housed the gates, and the sentries closed ranks behind them. Laurel was excited to see how Jamison would open her magical road home. She waited for him to do something amazing – a shower of sparks and flash of light or at least an ancient incantation – but all he did was reach out and pull on the gate, which glided on silent hinges. With a glance at the faeries behind him, he swung it all the way open and suddenly another group of sentries stood in a half-circle on the other side. At the centre of the arc stood Shar – grave and gorgeous – and to his right, Tamani. All were in full sentry armour; an intimidating sight, but one Laurel was getting used to.

Jamison extended his arm once more, inviting Laurel to step through the gate. At the last second he grasped her shoulder gently and leaned close to her ear. "Come back," he whispered. "Avalon needs you."

But as she glanced over her shoulder, he was closing the gate. Two more seconds and the sight of Avalon melted into shadows and was gone.

"I'll take that," Tamani said, startling Laurel. She smiled and handed Tamani the large pink bag. He glanced at it and laughed. "Females and their clothes."

Laurel grinned and turned to the gate for one last look. But it had already twisted into an average-looking tree again. She shook her head, still amazed at everything she'd seen this summer.

"As much as I wish we didn't, we do need to hurry," Tamani said. "We're expecting your mother to be here soon and it would be better if you were waiting for her." He placed a hand at her waist and Laurel sensed the other faeries melting into the forest as she and Tamani walked up the path.

Laurel felt awkward, the way she always did when it was time to say goodbye to Tamani. They walked in silence until they reached a spot just barely in sight of the cabin and the long driveway. "No one's here yet," Tamani said. "But I suspect it's only a matter of minutes."

"I—" Her voice caught, and she started over again. "I'm sorry there's not more time."

Tamani smiled softly. "I'm glad you're sorry." He leaned against a tree, lifting one leg up to brace himself against the trunk. He didn't look at her. "How long will you stay away this time?"

Guilt burned in Laurel's chest as she remembered what Jamison had said. "It's not what you think." She said. "I have to—"

"It's OK," Tamani interrupted. "I didn't mean anything by it. I simply wondered, that's all."

"Not as long as last time," she said impulsively.

"When?" Tamani said, and looked at her, his unaffected facade broken, if only for a moment.

"I don't know," Laurel said, not meeting his gaze. She couldn't look into his eyes, not when they were so open and vulnerable. "Can't I just come sometime?"

Tamani was quiet for a moment. "All right," he said. "I'll find a way to make it work. Just come," he added fervently.

"I will," she promised.

Both heads turned as they heard a motor turn off the highway and draw near.

"Your chariot," Tamani said with a grin, but his mouth was tight.

"Thank you," Laurel said. "For everything."

He shrugged, his hands jammed into his pockets. "I didn't do anything special."

"You—" She tried to find words to articulate how she felt, but nothing seemed right. "I—" This time her words were cut off by a series of short blasts on the horn. "That's my mom," she said apologetically. "I have to go."

Tamani nodded, then stood very still.

The ball was in her court.

She hesitated, then quickly stepped up to him and kissed his cheek, darting away before he could say anything. She hurried up the path and towards the car, which was now parked and silent. She stopped. It wasn't her mom's car.

"David." The name escaped her lips an instant before his arms enfolded her, pulling her to his chest. Her toes left the ground and she was spinning, the same way Tamani had spun her outside the Academy. The sensation of her cheek against his neck brought back memories of snuggling with him on the couch, in the grass at the park, in the car, on his bed. She clung to him realising – half ashamedly – that she had scarcely thought of him since she'd left. Two months of longing hit her all at once, and tears stung her eyes as her arms twined around his neck.

Gentle fingers lifted her chin and his lips found hers – soft and insistent. She couldn't do anything but kiss him back, knowing that Tamani must be just out of her sight, watching the reunion with that guarded expression he wore so well.

Chapter Nine

"Laurel?"

The tiny cylinder of sugar-glass shattered as she startled. "Up here," Laurel called wearily.

David strode through her doorway and slung an arm around her, dropping a kiss on her cheek. His eyes shot to the equipment in front of her. "What are you doing?" There was no disguising the excitement in his voice.

Letting the tiny shards of glass tinkle out of her hand and on to the table, Laurel sighed. "*Attempting* to make sugar-glass vials."

"Are they seriously made out of sugar?"

Laurel nodded as she rubbed her temples. "You can eat those pieces there, if you want," she said, not really expecting him to do it.

David looked dubiously at the pile of glass splinters, then picked up one of the larger pieces. He studied it for a moment before licking the flat side – far away from the sharp, pointed end. "Kind of like rock candy," he said, putting the piece back on the table. "Weird."

"Frustrating is more like it."

"What are they for?"

Laurel turned to her kit and removed a glass vial – one Yeardley had made, not her. She hadn't managed a decent one yet. She handed the vial to David. "Some potions or elixirs or whatever can't be stored in their final form. So you make them in two parts. As soon as they mix, whatever effect you're going for happens right away. So you store the different parts in sugar vials so you can mix them at the right time, or crush them in your hand in an emergency."

"Sounds painful," David said, handing the delicate vial back to Laurel with care.

Laurel shook her head. "It's usually not thick enough to cut you. But even if it does, the sugar would dissolve and you wouldn't have to pick bits of glass out of your hand or anything – that's why you don't use regular glass. Ideally you just dump them both into a mortar, or whatever, but you have to be prepared for anything." I *have to be prepared for anything*, she added to herself.

"Don't the potions dissolve the sugar?"

"They don't seem to."

"Why not?"

"I don't know, David," Laurel said tersely. "They just don't."

"Sorry," David said softly. He pulled a pink, padded stool over and joined her at her desk. "So how do you do it?"

Laurel took a deep breath and got ready to try again. "I have this powdered sugarcane," she said, pointing to a cloth bag of fine greenish powder, "and I mix it with pine resin." As she talked she followed her own directions, trying to concentrate despite David's breath near her ear, his eyes studying her hands. She could almost hear his mind whirring as he tried to take it all in. "It gets all thick and sticky like syrup," she said, stirring the mixture with a silver spoon, "and it heats up."

David nodded and continued watching.

"Then I get this little straw," she said, picking up what looked like a short drinking straw made of glass. She didn't tell David it was one solid piece of diamond. "I dip it in the sugar mix and blow it, just like regular glass." It sounded easy, and most of the Mixers her age had been making their own vials for years. But Laurel hadn't quite gotten the knack.

She breathed in, sucking just a tiny bit of the sugar mixture into the tube, and then blew out, very slowly, while picturing – concentrating on – what she wanted it to look like. She turned the tube as she blew, and the small bubble on the end elongated, stretching out – contrary to all laws of physics – not into a round bubble, but a long cylinder. The opaque, muddy mixture whitened, then grew translucent.

Laurel gave the tube a little more air and turned it once more before hesitantly pulling her mouth away. She usually did well up to this point.

"That's—"

"Shh," Laurel ordered, lifting a small silver knife that resembled a scalpel. She scored the sugar-glass all around the edge of the diamond tube, then pulled on the cylinder, slowly separating it from the straw.

The first side came easily and Laurel painstakingly rolled the cylinder in a circle, detaching the other edges. She held her breath as she pulled the tube away from the final point of connection. The still-flexible sugar bent, then stretched into a long string and, finally, broke away.

As it did, the cylinder shattered.

"Damn it!" Laurel yelled, slamming the tube down on her desk.

"Careful with that thing," David said.

Laurel brushed his concern away with an annoyed wave of her hand. "Can't break that," she muttered.

A long silence followed as Laurel studied the pile of glass shards, trying to decide what she had done wrong. Maybe if she sucked up a little more of the sugar syrup, it would make the vial thicker.

"Can… can I try it?" David asked hesitantly.

"If you must," Laurel said, although she knew it wouldn't work.

But David grinned and scooted over to the chair she had just vacated. She watched as he tried to imitate what she had done, sucking a small amount of the sticky syrup into the straw and then blowing carefully. For a second it looked like it would work. A tiny bubble began to form, although it was round, rather than oblong. But almost as soon as it had formed, the bubble popped with a faint *blurp* and the liquid ran uselessly out of the diamond tube.

"What did I do wrong?" David asked.

"Nothing," Laurel said. "You just can't do it."

"I don't see why not," David said, looking at the greenish blob hanging off the end of the tube. "It doesn't make sense that we should do this exact same thing with such drastically different results. At the very least they should be similar."

"This isn't physics, David; it's not science. It works for me because I'm a Fall faerie, and that's the end of the explanation. Well," she said, taking the tube from David, "it *almost* works."

"But, why?"

"I don't know!" Laurel said in exasperation.

"Well, do you blow it in a certain way? Is there a technique I can't see?" David asked, not catching her tone at all.

"No. What you see is what I'm doing. No secret method or whatever."

"Then what am I doing wrong?"

"What are *you* doing wrong?" Laurel laughed cynically. "David, I don't even know what *I'm* doing wrong!" She slumped down on her bed. "In Avalon, I spent an hour every day for the last three weeks practising blowing glass vials. And I haven't managed to make a single one without breaking it. Not a single one!"

David joined her on the bed. "An hour every day?"

Laurel knew he was wondering if practice would help him blow vials too, but at least he didn't say it. "My instructors keep telling me that if I've studied the components and the procedures, my intuition should do the rest, but that hasn't worked yet."

"So you're just supposed to *know* what to do?"

"That's what they keep saying."

"Like… instinct?"

At that Laurel flopped down on her back, a frustrated breath whooshing out of her. "Oh man, instinct, that's like the F-word in Avalon. Yeardley kept telling me, 'You are trying to rely on instinct, you need to trust your intuition instead.' But I looked up those two words and they mean the exact same thing."

David lay down beside her and she rolled over, snuggling into the crook of his arm, her hand draped across his chest. How had she lived without this for eight weeks? "It's just so frustrating. Everyone my age in Avalon is so far ahead of me. And they're just getting farther ahead. Right this minute!" She sighed. "I'm never going to catch up."

"Sure you will," David said softly, his lips tickling her neck. "You'll figure things out."

"No, I won't," Laurel said sullenly.

"Yes, you will," David repeated, his nose touching hers. His arms tightened around her waist and Laurel couldn't help but smile.

"Thanks," she said.

She closed her eyes, waiting for his kiss, but a rap on the doorway made her head jerk up.

"Can you at least not make out on your bed while I'm

148

home?" Laurel's mom said dryly. "You know, *pretend* you're following the rules."

David had already shot to his feet and stepped about three feet from the bed.

Laurel dragged herself up slowly. "I did leave the door open," she said.

"Oh, good," her mom responded. "Can't wait to see what's going on next time I walk by. I'm heading to the store," she continued before Laurel could respond. "I want both of you to come downstairs, please."

Laurel watched her mom walk away, wearing a nice skirt and blouse, with a very businessy-looking bag on her shoulder. Just one of the many changes that had greeted Laurel on her return from Avalon.

The first one had been awesome. David had driven Laurel back from the land yesterday and pulled into her driveway beside a black Nissan Sentra, complete with a red bow. "I figure, since you're responsible for our current financial situation, you should reap some benefit from it," her dad had said with a laugh as Laurel squealed and hugged him. The diamond Jamison had given Laurel last year to prevent her parents from selling their land had covered more than just her dad's medical bills. But Laurel had not anticipated such a personal perk.

The second big change was one she knew about. Her

parents had decided to renovate their very small house by adding on a rec room – with lots of big windows for Laurel – and enlarging the kitchen. Laurel being away for the summer had struck them as the perfect opportunity. The work was supposed to be done by the time she got back, but the first thing Laurel did after walking in the door yesterday was trip over a bunch of tools. The contractors promised to be out by the end of the week, but Laurel had her doubts.

The most drastic change, though, came as an even bigger surprise than her car. In the spring, Laurel's dad had acquired some shop space next to his bookstore, intending to expand his store. But shortly after Laurel left for Avalon her parents decided to open a new store, instead – a naturopathy store for her mom. Nature's Cure – which had opened just before Laurel got home – sold homemade remedies and a wide array of vitamins, herbs, and natural foods, as well as a nice selection of health and wellness books provided by the lovely bookstore next door. With all the time they both spent at their stores, her parents actually saw each other more now than ever before in their marriage.

This is great! Laurel told herself. After all, her mom should have something like this that was all her own. But in Laurel's absence her mom had grown... distant.

Her dad couldn't seem to hear enough about Avalon, but during those discussions her mom would suddenly remember something she needed to do in another room. Laurel felt like the new store presented an additional avenue of escape; in the twenty-four hours Laurel had been home, she'd only seen her mom for a short dinner and once or twice as she rushed in and out on errands.

She sighed and stood from the bed, pulling on David's arms to help him up. "Come on, let's go downstairs."

"Yeah, but…" David gestured at the glass-making supplies on Laurel's desk.

"I'm done for today," Laurel said. "Let's go do something fun. We've only got a few days before school starts again." Laurel pulled him towards the door. "My mom made cinnamon rolls this morning," she added, trying to give him incentive.

He let Laurel drag him away this time, but not before giving the desk a long look.

In the kitchen David pulled a cinnamon roll from the pan and slathered it with cream cheese frosting. As he bit into it, he turned towards the large kitchen window – a new addition Laurel was quite fond of.

"I haven't seen Chelsea yet. Should we call her and see if she wants to watch a movie or something tonight?"

Laurel secured the plastic wrap back over the bowl of frosting. The smell always made her a touch nauseated.

"Sure, if she's not hanging out with Ryan."

"Ryan?" Laurel asked, stowing the frosting in the fridge. "Tall Ryan?"

"Yep."

"Are they, like, together?"

"Chelsea's been a bit closed-mouthed about it – if you can imagine – but if they're not together now, they will be soon. Maybe you can worm something out of her."

"Maybe. That's weird." Not that Chelsea would have a boyfriend – Laurel was way excited about that – but that she would choose Ryan. Tall, gangly Ryan, who didn't talk a lot and was particularly unobservant. Laurel was all for the idea that opposites attract, but maybe there was such a thing as *too* opposite.

And then, of course, there was the issue that Chelsea had been enamoured with David for the last several years. But if she was over him now then, hey, all the better.

They were silent for several minutes, David finishing off his cinnamon roll and Laurel staring out the picture window, thinking about Chelsea. Finally David swallowed his last bite and took a deep breath. "I thought I saw Barnes yesterday, just before coming to pick you up."

An icy shudder of fear clutched at Laurel's chest. "You *thought?*"

"Yeah, wasn't him. It was just that guy who runs the bowling alley."

"Oh, I took a double take at him a few months ago too." Her laughter was tense, and it died away completely when she saw David's face.

"Why hasn't he come back, Laurel?" he asked quietly.

Laurel shook her head as she looked out the picture window at the woods behind her house. She wondered just how many faeries were living there, watching her right at this moment. Maybe now was the time to talk to David about her conversation with Jamison. "I don't know," she said, putting it off a little longer.

"We ruined his plans. Big, big plans. And he knows where you live."

"Thanks for reminding me," Laurel said wryly.

"Sorry, I'm not trying to scare you. But I feel like… I don't know, like a string getting stretched tighter every day. I keep waiting for *something* to happen. And it's just getting worse," he continued. "I see trolls everywhere. Every time I see an unfamiliar face in sunglasses, I wonder. As big as our tourist season was this summer, you can imagine it was a paranoid couple of months. And with you gone…" He took her wrist and pulled her to him, kissing the top of her blond head. "I'm just glad you're back."

"Good." She wrapped her arms around David's waist and pushed up on to her tiptoes for a kiss. It was quite a stretch these days – he was almost a foot taller than her now. He'd grown three inches the last six months and had started lifting weights, too. He hadn't said as much, but Laurel suspected his confidence had taken a beating from their encounter with Barnes. Whatever his motivation, she couldn't help but appreciate the results. She liked his stature; it made her feel safe and protected.

If she could only get the hang of the things she'd learned at Avalon, maybe she'd feel even safer.

Chelsea squealed and threw her arms around Laurel, who laughed into her hair, realising just how much she had missed her friend.

"I was going to come over yesterday," Chelsea said, "but I promised myself I'd give you a day with David first. He's been miserable without you."

Laurel grinned. She rather approved of that.

"He hung out with me almost every day and talked about you nonstop for the first month, but then I started hanging out with Ryan, and David got all weird, so I haven't seen him as much the last couple of weeks. Come upstairs," Chelsea said as a tangle of limbs crashed into the entryway where they had been standing. "The last week before school is always the worst," she said, pointing to her brothers wrestling on the floor.

Laurel couldn't tell for sure whether it was a real fight or just a fun one. In either case, it was probably safest to get out of the way. She followed the still chattering Chelsea upstairs to her faerie-bedecked bedroom. It always made Laurel a little uneasy to be in there, with traditional butterfly-winged faeries staring out at her from the walls, the ceiling, and the spines of Chelsea's impressive collection of faerie books.

"So, you don't look very tan," Chelsea said, pausing for a response.

"Uh," Laurel said, totally off guard. "What?"

"Tan," Chelsea repeated. "You don't look very tan. After almost two months at a wilderness retreat I figured you would have gotten pretty tan."

Laurel had almost forgotten the cover story David had invented – that she'd been on a wilderness retreat. A retreat that, conveniently, had no phone or internet access. Laurel felt awful lying to Chelsea, but Chelsea was just too forthright for keeping secrets. Ironically, it was one of her best characteristics. "Um, sunscreen," Laurel said elusively. "Lots and lots of sunscreen."

"And hats, apparently," Chelsea said dryly.

"Yeah. So tell me about you and Ryan," she said, anxious to change the subject.

Chelsea suddenly found something very interesting to study on the carpet.

Laurel laughed. "Chelsea, are you blushing?"

Chelsea laughed nervously and shrugged.

"You like him?" Laurel prodded.

"I do. I never thought I would, but I *do*."

"That's awesome," Laurel said sincerely. "So… are you guys officially together yet?"

"How do you get 'officially together'?" Chelsea asked. "Do you have to have some kind of special conversation where you say, 'Oh, gee, I like you and you like me, and we like to make out, so now let's be official'? How does that work?"

Laurel's eyes widened. "You make out with Ryan?"

"I think so."

"Either you do, or you don't," Laurel said with an eyebrow raised.

"Well, we kiss a lot. Does that count?"

"Not only does that count, I think that makes you officially together."

"Oh, good," Chelsea said with a sigh of relief. "I was all

stressed out because we hadn't had any special talk or anything."

"Kissing is better than talking," Laurel said with a grin. "So how did this happen?"

Chelsea shrugged. "It just did. Well, kind of. I mean, you know I liked David hardcore for forever."

Laurel nodded but thought it best not to actually say anything.

"It got to the point where he was all I could see. Ever. And I hated that you were with him, but I loved that you were both happy, and it was awful being so torn."

Laurel scooted a little closer and laid a hand on Chelsea's arm. It was a subject they'd never broached before, despite Laurel knowing it must have been difficult for her. Chelsea smiled and shrugged. "So I decided I needed to just stop. Stop everything David. Stop thinking about him, stop watching him, stop even liking him."

"How did you do that?" Laurel asked, thinking instantly of her issues with Tamani.

"I don't know, really. I just did. It was weird. I've spent years trying so hard to get David's attention, to *make* him like me. And it was like I couldn't see anything else. And then I didn't so much make myself stop focusing on David, as I *let* myself focus on other people. And it was really cool." Her eyes widened dramatically. "There are guys everywhere; did you know that?"

Laurel laughed. "I'm afraid I'm still pretty focused on David."

"You should be," Chelsea said seriously. "So, anyway, Ryan and I started hanging out more and then he asked me to a movie and then to lunch and soon we were hanging out all the time."

"And kissing."

"And kissing," Chelsea agreed enthusiastically. "Ryan is a great kisser."

Laurel rolled her eyes. "Now *there's* something I really wanted to know," she said sarcastically.

"Ah, come on – everyone wonders."

"Do not!"

"Sure. I've always wondered what kind of a kisser David is."

"Um, that's one of those questions you're not supposed to ask."

Chelsea laughed. "I didn't ask. I just said I've always wondered."

"That's asking."

"Is not." She leaned back against her headboard. "'Course, you could tell me anyway."

"Chelsea!"

"What? I told *you*."

"I didn't ask."

"Technicality."

"I'm not telling."

"That's code for *he sucks*."

"He does not suck."

"Aha!"

Laurel sighed. "You are so weird."

"Yeah," Chelsea said with a grin, tossing her springy curls. "But you love me."

Laurel laughed. "Yes, I do." She leaned over and tipped her head on to Chelsea's shoulder. "And I'm glad you're happy."

"I'd be happier if you told me what David's like in bed."

Laurel looked incredulously at Chelsea, then hit her with a pillow.

Chapter Ten

Laurel sat cross-legged in her room, sorting through school supplies and packing her backpack. David, who had been ready to go back to school for a week now – probably a month, Laurel just didn't have proof – was sprawled out on her bed, watching her. She pulled a four-pack of multicoloured highlighters out of her shopping bag and took a moment to hug them to her chest. "Oh, highlighters," she crooned melodramatically, "how I missed you!"

David laughed. "You can take them with you next year."

"Wow. Next year. At the moment I can't even imagine working that hard again." She looked up at him. "Wasn't this supposed to be summer *vacation*?"

David reached down and wrapped his arms around

her chest, lifting her up on to the bed beside him as she laughed. "Didn't feel like much of a vacation for me, either, with you gone the whole time," he said, leaning back against her pillows.

Laurel curled up against his chest. "And now it's over," she lamented.

"Day's not finished yet," David whispered, his breath tickling her ear.

"Well," Laurel said, holding her face straight, "my parents do tell me to make the most of every day."

"I'm quite in agreement with that," David said mockingly, but with a hint of growl in his voice. His fingertips pressed against her back as he softly kissed her shoulder, bare beneath the strap of her tank top. Laurel's arms twined around his neck and she ran her fingers through his hair. Silky curls would catch just a little on her fingertips, then slide through as she pulled a bit harder.

David's breath sounded in the back of his throat as his lips found hers and Laurel let herself slip into the pleasant satisfaction she always felt in David's arms. She smiled as he pulled back and rested his forehead against hers. "How did I ever get so lucky?" he asked quietly, his hand resting along her ribs.

"Luck had nothing to do with it," Laurel replied,

leaning closer and kissing him gently. Once, twice, and the third time she pulled him in harder, enjoying the feel of his mouth against hers. Her hand wandered under his shirt, feeling his rapid breath expand his ribs. She hesitated for a second – wondering what the chances were that either of her parents would come home early – then lifted his shirt with both hands, guiding it up his arms and over his head. It was her favourite indulgence; holding herself against his bare chest. He was always so warm – even in the summer, when her body temperature was almost as high as his. She loved to feel the heat spread into her from everywhere that touched him, slowly seeping through her until her whole body was pleasantly warmed, her foot lazily looped over his leg.

Her eyes were closed, waiting for his next kiss, and after a few seconds, she opened them. David was staring down at her, a half-smile on his face, but his eyes were serious. "I love you," he said.

She smiled, loving hearing those words. Every time he said it, it sounded like the first time.

"Hey, Miss Fae."

Laurel grinned as she walked down the stairs. Her dad had started calling her that after he had come home from the hospital. They'd always been close, but after almost losing him last year, it felt like every minute counted double. And even though his insatiable curiosity about all things faerie drove her up the wall sometimes, she loved how easily he accepted her for what she was.

"How was the first day of school?"

Laurel wandered over to the couch by way of the fridge, where she grabbed herself a Sprite. "It was OK. Better than last year. And I think I'm more prepared for chemistry than I was for biology."

"Sounds like an overall improvement," he said, looking up from his book.

"What are you reading?" she asked, glancing at the dog-eared paperback.

He looked a little chagrined. *"Stardust."*

"Again?"

He shrugged. Fantasy novels – especially ones involving faeries – had risen to the top of her dad's reading list, with Neil Gaiman's faerie tale numbering among his very favourites.

"Where's Mom?" Laurel asked, though she could guess at the answer.

"Taking inventory," came the expected reply. "She's got to get her order in tomorrow."

"I figured," Laurel said.

Her dad looked up into her sombre face and put his book down. "You OK?"

She shrugged. Her dad sat up a little and patted the spot beside him. Laurel sighed and joined him on the couch, leaning her head against his shoulder.

"What's the matter?"

"I don't know. It's just… it's kind of weird to suddenly have you around more than Mom. She's at the store all the time."

His arm tightened around her. "She's just busy right now. Starting up a store takes a lot of work. You remember last summer when I was getting the bookstore going. I was *never* home." He chuckled. "In fact, if I had been home more, I like to think I would have figured things out." He paused and squeezed Laurel's shoulders again. "You have to understand, when I… got sick, your mom felt completely helpless. We had almost no insurance, the hospital bills were piling up, and if anything had happened she would have had no way to support you. She's never quite gotten the knack of running my store. She might have been able to make ends meet, but only just. She's afraid to ever get into that position again, and let's face it – we're not young." He turned to face her. "She's doing this for you. So she can support you if anything ever happened again."

Laurel rubbed her toe along the couch cushion. "But sometimes I think…" She paused, then hurried on in a rush of breath before she could change her mind. "She hates that I'm a faerie."

Her dad scooted up a little. "What do you mean?"

After the first sentence, the rest tumbled out. "Everything started to change when she found out. She acts like she doesn't know me any more – like I'm a stranger living in her house. We don't talk. We used to talk all the time, about everything. And now I feel like she avoids my eyes and leaves the room when I come in."

"Sweetie, you need to give her a little time to get the store open. I really think—"

"It was before the store," Laurel interrupted, shaking her head. "She doesn't like to hear anything about me not being normal. When I got the invitation to go to Avalon I was so excited – the chance of a lifetime. And she almost didn't let me go!"

"In all fairness, that was because of the 'gone for two months with complete strangers' thing, not necessarily the faerie thing."

"Still," Laurel persisted. "I hoped that maybe things would change while I was gone. That maybe it would be easier to get used to the idea when I wasn't around, always putting it in front of her face. But nothing's changed," she said in a quiet voice. "If anything, it's gotten worse."

Her dad thought for a moment. "I don't know why she's having such a hard time dealing with this, Laurel," he said haltingly. "She just doesn't understand. This has knocked her whole worldview off-kilter. It may take some time. I'm just asking you to be patient."

Laurel took a long, shuddering breath. "She barely even hugged me when I got back. I'm trying to be patient, but it's like she doesn't even like me any more."

"No, Laurel," her dad said, holding her to his chest as she blinked back tears. "It's not like that, I promise. It's not about you; it's about her trying to wrap her mind around the idea that faeries exist at all." He looked Laurel full in the face. "But she loves you," he said firmly. "She loves you every bit as much as she ever did. I promise." He leaned his cheek against the top of her head. "Would you like me to talk to her?"

Laurel shook her head instantly. "No, please don't. She doesn't need more stuff to worry about." She forced a smile. "I'll just give her some time – be patient, like you said. Things will go back to normal soon, right?"

"Absolutely," he said with a grin and an enthusiasm Laurel couldn't match.

When Laurel stood and wandered back towards the

kitchen, her dad picked up his book again. She knelt by the side of the fridge and began loading more cans of Sprite into the refrigerator door. "Normal," she scoffed under her breath. "Right."

She looked up at the leftovers packed away in tidy Tupperwares in the fridge. "Hey, Dad, have you had dinner yet?" she asked.

"Um… no?" he said sheepishly. "I meant to just read the first chapter, but I got carried away."

"Big surprise," Laurel drawled. "Can I make you something?"

"You don't need to do that," her dad said, standing up from the couch and stretching. "I can nuke my own leftovers."

"No, I want to," Laurel said. "I do."

Her dad looked at her strangely.

"Just sit. I gotta run up to my room. I'll be down in a sec."

As she headed for the stairs, her dad shrugged and slipped into his chair at the kitchen table, opening his book up again.

Laurel grabbed her kit, forcing herself not to look at the latest batch of shattered sugar-glass vials strewn across her desk, and hurried back downstairs. There was a Tupperware of stir-fry and noodles, one of her dad's favourites. That would work. She opened her kit up beside the stove, dumped the stir-fry into a small saucepan, and lit a burner.

Laurel's dad looked up as the pan clanked on to the stove. "You don't need to do that," he said. "The microwave works just fine."

"Yeah, but I wanted to do something special."

Her dad raised an eyebrow. "Special like how?"

"You'll see," Laurel said, waving her fingers in the steam rising from the pan as the sauce started to bubble.

She didn't want to change the flavour – this wasn't like just adding spices. She wanted to enhance the flavour that was already there. Her teachers in Avalon had told her repeatedly that if she was familiar with the plant, and trusted her intuition, she could do almost anything. This should be easy. Right?

She relaxed and closed her eyes – glad that the stove wasn't facing the kitchen table – and soon the parts of the food seemed to come alive on her fingers, bathed in the vapour. She cocked her head to the side, feeling the garlic and soy, the ginger and pepper.

Crocus, she said to herself. *Crocus oil and a touch of sage. That will bring out the garlic and ginger.* She concentrated, feeling like there was one more thing she should add to make it perfect. *Stonewort*, she finally decided. Probably because it had high levels of starch that would emphasise the soy. And, well, pepper was pepper. It would be strong enough on its own.

She reached into her kit for a small mortar. She put in a few drops of crocus oil and a pinch of sage. The stonewort, however, came in a very small bottle with a tiny sprayer on it that would dispense less than a drop. Laurel sprayed a mist of stonewort into the stone bowl, considered, then sprayed once more. Using her pestle, she crushed the tiny sage seeds, mixing the three essences until the smell changed just a little. She turned the bowl over and let a couple of green speckled drops fall on to the bubbling noodles. A foamy vapour rose up, clearing as Laurel stirred the food, the extra drops blending into the brown sauce.

"Bon appétit," Laurel said, placing the meal in front of her dad with a flourish.

He looked up from his book a little startled. "Oh. Thanks."

Laurel smiled, then went back around to the stove to begin cleaning up. She kept sneaking glances at him, wondering if he would notice without her saying anything.

She didn't have to wait very long.

"Wow, Laurel, this is good!" her dad said. "I guess

stovetop really is better than microwave." He ate with vigour and Laurel smiled, irrationally proud that something had actually worked after messing up on so many things the last few weeks.

"Did you add something to this?" her dad asked after wolfing down about half the plate. "Because teriyaki has never tasted so good." He paused and put another forkful in his mouth. "And I had it two days ago when it was fresh," he said around the noodles.

Laurel turned with a conspiratorial smile on her face. "I may have added a little *something* to it," she said.

"Well, you gotta tell your mom because this is the most amazing stir-fry I have ever had."

Laurel grinned as she turned and put the pan and Tupperware in the sink and started running some warm water. She put her rubber gloves on, then began cleaning the two dishes. "See, this is what I wish Mom would understand," Laurel said, her voice just audible above the running water. "The things I can do, they aren't just for faeries, I can do stuff for you guys too. Make your food taste better, for example, in ways no one else can. And I make great vitamins. My version of vitamin C is awesome." She shut off the water after rinsing the few dishes. "Or it will be, once I get it right. I just wish Mom could see that I'm no different from how I was before. I didn't become a faerie, I've always been a faerie. I'm still the same person. I mean, *you* realise that," she said, turning around. "Is it—" Her mouth fell open.

Her dad was asleep – snoring softly – with his cheek sitting in the last few bites of stir-fry.

"Dad?" Laurel walked over and touched his shoulder. When he didn't respond she shook him, lightly at first, and then harder. *What did I do!* She was halfway up the stairs after the small blue bottle of healing tonic when she remembered *all* the uses of stonewort. She slumped down on the stairs and recalled the passage from her textbook. *Should you ever need it, a sprinkle of stonewort will put any animal into a deep sleep. Not instantaneous but perfect for escapes when you have ample time.* Until now, Laurel hadn't applied any of the things she'd learned about plant uses for animals to her parents. But technically, that's what they were.

Slowly, Laurel stood and returned to the kitchen. Her father was snoring louder now. Grabbing a washcloth, she carefully lifted his head and cleaned the sticky sauce from his cheek. Then she slid *Stardust* under his hands and laid his head back down on to his arms. It certainly wouldn't be the first time he'd fallen asleep reading. At the kitchen table was a new one, but she suspected no one would ask questions. He had been working hard lately.

She took the plate to the kitchen and scraped the remaining stir-fry into the trash. She'd have to wash the plate too. Couldn't have her mom finding out just how badly she'd screwed up while trying to show off. After stowing the plate in the cabinet, Laurel took one more look at her father, snoring away at the table. She hoped he would wake up in the morning. She had no idea what she would do if he didn't.

"I am the lamest faerie *ever*."

Chapter Eleven

A week into school, Laurel walked towards Mark's Bookshelf with David, her hand in his, their arms swinging in the last warm gasps of summer. With a kiss he peeled off to head to his job at the pharmacy and Laurel opened the door to the bookstore, a cheery chime sounding as she did.

Maddie looked up at her with a broad smile. "Laurel," she said brightly, the way she did every time she saw her. It was a constant in her life that Laurel loved. No matter what was happening with her parents, or trolls, or Avalon, or whatever, Maddie was always behind the counter at the bookstore, ready with a smile and a hug.

Laurel laughed as Maddie squeezed her tightly. "Where's my dad?" she asked, looking around.

"In the back," Maddie said. "Inventory."

"As usual," Laurel said, heading towards the swinging doors at the back of the store.

"Hey, Dad," she said with a smile as he looked up at her. Even though she doubted it was necessary, she'd been watching him closely. He hadn't come out of his stonewort-induced nap until eight o'clock the following morning. Aside from a sore neck, he seemed unaffected. Her mom had chastised him for both working too hard and staying up too late, but luckily she hadn't seemed suspicious beyond that. Still, Laurel had stayed out of her parents' food since then. Better safe than sorry.

She slid on to a chair across from the computer and fingered a small stack of bookmarks.

"How was school?" her dad asked.

"Fine," Laurel said with a grin. "Easy." After Avalon, everything seemed easy. Seven hours of school a day? No problem. An hour or two of study each night? Piece of cake. Her trip to Avalon had improved Laurel's entire attitude towards human schooling. If only they had more skylights.

"Do you need any help today?" Laurel asked, looking around at the back room.

"Not really," her dad said, standing straight and stretching his back. "Actually, I've been catching up on my paperwork, it's been so slow." He looked out the small window behind his desk. "Gorgeous day. Apparently people would rather be outside enjoying the weather instead of finding something to read at the stuffy old bookstore."

"Your store's not stuffy," Laurel said with a laugh. She paused for a moment. "Do you think maybe Mom needs some help?" she asked without meeting his eyes.

He looked up at her for a second, then asked casually, "Do you need money?"

Laurel shook her head. "No, I thought... I thought maybe... it could help make things better between us, less tense. Maybe we've both been waiting for the other to make the first move," she said, her voice low.

He dad paused, his fingers poised above the keyboard. Then he took off his glasses, walked around the desk, and hugged her. "Way to be proactive," he said in her ear. "I'm proud of you."

"Thanks." Laurel shouldered her backpack and turned to wave just before heading towards the front of the store. She took a deep breath, forced herself not to hesitate any longer, and walked next door to Nature's Cure. In the weeks since Laurel returned from Avalon she'd only been in her mom's store a few times, and the attention to detail never failed to impress her. She pushed the front door open and instead of a mechanical chime, the corner of the door hit a small silver bell that tinkled softly. Potted plants filled the windowsills, and a serenity fountain gurgled in the corner where it sat in a small Zen garden. There were even sparkly crystal prisms strung up in the window. Laurel took a moment to touch one, pleased that her mother had taken a decoration idea from Laurel's room to use at her store. Despite the current tension with her mom, Laurel suspected she would enjoy working here even more than at the bookstore – which was saying something.

Laurel turned as her mom came through a bead curtain from the back room, lugging a large box. Her face was a little red and she was breathless. "Oh, Laurel, it's you. Good. I can put this down for a second." She plopped the large box down in the middle of the floor and wiped her brow. "You'd think they would send this stuff in smaller boxes. So what did you need?" her mom asked, bending over and sliding the box across the floor instead of lifting it.

"I just came to see if you needed help. Things are slow next door," she added, and then wished she hadn't. She didn't want her mom to feel like her second choice.

"Oh," her mom said, smiling in a way that at least *looked* genuine. "That would be perfect. I'm stocking today and I can always use an extra hand." She laughed. "Your dad gets employees; I'm not to that point yet."

"Great," Laurel said, shedding her backpack and coming to stand by the new shipment. Her mom explained the contents of the box – most of which Laurel was familiar with from years of living with a naturopath – and then showed her the system of tags on the shelves that she could match with the bottles and boxes.

"I'm going to go fill out the invoice and start preparing my order for next week, but you just holler if you need any help, OK?"

"I will," Laurel said, and smiled. Her mom smiled back. So far, so good.

Laurel was surprised by how many of the elements in the herbal remedies she could remember from her summer of intense study. The note cards *were* worth it. As Laurel pulled the different items out of boxes and placed them on their appropriate shelves she recited their uses in her head. *Comfrey, use as an oil to calm inflammation, reduce the life span of weeds, and for the eyes when sight is failing. Winter savory, for clarity of mind and sleeplessness. Also good for koi, if you add it to their water. Promotes oxygenation. Raspberry leaf tea, for seedlings who refuse to eat. Add plenty of sugar to increase the nutritional value. Energising when you have to be up late at night.*

She particularly liked sorting the homeopathics, which were completely safe for faerie consumption since they were generally preserved in sugar, but almost always did the opposite thing for humans as for faeries. St Ignatius Bean, for example, could be used as a remedy against grief for humans. For faeries, it was used as a sedative. And white bryony would reduce fevers in humans, but for faeries it was extremely effective in staving off freezing. Tamani had told her that the sentries who guarded the gate in Japan drank a cold tea made from white bryony every day during the winter months, when it could get very cold in the high mountains.

Thinking of Tamani distracted Laurel for a while and her hand was still – clutched around a cylinder of Natrum muriaticum – for almost a minute before her mom walked over and pulled her from her thoughts.

"Everything OK, Laurel?"

"What? Oh, yeah," she mumbled, looking up at her mom before bending back down to grab more cylinders from a small box. "Just lost in thought."

"OK," her mom said, looking at her a little funny. She turned, then stopped for a second. "Thanks for coming in to help out," she said. "I appreciate it." She put one arm around Laurel and hugged her sideways. It was an awkward hug, the kind you give someone when you'd rather just shake their hand. An obligatory kind of hug.

The phone rang, and with a hollow longing in her chest Laurel watched her mom walk back up to the register. It was strange to miss someone who was standing right in front of her, but that was how Laurel felt. She missed her mom.

"Excuse me," said a voice just behind her.

Laurel turned to see an older woman she vaguely recognised from town. "Yes?"

"Could you help me?"

Laurel looked up towards her mom, who was still on the phone. She turned back to the woman. "I can sure try," she said with a smile.

"I need something for my headaches. I've been taking Advil, but it's not helping as much any more. I think my body's getting used to it."

"That happens," Laurel said, nodding sympathetically.

"I want something a little more natural. But effective, too," she added.

Laurel was trying to remember what it was she had put on the shelves just a few minutes earlier. She had held the small bottle for several seconds, wondering if she should get some for herself – with the stress of the last few months, Laurel had more than a few headaches of her own. She moved an aisle over and found the bottle. "Here," she said, handing it to the woman. "It is a little pricey" – she pointed to the price tag—"but it will be so worth it. I'm considering getting some for myself. It will be much better than Advil."

The woman smiled. "Thanks. It's certainly worth a try."

She carried the bottle up to the register as Laurel went back to sorting homeopathics. After a minute Laurel's mom led the woman over to Laurel's display and, after a pointed look at Laurel, grabbed one of the green cylinders. "This will work much better," she said. "It's cyclamen, and I've given it to my husband for years for his migraines. Works like a dream." As they were walking back up to the register Laurel's mom explained how to use the homeopathic pilules and soon the woman was on her way.

Her mom stood by the door for a few seconds to wave at the woman, then walked towards Laurel. "Laurel," she started, and Laurel could hear the frustration she was holding carefully in check, "if you don't know what to recommend, come get me. Don't just pull random bottles off the shelf. I wish you had waited for me to finish my phone call. These people are looking for help, and all of these herbs work very differently."

Laurel felt like a little child being scolded by an adult who was being very careful not to hurt her feelings. "I didn't just pull a random bottle," Laurel protested. "That stuff's really good for headaches. I picked it on purpose."

"Really?" her mom said dryly. "Somehow I don't think it's *that* kind of headache."

"What?"

"Pausinystalia yohimbe? Do you even know what Pausinystalia yohimbe is marketed for? It's a male-enhancement herb."

"Eww, gross!" Laurel said, repulsed now by her thought that she should get a bottle for herself. She knew most herbs affected faeries differently, but that was just wrong!

"Exactly. I only carry it because there's a guy who came in last week and asked if I could special-order it. There's something I didn't need to know about my sixty-year-old banker," she added.

"I'm sorry," Laurel said genuinely. "I didn't know."

"I don't expect you to. But that's what I'm here for. I'm really glad you came in to help, but handing out sex pills for headaches isn't helping. You need to ask for advice when you need it, Laurel. You could potentially kill someone by giving them the wrong herbs, depending on their health conditions. Please think about that next time."

"I did think," Laurel retorted, suddenly angry at her

mom's attitude. "It would have helped *me*!" she added impulsively.

Laurel's mom sighed heavily and turned away.

"I got mixed up," Laurel said, following behind her. "I forget that herbs don't work the same for humans as for fae. I just made a little mistake."

"Laurel, not now, please." She walked around to the other side of the counter.

"Why not now?" Laurel said, slapping her hands down on the counter. "When? At home? Because you don't ever want to talk about me being a faerie there, either."

"Laurel, lower your voice." Her mother's voice was sharp – a clear warning to watch her tongue.

"I just want to talk, Mom. That's all. And I know this isn't the ideal place, but I can't wait for ideal any more. I'm tired of what's been happening to us. We used to be friends. Now you never want to hear anything about my faerie life. You don't even like to look at me any more! Your eyes slide right by me. It's been *months*, Mom." Tears welled up in her throat. "When are you going to get used to me?"

"That's ridiculous, Laurel," her mom said, raising her eyes to meet Laurel's as if to prove her wrong.

"Is it?"

Laurel's mom held her gaze for a few seconds and Laurel saw something change in her eyes. For just a second, she thought her mom would give – would really talk to her. But then she blinked and cleared her throat and it was gone. Her mom looked down and began sifting through receipts on the counter. "I can put the rest of the homeopaths away later," she said quietly. "You can go."

Feeling as though she'd been slapped, Laurel stood still, dazed. Her mom had dismissed her. After taking a couple of quick breaths, Laurel spun on her heel and opened the door, the cheerful bell mocking her.

A strong gust of wind hit her in the face as the door closed, and Laurel realised she had no idea where to go. David was working; Chelsea was at cross-country practice. Her next instinct was to go talk to her dad, and she even got as far as putting her hand on the door handle before she stopped. It wasn't fair to pit her parents against each other, to run to one when the other had hurt her feelings. She stood just out of sight, behind a big poster announcing the newest Nora Roberts novel, and watched her dad and Maddie help a customer with a big stack of books. The man said something Laurel couldn't hear, and her dad threw back his head and laughed as he wrapped the books in tissue paper while Maddie looked on with a gentle smile.

After one last look at her dad, Laurel turned away and headed to her empty house.

Chapter Twelve

Laurel and David stood together in their chemistry lab, watching their first graded experiment fail miserably. David was scouring their calculations, looking for a step they'd missed or math they'd done incorrectly. Laurel wrinkled her nose at the pungent mixture bubbling over their Bunsen burner.

"Did we put in the sulphuric acid?" David asked. "We did, didn't we?"

"Yes," Laurel said. "Fifty millilitres. We balanced the equation three times."

"I don't understand!" David vented under his breath. "It should have turned blue, like, two minutes ago!"

"Give it a few more minutes. Maybe it will."

"No. It's definitely too late. Look, it says right here, 'The solution should turn blue within one minute after reaching boiling temperature.' We totally screwed up. And she said this was just a simple lab." He raked his hands through his hair. For some reason David had decided that four AP classes weren't too much for one semester; Laurel wasn't convinced. Just two short weeks into the school year and already he was more than a little high-strung.

"David, it's OK," she said.

"It is *not* OK," he whispered. "If I don't get an A in this class, Mr Kling won't let me into AP physics. I *have* to get into AP physics."

"You'll be fine," Laurel said, a hand on his shoulder to soothe him. "I hardly think one funky experiment is going to keep you out of Mr Kling's class."

David hesitated for a moment, then his eyes darted back to their shared paper. "I'm going to balance this one more time, see if I can find where we made our mistake."

It was so unlike David to freak out over anything, but here he was on the verge of melting down. Laurel sighed. She took a deep breath and put her fingers over the steaming beaker, far enough away that it didn't burn her fingertips. "It's just supposed to turn blue?"

David looked up at her even tone. "Yeah, why?"

Laurel shushed him as she concentrated, wiggling her

fingers in the steam for a few more seconds. After a quick glance at David, still bent over their calculations, Laurel closed her eyes and took several deep breaths, trying to clear her mind the way her instructors in Avalon had taught her. Her fingers tingled vaguely as she tried to sift through the elements of the solution, but there was no plant material to identify. This was going to be tricky.

"Laurel," David whispered close to her ear, "what are you doing?"

"You're distracting me," Laurel said levelly, trying to maintain her tenuous hold on her concentration.

"Are you doing faerie stuff?" he asked.

"Maybe."

David's eyes darted around the room. "I don't think that's a good idea."

"Why, because I might ruin our *perfect* experiment?" she said sarcastically.

"I'm a little concerned you're going to blow up the school," he said, his voice still a low murmur.

She yanked her hand out of the steam. "I'm not going to blow up the school," she said, just a little too loudly. The team at the table behind them looked up and exchanged amused glances.

"Come on," David said, his hand on her arm. "Things

haven't exactly been going well in the potion-making department."

He had a point. She didn't feel like she'd made any progress since returning from Avalon, despite practising for at least an hour every day. Jamison had told her to be vigilant, and she was doing the best she could. But it wasn't working. Yet. "So I should just give up?"

"No, of course not. But should you really be experimenting on a *graded* assignment?"

Laurel wasn't listening. "Be my lookout, OK?"

"What?"

"Just tell me if Ms Pehrson looks over."

"What are you doing?" he asked, but his eyes stayed locked on their teacher.

Laurel reached into her backpack and unlatched the lid of her kit – a permanent fixture at the bottom of her bag. She sifted through its contents and unscrewed a small bottle of valerian oil and squeezed a drop on to her fingertip. She grabbed another bottle and shook a sprinkle of powdered cassia bark into her palm. After blowing on it, Laurel rubbed the oil on to the palm of her hand, mixing it with the gritty powder. "Give me our little spoon thingy," she whispered to David.

"Laurel, you can't do this."

"I can! I really think I've got it this time."

"That's not what I meant. This is an assignment. We're supposed to—"

Laurel cut him off by reaching across the table for the long-handled, stainless-steel spoon he'd refused to hand her. She scraped the mixture off her palm and, before David could stop her, popped it into the boiling mixture, stirring carefully in one direction and then the other.

"Laurel!"

"Shh," Laurel ordered, concentrating on the mixture.

As she watched, the mixture slowly began to take on a bluish tinge. The longer she stirred, the bluer it became.

"Is that good?" Laurel asked.

David just stared.

Laurel glanced behind her where two other students had completed their project. The blues looked about the same. She went ahead and stopped stirring.

"See if you can get her to come to our table next," Laurel said. "The mixture's too hot for the colour to hold very long."

David stared at her with an expression Laurel couldn't quite identify, but he didn't seem pleased.

"Very good, David and Laurel," Ms Pehrson said, catching them both off guard as she walked up behind them. "And just in time. Bell's about to ring."

David looked up as Ms Pehrson marked something

down on her clipboard and turned away. "Wait, Ms Pehrson!"

Ms Pehrson turned, and Laurel shot David a warning look.

"Um…"

Laurel and Ms Pehrson both stared at David.

His eyes looked determined for a second, then relaxed. "I just wondered if it's safe to dump this stuff down the sink."

"Yes. Didn't I put that on the handout? Just make sure you don't burn yourself," she said, moving on to the next lab table.

Laurel and David cleaned up in silence, both jumping when the bell rang. As they walked into the hall Laurel slipped her hand into David's. "Why are you mad?" she asked. "I just got you an A."

"You cheated," David said quietly. "And I let her give me an A for it because there was absolutely no way to explain *why* it was cheating."

"I didn't cheat," Laurel said, offended now. "I figured out how to make the solution turn blue. Wasn't that the whole point?"

"The point was to follow the directions."

"Was it? I thought the point was to figure out what to mix together to get blue stuff. Isn't that just as important?"

He sighed. "I don't know. I suck at chemistry."

"No, you don't," Laurel said, but her tone wasn't very convincing.

"I do. I just don't get it like I get biology. It doesn't make sense to me. We're two weeks in and I already feel overwhelmed. What's the rest of the semester going to be like?" He sighed. "I study so much for this class."

"I know you do," Laurel said. "And you deserve a good grade. So what if I helped a little? I think all the studying you put in justifies a little tampering. Besides," she added after a pause, "you're the only reason I got into AP chemistry. I think it's only fair that I help you get into AP physics." They were silent for a moment before Laurel elbowed his ribs gently. "She did say that we should think of our lab partner as a team member."

"Are you sure it's not really cheating?"

"David, for all I know, the reason the experiment failed is because something about my" – she lowered her voice—"Fall faerie abilities was interfering. She said she gave us an easy one for the first lab. All we had to do was follow the directions. It should have worked. I really think I made it *not* work."

He stared at her for a long time. "You may have a

point," he said. "The directions have never failed me before."

"See?"

Now David started to laugh. He backed up against his locker and slid down on to the floor. Laurel joined him warily. "How bad is it that I don't know whether to be mad or think that's the coolest thing ever?" David asked. He slung an arm around her. "You did it, though. You did it right."

Laurel smiled. "I did, didn't I?" She laughed now. "I don't suck."

"You don't suck," David agreed, then pulled her in, kissing her forehead. "Good job."

"Get a room!"

David's head jerked up, but it was just Chelsea, who grinned at them from across the hallway before turning back to Ryan. .

"I'm still not used to that," David said, shaking his head with a smile.

"I know," Laurel said, feeling intrusive watching someone else kiss, but unable to tear her eyes away.

"I wonder how long before they have to come up for air."

"Be nice," Laurel said, just a touch of seriousness to her tone. "She's happy."

"I hope so."

"We should do something with them. I mean, the four of us."

"Like a double date?"

"Yeah. We haven't done anything all together since they hooked up. I think we should. I like Ryan. He has great taste in girls."

David laughed. "My taste is better."

Laurel raised her eyebrows. "I think anyone who has kissed me would have to agree that I have the best taste of all."

"Not all of us can taste like nectar," David said teasingly, his hand at the back of her neck as he kissed her. "You have an unfair advantage," he murmured against her mouth, his hand sliding down her back and pressing her against him.

"Ow!" she said, pulling away.

David looked down at her, confusion plain on his face. "I'm sorry?" he said – both a pronouncement and a question.

Laurel glanced around the hall. "I'm getting ready to blossom," she whispered. "Another two or three days, I think."

David grinned, then coughed to try to hide it. It didn't work.

"It's OK," Laurel said. "I know you like it. And since I know what it is this time around, it doesn't bother me, really. It's just sensitive."

"Well, I'll be careful," he promised, leaning in for another kiss.

They both jerked as the door to the chemistry lab flew open, smacking loudly against the wall beside it. The earsplitting clang of the room's smoke detector filled the hall as blue smoke billowed out of the doorway and several students emerged from the cloud, coughing. "Out, out!" Ms Pehrson's voice sounded above the din as she shooed a bunch of sophomores from the classroom. The blue haze spread down the hallway and somebody pulled the fire alarm, setting off the entire building's cacophonous alert system.

David looked at the blue haze and the students running towards the exits. He stood and helped Laurel to her feet. "Well," he said wryly, his mouth close to her ear, "whose experiment do you think *that* was?"

They looked at each other and burst out laughing.

Laurel stood in front of the mirror in her room, staring at the pale blue petals that rose just above her shoulders. After her dad's return from the hospital last year, their family had decided that home would be a safe haven for

Laurel – that she would never have to hide what she was. But agreeing to that and actually walking downstairs without hiding her blossom were two very different things. She had to leave for school in half an hour; maybe it would be understandable if she came down with her petals already bound.

But her dad would be disappointed.

Of course, her mom might be relieved.

Laurel looked down at the sash in her hand. This year she was spared the fear of having some strange disease, but for some reason, the trepidation she associated with her blossom hadn't really abated.

Clenching her teeth, Laurel wound the sash around her wrist. "I'm not ashamed of what I am," she said to her reflection. But her stomach still twisted as she turned the doorknob and opened the door, her petals spread out behind her for everyone to see.

She tiptoed halfway down the stairs, then changed her mind – not wanting to appear as though she were sneaking around her own house – and clomped down the rest of the stairs.

"Wow!"

Laurel's eyes shot up to meet David's. His gaze flitted to her exposed navel and snapped back up to her face. Leaving her petals unbound had a tendency to slightly raise the front of her shirt as well as the back. David seemed to appreciate the effect, but Laurel had forgotten how uncomfortable it was to have her shirt bunched up around her ribs, crowding the tiny leaves at the base of her blossom. Several of the tops she'd brought back from Avalon had low-cut backs, perfectly suited for wearing while in bloom, but what she needed today was concealment.

"What are *you* doing here?" she asked.

"I'm glad to see you, too," David said, raising one eyebrow.

"Sorry," Laurel said, squeezing his hand. "You surprised me."

"I knew you were close yesterday; thought I'd stop by and offer support. Or whatever."

Laurel smiled and hugged him. It did feel better to have him here. Even if he was really here to get an early peek at her new blossom.

In the kitchen, Laurel's mother fussed with the coffeemaker, studiously avoiding Laurel's gaze. From the corner of her eye, however, Laurel caught her mother sneaking furtive glances as she poured fresh coffee into a take-along cup. Nothing had changed after their fight at the store. No apology but no added awkwardness, either. It was as if Laurel had never showed up that day, which was somehow worse. Their relationship seemed to increasingly revolve around ignoring problems in hopes that they would go away. But they never did.

"Where's Dad?" Laurel asked.

Her dad shook his paper from the couch, just out of sight through the living room doorway. "I'm here," he said distractedly.

"She blossomed," David called.

Laurel brought one hand to her forehead as she heard her father get quickly to his feet. "Oh, yeah? Let's see."

"Tattletale," she whispered to David.

Her mom grabbed a canvas tote and passed by as her dad was coming through the doorway. "I'm headed to the store," she said, her eyes avoiding his.

"But don't you – ?"

"I'm late," she insisted, though her voice wasn't sharp. It sounded strange to Laurel, almost like she wanted to stay and couldn't bring herself to. She and her dad both watched her all the way out the door.

Laurel's eyes stayed glued on the door, willing it to open; for her mom to come back.

"Whoa," her dad said, refocusing on Laurel. "That... that's huge."

"I did tell you," Laurel said, knowing that if she were

human her face would be bright red right now. Being a plant was not without advantages.

"Sure. But, I thought…" He scratched the back of his neck. "Honestly, I thought you were exaggerating a little." He circled Laurel as her embarrassment grew. "How did you hide this from us?"

Excellent timing. "Like this," she said, pulling her sash off her wrist and binding the petals around her ribs and waist. She pulled her blousy peasant top down over it and dropped her waist-length hair over the whole thing. "Ta-da!"

He nodded. "Impressive."

"Yeah," Laurel said, grabbing David's hand. "Let's go."

"What about breakfast?" her dad said as she picked up her backpack off the table.

Laurel shot him a look.

"Sorry, habit."

"My car or yours?" David asked after Laurel shut the door.

"Yours. Driving with a smooshed blossom can't be very comfortable."

"Good point." David held the passenger door open for her. Even after almost a year, he never forgot.

"Well," David said, firing up the engine, "we've got almost half an hour before first bell. Shall we go straight to school?" His hand slid on to her thigh. "Or somewhere else first?"

Laurel smiled as David leaned over and kissed her neck.

"Mmm, I have missed that smell." His lips travelled up her neck to her jawline.

"David, my dad is peeking through the window at us."

"That's OK with me," he murmured.

"Yeah, 'cause he's not *your* dad. Get off!" she said, laughing.

David leaned back and shifted into reverse. "I guess I can hold on till I get a block or two away." He looked at the house and waved at the small gap in the living room curtains.

"David!"

The gap disappeared.

"You are so bad."

He smirked. "Your parents love me."

And they did. Laurel had always thought that would be a good thing. Sometimes, though, she wasn't so sure.

Chapter Thirteen

The next day, Laurel and Chelsea sat on the porch swing in front of Laurel's house, lazily swaying back and forth. "I hate Saturdays," Chelsea said, her head hanging over one arm of the swing, her eyelids closed against the sun.

"Why?" Laurel asked, similarly draped.

"'Cause boyfriends always have to work."

"Sometimes you have races."

"That's true."

"And besides, you get to come over and hang out with me. Isn't that worth something?" Laurel said, poking her.

Chelsea opened her eyes and looked at Laurel sceptically. "You don't kiss as good as Ryan."

"You don't know that," Laurel said with a smile.

"Not yet," Chelsea said, leaning towards Laurel.

Laurel swatted at her arm and they both leaned back again, giggling.

"You do have a point," Chelsea said. "We don't hang out as much any more; aside from lunchtime, I mean."

"And you *mysteriously* disappear about half the time," Laurel said with a laugh.

"I'm a busy girl," Chelsea said in mock defence. "Oh, hey! Ryan's having a big party at his house next Friday. You and David are invited. It's the old 'say goodbye to summer' thing but minus the cold water, scratchy sand, and smoky fire."

"He's a little late," Laurel said, forgetting that not everyone was hyperaware of the change from summer to fall.

"Meh. Close enough. It's still a good enough reason to have a party. Ryan has the best party house. Surround sound, big rec room. It'll be awesome. You guys should come."

"Sure," Laurel said, accepting the invitation for the both of them. David wouldn't mind; she was the one who usually didn't like late-night things.

"Awesome." Chelsea squinted at the sun. "Is it five o'clock yet?"

Laurel laughed. "I'd be surprised if it's even three."

Chelsea stuck out her bottom lip dramatically. "I miss Ryan."

"That's good. You should miss your boyfriend."

"I used to mock girls who practically swooned when their boyfriends walked by. I always wanted to tell them to grow a personality and stop letting someone else define them. Sometimes I did tell them."

Laurel rolled her eyes. "Why am I not surprised?"

"And now I'm one of them," Chelsea said with a groan.

"Except that you have a personality." Chelsea had more personality than almost anyone Laurel knew.

"I hope so. But, seriously, he's become such a big part of my life." She lifted her head to look at Laurel again. "Did you know that the two races he's come to this year have both been personal bests for me? I *run* faster when he's around. And, before, I thought I was running as fast as I could. I'm a scoring runner on our team now. He did that to me!" She put her hand to her forehead and mocked fainting back against the swing. "He's wonderful."

"I am so glad, Chelsea. You deserve a great guy, and Ryan seems to really like you."

"Yeah, he does. Weird, huh?"

Laurel just snorted.

"Do you think we're moving too fast?" Chelsea asked seriously.

Laurel raised an eyebrow. "Well, that depends. How fast are you moving?"

"Oh, nothing like that," Chelsea said, waving away her concern. "I mean more like maybe I'm getting in too deep too quickly."

"How so?"

"I was registering for the November SAT the other day—"

"November?" Laurel interrupted. "How come November? David and I aren't taking it till spring."

"Chronic overachiever," Chelsea said dismissively. "Anyway, it asked which schools I wanted my scores sent to. And I said… ?" She looked at Laurel.

"Harvard. You've always wanted to go to Harvard," Laurel said without even having to think about it.

"I know, exactly," Chelsea said, sitting all the way up now and crossing her legs beneath her. "But I went to write Harvard and I was like, Well, wait. Ryan's going to UCLA; Boston's really far away from UCLA. Do I want to go that far away from him? And I totally didn't write it down."

"You had your scores sent somewhere else?" Laurel sat up straight. "Where? Stanford? You hate Stanford."

"No, I just left it blank. I haven't finished it yet." She paused. "Do you feel this way? About David?"

"Yep," Laurel said. "I would totally not go to Harvard for David."

"Sure," Chelsea drawled. "That's because you want to go to Berkeley, like your parents, right?"

The question took Laurel completely off guard. She nodded, vaguely, but her thoughts were in Avalon. There was a place for her at the Academy – tuition-free, room and board, no SATs required, and even though Jamison wanted her to help watch for trolls now, she assumed the faeries would expect her at the Academy full-time pretty soon. But how could she tell Chelsea that?

"Let's say David goes back East. Would you throw away your plans and follow him there?"

That's two years away, Laurel told herself, attempting to quell her rising discomfort. She gave a little shrug.

"But you'd think about it, right?"

"Maybe," Laurel said automatically. But it was so much more than just a question of following David a thousand miles. Following David would mean leaving behind Avalon, the Academy, everything. Would going to the Academy mean not choosing David? It was a new thought, and not one Laurel liked.

"So do you think you and David will be together forever? Because some people do that," Chelsea added in a rush, speaking more to herself than to Laurel. "They meet in high school and it's just like – click! – soul mates."

"I don't know," Laurel said honestly. "I can't picture myself ever not loving David. I just don't see us breaking up." *But torn apart?* Suddenly that seemed like a distinct possibility.

"You said the L-word," Chelsea said with a grin, pulling Laurel away from her dreary thoughts.

"Why, yes – yes, I did." Laurel laughed.

"You're in love with David?"

Just thinking about it made Laurel's whole body feel warm. "Yeah. I am."

"So do you guys… you know?"

There went that fuzzy moment. "Not… exactly."

"What does *that* mean?"

"It means not exactly," Laurel insisted stubbornly.

Chelsea was silent for a while. Laurel hoped she wasn't dwelling too hard on the precise state of Laurel and David's physical relationship. "I think I might love Ryan," Chelsea finally said, relieving Laurel's tension. "That's why this whole Harvard thing is throwing me. It's what I've wanted to do since I was, like, ten. Go to Harvard, major in journalism, be a reporter. But now, I can hardly bear the thought of being away from Ryan."

"Maybe *he* should follow *you* to Harvard."

"Don't think I haven't considered that," Chelsea

retorted. "He wants to be a doctor like his dad, and Harvard's got a great med programme."

"So send your scores to Harvard," Laurel said, doing her best to focus on Chelsea's problems instead of her own. "You have almost two years before you have to decide. A lot can happen in that time. And, seriously, if you have to give up a dream to be with a guy, maybe you've chosen the wrong guy."

Chelsea's brow furrowed and she fiddled with her fingers. "And what if the time comes and the dream doesn't seem worth it?"

David's and Tamani's faces seemed to float before Laurel's eyes, the Academy looming in the background. She shrugged and forced the images from her mind. "Then maybe it was the wrong dream."

Ryan's house was vibrating with music when Laurel and David pulled up on Friday night. "Wow," Laurel said. The three-storey, bluish-grey house had a slate roof and bright white shutters. A large set of picture windows adorned the front and looked out on to a beautifully landscaped yard with dogwoods lining a rock-paved walk and ivy crawling up the south wall. The house was right up against the rocky shoreline, and Laurel suspected they had an incredible view off the back deck. "This is really beautiful."

"Yep. It's nice to be the only child of the town cardiologist."

"I see that." They walked hand-in-hand up the walk and through the front door. Since it was a small town and a big house, the party wasn't too crowded, but it was full enough. And where people didn't fill the corners, music did. Laurel already felt a dull ache in her ears.

"Over there," she said, raising her voice over the music and pointing towards Ryan and Chelsea. Ryan looked fairly normal in a bright red T-shirt and Hollister jeans, but Chelsea had outdone herself. She had pulled her curls up in a high ponytail and was wearing long, swinging gold earrings. Dark blue jeans with cute black sandals and a black tank top with shiny beading set off the tan she'd gotten that summer.

Probably on the deck of Ryan's pool.

"Look at you!" Laurel said as they approached. She pulled Chelsea into a hug. "You look awesome!"

"You too," Chelsea said.

But Laurel was already wishing she hadn't had to wear the long, empire-waist, tie-back blouse with a rather large bow that covered up the bump from her blossom. It was warm, and she was already starting to feel confined.

"Don't you just adore this house?" Chelsea exclaimed, pulling Laurel a little off to the side.

"It's gorgeous."

"I love to come here. With three brothers under twelve, we can't have very many breakable things at my house," Chelsea said. "But here? They put statues on the coffee table. At dinner the glasses are made of – would you believe it – *glass*."

They both laughed.

Chelsea turned her head to watch David and Ryan talking and laughing together. As if feeling themselves being observed, they both turned to look over at the girls. Ryan winked.

"Sometimes when I see the two of them together like this I wonder how Ryan could have been there for so many years and I never saw him." She turned to Laurel. "What was I thinking?"

Laurel laughed and put her arm around Chelsea. "That David was hotter?"

"Oh yeah, that's right," Chelsea said, rolling her eyes. "Come on," she said, pulling Laurel towards the back of the house. "You have got to see this view."

Chapter Fourteen

By eleven Laurel was thoroughly exhausted from
dancing and the rather distinct lack of sunlight. She
smiled in relief when David elbowed his way through the
crowd and brought her a plastic cup with some kind of
red punch in it.

"Thank you," Laurel said, taking it from him. "Seriously,
I am parched and exhausted."

"Your knight in shining armour comes through again,"
David said.

She brought the cup up to her mouth, then made a
face. "Yuck. Someone totally spiked this."

"Really? What is this, a fifties sitcom?"

"No kidding." Laurel couldn't even sit at the same table
with her parents when they had wine without growing

nauseated. The smell of any kind of alcohol made her queasy.

"Well, I guess I'll do my date-ly duty and drink them both," David said, taking Laurel's cup from her.

"David!"

"What?" he said after taking a long swallow.

Laurel rolled her eyes. "I'm driving home."

"Fine with me," David said, after taking another drink. "Means I can go back for seconds."

"You're going to get totally sloshed."

"Oh, please. My mom serves wine with dinner at least once a week."

"Does she really?"

David grinned.

"Give me that," Laurel said, taking her cup back.

"Why? You can't drink it."

"I most certainly can," she said, reaching into her bag for a small bottle she had taken from her Fall faerie kit.

"What is that?" David asked, scooting close to her.

"Water purifier," Laurel said, squeezing one clear drop into her cup and swirling the contents gently.

"Did you make that?"

"I wish," Laurel said darkly. "They gave it to me at the Academy."

Laurel looked down into her cup. The red punch had

turned clear. "Huh," she said. "I guess the dye is considered an impurity as well."

David tilted the cup in his direction and sniffed. "You know, most people pay to *add* alcohol to their beverage, not the other way around."

"I march to my own beat."

"So what have you got left? Sugar water?"

Laurel shrugged and took a sip. "Yeah, basically."

"Appetising as that sounds, I think I'm going to grab my refill at the punch bowl, thank you."

"Lush," Laurel called teasingly after him.

She wandered into an empty hallway with her cup of sugar water. It was nice to get away from the stifling crowds. If she were being completely honest with herself, she was ready to go home and go to bed. There was at least another hour – probably two to three – of the party left and she knew David would want to stay for the whole thing.

Still, she could tough it out for one more hour. Probably.

She wandered over to a long, tall window between two matching paintings of ballerinas and leaned her forehead against the cool surface as she looked out at the night sky. A flicker of movement outside the window caught Laurel's eye. A dark shape, barely illuminated by the glow from inside the house, moved again. She focused on it, trying to make out what it was. Could it be an animal? A dog, maybe? It seemed too big for that. It was standing halfway in the shadow of a large tree that kept her from discerning more than an outline. Then it lifted its head, and the dim beam illuminated a pale, deformed face with grotesque clarity. Laurel threw herself back from the pane, her chest tight and her breathing rapid. After slowly counting to ten she peeked around the sill again.

It was gone.

Its absence was almost as formidable as its presence, as if a hole in the light itself sat empty where the hulking form had been.

Did I imagine it? Her hands were still shaking as she pictured the mismatched face – one eye more than an inch lower than the other, a twisted snarl of a mouth, an impossibly crooked nose. No, she'd seen it.

Fear clutched at her chest. She had to find David.

Forcing herself to remain composed, Laurel moved from room to room, looking. Panic welled up inside her as she seemed to find everyone *but* him. Finally, she spotted him in the corner of the kitchen with a snack in one hand and a cup in the other, talking with a bunch of guys. She walked up to him, feigning calmness. "Can I talk to you?" she asked with a tight smile, leading him a few feet away from the crowd. She leaned in close to his ear. "There's a troll outside," she said, her voice shaky.

David's smile disappeared. "Are you sure? I mean, we've both been pretty jumpy. But we haven't seen an actual troll in months."

Laurel shook her head almost convulsively. "No, I saw it. It's not a mistake. It's here for me. Ah!" She groaned softly. "How could I be so stupid?"

"Wait, wait," David said, his hands on her shoulders. "You don't know that it's here for you. Why would they attack you *now*, all of a sudden? It doesn't make sense."

"Yes, it does. Jamison told me this would happen. And it has!" Her hands shook, and words kept spilling out of her mouth as her fear grew. "I've been so careful, and the one night I let my guard down, they're there. Just like Jamison said. They must have been watching – waiting for me to forget my kit. I'm the fly, David. I'm the stupid, stupid fly!"

"What fly? Laurel, you've got to calm down. You're not making any sense. You don't have your kit?"

"No! I don't! That's the problem. I threw a couple of basics in my bag and I meant to bring my backpack and leave it in your car, but I totally forgot."

"OK," David said, pulling her farther from the crowd.

"Let's just think about this for a moment. What have you got on you?"

"I have two monastuolo serums. They put trolls to sleep."

"Perfect, then we should be fine."

Laurel shook her head. "They only work in an enclosed space and they don't work instantly. It's for escape scenarios, not like this. If a troll got in the house, half of these kids would be dead before the serum even started to work."

David took a deep breath. "So what do we do?"

"They want me, but they'll kill everyone else in a heartbeat if they think it will do any good. We have to lure him away, and we have to do it fast."

"Lure him where?"

"My house," Laurel said, hating the idea. "My house is safe. It's warded against trolls, and the sentries are there. It's the safest place in the world for us right now."

"But—"

"David, we don't have time to argue."

David set his jaw. "OK. I trust you. Let's get out of here." He pulled his keys from his pocket.

"I'm driving."

"Believe me, Laurel, I'm feeling *very* sober."

"I don't care. Give me your keys."

"Fine. What do I tell Chelsea?"

"I'm feeling sick. Something I ate. She knows my stomach's weird."

"OK."

They spotted Chelsea and Ryan, dancing to a slow song. Chelsea's head rested on Ryan's shoulder, and he held her tight against his chest.

"Let's just go," Laurel said. "I don't want to interrupt this."

David hesitated. "You know Chelsea. She'll worry if we're just gone." He turned to look at Laurel. "She might even stop by your house on her way home from the party to check on you."

"You're right. I'll go tell her."

Laurel felt bad butting in, but there was nothing else to be done. She apologised profusely and assured Chelsea three times that she didn't need anything but to go home and rest.

Chelsea smiled and threw her arms around Laurel. "Thanks so much for coming. I'll see you guys later."

Hugging Chelsea back, Laurel desperately hoped she could get the trolls to follow her. She would regret this night for the rest of her life if anything happened to Chelsea – or any of the other people at the party.

David took Laurel's hand and they headed towards

the kitchen. "The side door is closest to my car," David said, pointing, "but it's still going to be a bit of a run."

"OK, let's go."

They stood at the kitchen door for a few seconds and David tucked Laurel tightly under his arm. After pressing a quick kiss to her forehead, he asked, "You ready?"

"Yeah."

They both took a few deep breaths, then David grabbed Laurel's hand and pushed the door open. "Go!" he commanded in a hissing whisper.

Hand in hand they ran towards David's Civic, about fifty feet away. They ducked around several cars before throwing open the doors and jumping into their seats. "Do you think he saw us?" she asked as she shoved the key in the ignition and cranked the engine.

"I don't know."

"I can't leave if they didn't see us."

"Well, what do you propose we do?" David asked, peering out his window into the darkness.

Laurel took a quick breath, hardly daring to even think about what she was about to do. Before she could change her mind she slipped out of the driver's seat and jumped up and down, waving her arms. "Hey! You looking for me?"

A dark shape rose up twenty feet in front of them.

Laurel gasped and threw herself back into the car and shoved the gearshift into reverse. The troll rushed forward, its navy coveralls and fearsome visage illuminated by the Civic's headlights. It slammed its hands down on the hood of the car just as the stick shift popped into place.

"Go, go, go!" David screamed.

Laurel slammed one foot on the gas and popped her other off the clutch so fast the car shot backward, almost hitting the truck parked behind them. The troll stumbled into the spot where the car had just been, but it was already getting to its feet. Laurel shoved the stick into first gear and peeled out of the driveway. David was twisted around in his seat, staring out the back window.

"David!" Laurel shouted. "Watch for cars for me. I can't stop at the stop sign up here."

David turned forward and peered into the darkness in both directions. As they approached the intersection Laurel's foot hovered over the brake.

"You're all clear. Go!"

Laurel pressed on the gas, carrying the car through the intersection. She stepped hard on the brake as she turned off the road that led to Ryan's house and on to Pebble Beach Drive. The car skidded and the tyres protested noisily, but Laurel managed to keep the headlights facing the right direction.

"It just came around the corner," David said when they were less than ten seconds up the road. "It's wicked fast."

"The speed limit's thirty-five here. How fast can I get away with going?" Laurel asked, the needle on the speedometer already creeping towards forty-five.

"Cops are the least of our worries tonight," David said. "You can just – Laurel, look out!"

A hulking shape darted in front of them, stopping in the middle of the road. Laurel slammed on the brakes and the car slid over the pavement as she fought to keep control. They skidded, barely missing the large animal – a troll, surely – and slid off the shoulder into a crumbling ditch on the other side. The car lurched to a stop, its wheels spinning uselessly in the mud and gravel.

David groaned as he tried to right himself after being thrown against the dashboard. Laurel peered into the darkness but couldn't make anything out. Then her eyes focused on the jagged outline of the forest's edge, only a hundred yards away. "The trees, David," Laurel said urgently. "We have to run for the trees."

"I don't know if I can run," David said. "My knees got hit really hard!"

"You can do it, David," Laurel said desperately. "You have to. Let's go!" She threw the door open and dragged

David out behind her. After a few wobbly steps he managed to find his bearings and they ran, hand in hand, towards the forest.

"He's going to smell me," David said. "My left knee is bleeding."

"You're no worse off than me," Laurel said. "He'll totally smell my blossom. We stick together. No arguing." Suddenly she realised her mistake – the trolls must be making their move because she had blossomed. There was no way she could evade them, not when they could track her inescapable scent. She hated that she'd so easily let down her guard. She'd *let* this happen.

As they ran, Laurel dug into her bag and pulled out a set of vials that would make the monastuolo serum when crushed together. She knew it wouldn't be very effective in the open air, but she had to try something; maybe it would slow them down. Her sash loosened and her blossom slipped free as she and David tore through the bushes, but she wasn't about to stop to fix it; she could hear one troll right behind them and another approaching from their right. David stumbled, betrayed by his injured knee, and the troll behind them growled and sprang. A stabbing pain shot up Laurel's back from her blossom. Biting off a scream, she whirled and, with an open palm, smashed the monastuolo vials against the troll's forehead. He reeled back, howling in pain, enormous hands clapped to his face. Laurel leaped away, her back throbbing so badly a sob built in her throat and she fought to quell a wave of nausea.

Her legs ached almost unbearably when they reached the tree line at the top of the hill. "Come on, David," she urged.

They stumbled into the forest, branches clinging to their clothes and whipping against their skin, scratching their faces. When they reached a small break in the trees they jolted to a stop, turning in circles.

"Which way?" David asked.

A low growl sounded from one side of the clearing.

"That way," Laurel said, pointing away from the sound. But even as she pointed, another growl sounded from the other side. They spun again, only to be confronted by the shadowy silhouette of a third troll, his warm breath steamy in the brisk autumn air.

David pulled Laurel back against his chest, crushing her blossom painfully between them. They tried to keep their eyes on the trolls as they circled, but the creatures were too fast, whirling around, then switching directions and spinning the other way, circling them like sharks.

The sound of metal scraping against metal filled the air, and the flash of a knife glinted in the moonlight.

Laurel felt David's breath catch in his chest.

David squeezed Laurel in a quick hug, then stepped away with his hands raised. "I give up," he called loudly. "Take me and let her go. She's harmless."

Laurel gasped and grabbed the back of his shirt, trying to pull him back, but he continued walking forward.

Raucous laughter filled the air. "Harmless?" a harsh, gravelly voice said. "How stupid do you think we are, human? If anyone is going to live tonight, it is not going to be her."

Before David could get back to Laurel, two trolls stepped between them. One was taller than David, his broad shoulders straining his faded coveralls. The other was hunchbacked, her hair long and stringy, and even in the moonlight Laurel could see that her bone-white skin was cracked and bleeding at the joints. Laurel forced herself not to squeeze her eyes shut as the tall troll closed in on her, knife raised.

Chapter Fifteen

Laurel covered her head with her arms and wished that David would run – save himself – even though she knew he wouldn't. Then a loud clang reverberated in her ears and it took a few seconds for her to realise she was still alive.

The trolls were shouting and grunting as they looked around for their assailant. Their blades had been knocked to the ground by a strange-looking metal disc, now buried in the trunk of the tree right behind Laurel, a scant six inches above her head. Laurel's whole body shook with relief and for the first time in her life she thought she might faint – but the danger wasn't over yet. Taking advantage of the trolls' momentary distraction, Laurel dropped to her stomach and slithered towards the edge of the clearing. Something big and heavy slammed into her, carrying her away from the clearing and behind a large tree. A hand covered her mouth as she tried to scream.

"It's me," David hissed into her ear.

David. He was alive, too. Her arms wrapped around him, her ear close against his chest, where she could hear his heart racing in loud thumps. It was a beautiful sound. "Do you think we can sneak away?" Laurel asked as quietly as she could.

"I don't know. We have to wait for a good chance or they'll just catch us again."

Laurel had an iron grip on David's arm as the trolls started moving in their direction, noses aloft. Laurel heard a hollow click and, before she could even guess what it was, David's hand came down hard on the top of her head, forcing her to the ground, where he settled in beside her. No sooner had her belly hit the dirt than a volley of gunfire filled the forest with its sharp, staccato rhythm. Laurel threw her arms over her ears and pressed her face against the damp leaves as she tried to blot out the sound of the gunshots and, with them, a flood of memories from last fall.

Pained yelps sounded between gunshots, and Laurel

peeked up to see the three trolls fleeing into the forest, a hail of bullets at their backs.

"Cowards," a woman's voice said softly, calmly.

Laurel rose from the ground, her mouth slightly agape.

"You can come out now," the dark form said, still staring after the trolls. "They won't be back – it's a shame I didn't come prepared for a real chase."

Laurel and David scrambled to their feet. Laurel pulled her blouse as securely as she could over her blossom, wincing against the pain. The heat of the moment had chased her injury from her mind; she wondered how much damage the troll had done, but an examination would have to wait. David started to step out from behind the tree, but Laurel held his hand, pulling him back.

"I won't bite," the woman said in a clear voice.

It was pointless, Laurel realised, to try to stay hidden. Whoever this was, she knew they were there. Laurel and David took a few tentative steps out from behind the tree to get their first good look at the woman who had saved them. She was several inches taller than Laurel, and dressed from head to toe in black, from her long-sleeved shirt and running trousers to her black leather gloves and combat boots. Only the mirrored sunglasses resting casually atop her head departed from the scheme, setting off the gelled strands of auburn hair that surrounded her face and stuck up just right in the back. She looked about forty, and in excellent shape, but she wasn't built as thickly as a troll.

"I don't blame you for being nervous," the woman said. "Not after what you've just been through, but trust me: I'm one of the good guys." She raised her gun and performed a series of actions that made a lot of clicks before she stowed it back in a holster at her hip.

"Who are you?" Laurel asked bluntly.

The woman smiled, her white teeth bright in the moonlight. "Klea," she said. "Klea Wilson. And you are?"

"That was... that was, wow!" David stuttered, ignoring her question. "You were amazing. I mean, you just came in and they... well, you know."

Klea stared at him for a long time, one eyebrow arched. "Thank you," she said dryly.

"How did you—" David started to ask, but Laurel cut him off with a quick yank on his arm.

"What were those things?" Laurel asked, trying to sound innocent without being too fake. "They didn't look... human."

David looked down at her, confused, but a quick glare wiped the question off his face. Despite everything,

Laurel was determined to keep her wits about her, and the most important thing was not to reveal who she was to this stranger – even if she was, as she claimed, "one of the good guys."

Klea hesitated. "They were… a species of animal like you've never encountered before. Let's just say that." She crossed her arms over her chest. "I still haven't caught your names."

"David. David Lawson."

"David," she repeated, then turned to Laurel.

Laurel wondered if there was any point in trying to withhold that information. But it wasn't like it would be hard to find out. Finally she murmured, "Laurel."

Klea's eyes widened. "Laurel Sewell?"

Laurel looked up sharply. How did this woman know who she was?

"Well," Klea said softly, almost to herself, "that explains a lot."

David rescued Laurel from her bafflement by changing the subject. "How did you know we were – ?" David gestured wordlessly to the centre of the clearing.

"I've been tracking these… subjects for several hours," Klea said. "It was only when they started chasing your car that I realised what they were doing. Sorry for cutting it so close, but I can't run as fast as you can drive. Good thing they forced you off the road when they did; I'd have never gotten here in time."

"How do you – ?" Laurel started.

"Listen," Klea said, "we can't just hang around here talking. We don't have any idea how far their reinforcements might be." She walked over to the tree where her metal disc was stuck. She retrieved it, then looked up at David, meeting his eyes for the first time. "Would you two mind giving me a ride? I'll take you somewhere safe and we can talk." She turned her gaze to Laurel. "We really need to talk."

Laurel's mind was screaming out against the idea – to not trust whoever Klea was. But she *had* just saved their lives. Besides, David was only too eager to agree.

"Yeah. Sure. Of course!" he said. "My car… it's just down – well, you know where it is. I can totally give you a ride – um, except, well, it's kind of stuck, but…" His voice trailed off, and an awkward silence filled the clearing.

Klea stowed the metal disc in a wide case that attached to her back. "I imagine the three of us can push your car free. Let's go." And she strode off in the direction of the car.

David turned to Laurel, both hands on her shoulders.

"Are you OK?" he asked, his eyes darting over her, looking for wounds.

Laurel nodded. *OK* probably wasn't the best word, but she was alive. He gave a relieved sigh and wrapped his arms around her, his hand pressing painfully against her blossom. But Laurel didn't care. She burrowed against his shoulder, wishing she could burst into relieved tears. But that would have to wait. "I'm so glad you're safe," he whispered.

"I'm alive," she said sceptically. "I don't know about safe yet. How are your knees?"

David shook his head. "They're going to be way sore tomorrow, but at least I'm walking."

"Good," Laurel said, her breathing still a little fast. Then, remembering his moment of idiocy, she slapped her hand against his chest. "And what the hell was that giving-yourself-up thing?" she demanded.

David grinned sheepishly. "It was all I could think of at the moment."

"Well, don't you ever do anything like that again."

David didn't say anything for a long moment, then he shrugged and turned towards the car. "We'd better go."

"Hey," Laurel said, one hand reaching up to touch David's cheek. "You go ahead, I'll be there in a second," she whispered. "I have to tie up my blossom. But," she said sharply, "don't tell her anything. I don't trust her."

"She just saved us from the trolls," David countered. "She was awesome!"

"I don't care! She's a stranger and she knows something. You can't tell her anything!" It was different for David – he wasn't the one who had something to hide. "Now go, before she gets suspicious. Tell her I dropped my bag."

"I don't want to leave you alone," he said firmly.

"I'll just take a second," Laurel said. "I have to tie up my blossom. Now please go. She's looking up at us." Klea had reached the bottom of the hill and was peering up at them through the darkness. "She's going to come back up here if she doesn't see you soon."

With a long look and a squeeze of her hand, David reluctantly headed out of the trees and down the hill.

Laurel untied the knot around her waist and bent her petals down. The spot on her back still stung like an open wound. She gritted her teeth and bound the petals tightly. As soon as she pulled her shirt down over the blossom, she hurried out of the trees, forcing herself not to run. She picked her way down the hill in the dim moonlight and almost shrieked when she tripped and found herself face-to-face with a troll. She threw herself backward and started to scramble to her feet when she realised the troll wasn't moving. She crept back to it and realised it was the troll who had gotten a face full of monastuolo serum. Apparently there were ways around the open-air limitation.

She had only seconds to make her decision. Klea would want to see the unconscious troll – maybe kill it. But bright red lines streaked across the troll's face where the serum had splashed and burned him; Klea would know Laurel or David had done something. And if Klea knew anything about Laurel at all, it would just make things worse. Laurel couldn't alert Klea to the troll's presence without also exposing her faerie potion. Trembling, Laurel stood, continued down the hill, and didn't look back, wondering how long the serum would last. The sooner they were out of there, the better.

David's car sat right where they had abandoned it, front tyre wedged into the mud, with its headlights shining into the dark night and the passenger doors wide open.

"It's pretty mired," Klea said, her eyes lifting only briefly to acknowledge Laurel's return, "but I think you and I can push it out, David." She reached out and punched his arm lightly. "You look like a strong guy."

David cleared his throat like he was going to say something, but nothing came out.

"Laurel, would you steer?" Klea asked as she pushed up the sleeves of her shirt.

After slipping into the driver's seat, Laurel watched as David followed Klea to the hood of the car and they braced their hands against the bumper. She still wasn't sure what to think. Five minutes ago she had thought her life was over – and, without Klea, she had no doubt it would have been. So really, what were they supposed to do? Leave the woman who had saved their lives stranded on the side of the road just because she knew Laurel's name somehow? There was nothing to do but take her wherever it was she wanted to go. Once the car was out, anyway. But it was all too weird. Laurel wished she had more time to process the situation.

Laurel cranked the wheel as David and Klea pushed. After a few tries, the Civic slowly came loose and Laurel backed it up on to the road. After putting on the parking brake, she joined them as they stood studying the car, looking for damage. Or, more precisely, Klea studied the car while David stared at Klea.

"It could definitely use a good wash," Klea said, "but it looks like you're not going to have any souvenirs."

"All the better," Laurel said.

"So," Klea said, stepping out of the glare of the headlights, "shall we go?"

David and Laurel exchanged looks, and Laurel gave him a nod. There was no way to silently indicate that there was an unconscious troll not fifty feet away.

They loaded into the car, David hurrying to open their doors for them as if it were just another night, and they were off. It took a short, silent argument with David, but Laurel remained at the wheel.

Klea directed her as they drove along. "It's only about a mile or so," she said. "We move our camp constantly. The only reason I'm letting you guys see it tonight is that it will be somewhere else tomorrow."

"What kind of camp?" David asked.

"You'll see," Klea said. "Turn right here."

"I don't see a road," Laurel said.

"You're not meant to. Start turning, and you'll see it."

With a stoic nod Laurel began edging the Civic to the right. Just behind a large clump of bushes she spotted a hint of a road. She eased on to it and drove through a thin curtain of branches that scraped at the doors and windows. But as soon as she had passed through that, she found the Civic on two parallel tracks, obviously recently cut.

"Cool," David said, leaning forward in his seat.

For about a minute they travelled silently up the dark, narrow road, Laurel becoming more and more certain that they were driving into a trap. If only she hadn't forgotten her backpack! Then the road turned sharply to the right, revealing three camping trailers in a well-lit circle. In front of two of the campers sat two black trucks that would have been at home in a monster truck arena. Their deeply tinted windows reflected the glare from several bright floodlights, mounted on tall poles, that filled the camp with a stark, white light. Smaller lamps hung over each of the entrances to the trailers. Just outside of the light two brown horses were tethered to a stake and several swords and large guns were laid out on an aluminium picnic table. The sinking pit in Laurel's stomach told her that she and David had just gotten in over their heads.

"Whoa," David said

"There's no place like home," Klea said wryly. "Welcome to camp."

They all got out of the car and walked towards the camp – Klea purposefully and Laurel and David more tentatively. A handful of people buzzed around, completing various tasks with hardly a glance at Laurel and David. Like Klea, they wore mostly black.

"Laurel, David, this is my team," Klea said, gesturing to the people meandering about. "We're a small lot, but we work hard."

David took a step towards a low, white tent that glowed from within, as though a dozen lanterns were burning inside. "What do you have in there?" he asked, craning his neck as a man slipped in, releasing a bright beam of light over the entire area for just a moment before the flap fell shut.

"As they say, I could tell you, but then I'd have to kill you," Klea said with just a touch more seriousness than Laurel was comfortable with. Klea paused beside one of the black trucks and reached into the bed to grab a khaki-coloured shoulder bag. "Come on over here," she said, gesturing to a picnic table set up near the centre of camp.

Laurel gripped David's hand as they followed Klea to the table. Now that they were there, they might as well get what answers they could. There was no way they could make a break for it. Laurel wasn't sure whether she was now in more or less danger than when the trolls were chasing them.

They sat as Klea pulled a manila envelope out of her bag and slipped her mirrored sunglasses down from her head to cover her eyes. The camp *was* brightly lit, but Laurel found the gesture weirdly melodramatic. Klea riffled through the contents of the envelope, removing a glossy photograph that she slid over

towards Laurel. "What do you know about this man?"
she asked.

Laurel looked down at the snarling face of Jeremiah
Barnes.

Chapter Sixteen

Suppressing a shudder, Laurel stared in shock at the face that had haunted her nightmares for almost a year. Her hand, wrapped around David's, convulsed into a tight grip.

"I've spent several years looking for him…." Klea said. "Well, him and others like him. But the last time we caught up with him – a couple months back – he had a business card in his pocket with some names on it." She looked up at Laurel. "One of them was yours."

Laurel's hands started to shake at the thought of Barnes carrying her name around with him. "And you just took down my name and sent him on his merry way?" Laurel kept her voice low, but there was a hefty dose of hiss in it.

"Not... exactly." Klea's eyes flitted back and forth before she leaned forward, sliding the picture back into its envelope. "He... was stronger than we expected. He escaped."

Laurel nodded slowly, struggling to keep her trembling to a minimum. Despite what Jamison had said, Laurel held on to a tiny hope that Barnes really had died after getting shot last year. But this was proof – undeniable proof – that he was still around. And hunting her.

"You don't seem surprised. So you do know him?"

Lie, lie, lie! her mind was shouting. But what good would that do? She'd tipped her hand the moment she recognised Barnes. It was too late to deny everything. "Sort of. I had a run-in with him last year."

"Not many people walk away from run-ins with this guy." Klea's tone was flat, but the implied question was painfully obvious. *Why are you still breathing?*

Laurel's thoughts immediately centred on Tamani, and she almost smiled. She forced herself to look down at a spot on the table. "I just got lucky," she said. "He put his gun down at the wrong time."

"I see." Klea was nodding now, almost sagely. "Cold steel is about the only thing this man fears. What did he want with you?"

Laurel stared up into Klea's reflective shades, wishing

she could see the woman's eyes. She had to come up with something – anything – to conceal the truth.

"You can tell her," David said after a long pause.

Laurel shot him a glare.

"I mean, they sold it already; no one can take it from you." What was he talking about? His hand squeezed her thigh meaningfully, but cover stories were David's thing – Laurel was no good at lying. The best she could do was play along. She covered her face with her hands and leaned against David's chest, pretending to be too distraught to talk.

"Her parents found this diamond when they were… renovating their house," David explained.

Laurel hoped Klea didn't catch the tiny pause.

"A huge one. This guy tried to kidnap her, for ransom or something." David stroked her shoulder and patted her back. "It was a very traumatic experience," he assured Klea.

David, you are brilliant.

Klea was nodding slowly. "Makes sense. Trolls have always been treasure hunters. By their very nature, and because they need money to blend into our world."

"Trolls?" David asked, propping up their charade. "Like, live-under-bridges, turn-to-stone-in-sunlight trolls? Is that what those creatures were?"

"Did I say trolls?" Klea asked, her eyebrows arching comically over the rims of her sunglasses. "Oops. Well" – she sighed, shaking her head—"I guess once you've seen them, you may as well know what they really are." She looked at Laurel, who was sitting back up again, wiping away pretend tears. "It's a good thing your parents sold the diamond. At least Barnes probably won't be hunting them. However," she said, "you seem to have found a permanent spot on his radar. There's no way those trolls were at your party tonight by chance." She paused. "I don't believe in coincidences that big."

"What would he want with me now?" Laurel asked, exchanging a quick glance with David. "The diamond is gone."

"Revenge," Klea answered simply. She turned her face to Laurel, and Laurel could feel the intensity of Klea's gaze even through the sunglasses. "It's pretty much the only thing trolls love more than treasure."

Laurel recalled Jamison saying almost the same thing on her last day in Avalon. It seemed rather absurd to find truth in this bed of lies.

Klea reached back into her bag, removed a small grey card, and held it out to Laurel, who took it tentatively. "I belong to an organisation that… tracks… supernatural beings. Trolls, mostly, because they're the only ones that work to infiltrate human society. Most of the others avoid it at all costs. This here is my team, but our organisation is international." She leaned forward. "I believe you are in great danger, Laurel. We'd like to offer our assistance."

"In exchange for what?" Laurel asked, still suspicious.

A hint of a smile played at Klea's lips. "Barnes escaped me once, Laurel. He's not the only one with a score to settle."

"You want us to help you catch him?"

"Certainly not," Klea said, shaking her head. "Untrained children like you? You'd only get yourselves killed. And, no offence, but you're kind of... small."

Laurel opened her mouth to retort, but David squeezed her leg sharply and she bit her tongue.

Klea was pulling another piece of paper out of her bag; this time, a map of Crescent City. "I'd like to place some guards around your house – yours, too, David – just in case—"

"I don't need guards," Laurel said, thinking of the sentries stationed near her house.

Klea startled. "Excuse me?"

"I don't need guards," Laurel repeated. "I don't want them."

"Now really, Laurel. It's for your own protection. I'm

sure your parents would agree. I could speak with them, if you like—"

"No!" Laurel bit her lip when two of the men working a few yards away paused and looked over at her. She'd have to tell the truth now. "They don't know about him," she admitted. "I never told them anything about Barnes at all. I got back before they realised I was gone."

Klea grinned openly. "Really? Resourceful little thing, aren't you?" Laurel managed not to throw Klea a dirty look but only barely. "But seriously, Laurel. There's been a lot of troll activity around Crescent City lately. Way more than I'm comfortable with. Luckily," she continued, a touch of amusement in her voice, "we're dealing with the kind of being who is easily… stopped." She rubbed at her temples briefly. "Not like some of the other creatures I've had the singular experience of hunting down."

"Other creatures?" David asked.

Klea stopped rubbing her head and looked at David with a pointed expression. "Oh, David, the things I have seen. There's more out there than anyone dares to believe possible."

David's eyes widened, and he opened his mouth to speak.

"But I'm afraid we don't have to time to discuss that tonight," she said, shutting down his questions. She looked at Laurel. "I'd like you to reconsider," she said seriously. "Because you managed to escape from your last encounter unscathed, I think you underestimate these creatures. But they are fast, cunning, and amazingly strong. We have a hard enough time keeping them in line and we're trained professionals."

"Why do you do it then?" Laurel asked.

"What do you mean, why? Because they're *trolls*! I hunt them to protect people, like I protected you tonight." She hesitated, then continued. "Some time ago, I lost everything… *everything*… to inhuman monsters like these. I have made it my life's work to end the suffering they cause." She stopped talking for a second, then focused back on Laurel. "A big dream, I know, but if no one tries, it will never happen. Please help us by *letting* us help you."

"I don't need bodyguards or whatever it is you're offering," Laurel insisted. She knew she sounded petulant, but there was nothing else she could say. Faerie sentries were one thing, but this? This stranger with her army camp and big guns – Laurel didn't need them stumbling upon her real guardians. The sooner she and David could get out of there, the better.

Klea pursed her lips. "OK," she said softly, "if that's the way you feel. But if you change your mind, you have my card." She looked back and forth between David and Laurel. "It's only fair to tell you that I'm still going to keep my eye on you two. I don't want anything to happen. You seem like good kids." She paused, her finger near her chin, thinking for a few seconds. "Before you go," she said slowly, "I have something for you. And I hope you'll understand my reasons for giving them to you, as well as my request that you keep them a secret. Especially from your parents."

Laurel didn't like the sound of that.

Klea gestured to one of the passing men, and he brought her a large box. She sifted through it for a few seconds before pulling out two handguns in black canvas holsters. "I don't anticipate your needing these," she said, holding one out to each of them. "But if you won't consent to guards, then this is the best I can do. I prefer to be overly cautious rather than... well, dead."

Laurel looked down at the gun Klea had extended towards her, grip-first. In her peripheral vision she saw David take his without hesitation and murmur, "Sweet!" but her eyes stayed locked on the gun. Very slowly, she reached out her hand and touched the cool metal. It didn't look quite like the gun she'd pointed at Barnes last year, but when she wrapped her fingers around the grip, it *felt* the same. Visions of Barnes flashed through her head, all tinted the scarlet of blood – David's blood on her arm, the blood that blossomed on Barnes's shoulder when she shot him, and worse, the look on Tamani's face when he'd been shot, twice, by a gun not unlike this one.

She jerked her hand back as if she'd been burned. "I don't want it," she said quietly.

"And that does you credit," Klea said calmly. "But I still think—"

"I said I don't want it," Laurel repeated.

Klea pursed her lips. "Really, Laurel—"

"I'll take it for now," David said, his hand reaching out for the second gun. "We'll talk about it later."

Klea looked up at David, her expression unreadable behind those stupid mirrored glasses. "I suppose that will do."

"But…" Laurel began.

"Come on," David said, his voice soft and gentle. "It's almost midnight; your parents will be worried." He put an arm around Laurel and started to lead her towards the car. "Oh," he said, stopping and turning back to Klea, "and thanks. Thanks for everything."

"Yeah," Laurel mumbled without turning back. "Thank you." She hurried to the car and slipped in before David could open her door. Her back was aching now and all she wanted was to get away from Klea and her camp and get home. She started the car before David even had a chance to get in and the moment his seat belt clicked, she shifted into reverse and turned the car around. She drove back down the makeshift road as quickly as she dared, and watched Klea in her rearview mirror until the road curved and she blinked out of sight.

"Wow," David said as they pulled back on to the highway.

"I know," Laurel agreed.

"Wasn't she awesome?"

"What?" That was *not* what Laurel had in mind.

But David was already distracted. He took out the gun Klea had given him and unsnapped the holster.

"David! Don't take that out," Laurel said, trying to look at David and the gun and the road all at once.

"Don't worry. I know what I'm doing." He took the gun out and turned it around in his hands. "SIG SAUER," he said.

"Sig what?"

"SAUER. It's the brand name. It's a really good gun. Expensive," he added. "Although not nearly as cool as Klea's gun. Did you see that thing? An automatic. I bet it was the Glock eighteen."

"Hello! NRA David," Laurel said peevishly. "Where did

you come from? I didn't know you were so into guns."

"My dad's got a bunch," he said distractedly, still petting the firearm in his hand. "We used to go hunting a little, when I was younger, before they split. He still takes me shooting at the range, sometimes, when I'm visiting. I'm a pretty good shot, actually. Mom's not a fan; she prefers the microscope. Just one more reason they weren't meant to be together, I guess." He pulled on the barrel and Laurel heard a click.

"Be careful!" she yelled.

"The safety's on – no worries." He clicked something else and the magazine came sliding out. "Extra-long magazine," he said, rattling off facts in the same tone of voice her dad might use to check off inventory. "Ten shots instead of eight." He ejected one bullet and held it up to the window. "Forty-five calibre." He whistled softly. "These bullets could do some serious damage."

The phrases ran through Laurel's head like a grotesque broken record. *Forty-five calibre, extra-long magazine, ten shots, serious damage. Forty-five calibre, extra-long magazine, ten shots, serious damage.*

"That's it," Laurel said through gritted teeth. Her foot slammed on to the brake, and she lurched to a stop on the side of the road.

David looked up at her with a combination of confusion and what almost looked like fear. "What?"

"What do you mean, what?"

"What's wrong?" His innocent, genuine tone told her he really had no idea why she was upset.

Laurel folded her arms over the steering wheel and laid her forehead against them. She took several deep breaths and forced herself to be calm. David said nothing, just waited as she took hold of her temper and gathered her thoughts.

Finally she broke the silence. "I don't think you understand what all of this means for me." When David didn't respond, she continued. "They're watching us now. Maybe they've always been watching us, I don't know. And truth be told, I really think *you* are going to be safer. But how do we know she's not hunting faeries as well?"

David snorted in disbelief. "Oh, come on, she wouldn't do that."

"Wouldn't she?" she asked, turning to face David, her tone deadly serious.

"Of course not." But his voice had lost a little of its confidence.

"Did she ever say why she wanted to catch the trolls? Or kill them, I think we can safely assume?"

"Because they're trying to kill *us*."

"She never said that. She only said it was because they are trolls."

"Isn't that enough of a reason?"

"No. You can't hunt things just because of what they are, or what others like them have done to you. I can't assume there are no good trolls out there any more than I can assume there are no bad faeries. The fact that she's hunting the right thing doesn't mean it's for the right reason."

"Laurel," David said calmly, one hand on her shoulder, "you're arguing semantics here. I really think you're blowing this all out of proportion."

"That's because you're human. That gun you're so impressed by? I can't be as impressed because I'm afraid it will be pointing at *me* someday if she finds out what I am."

David stopped, shock written across his face. "I wouldn't let it happen."

Laurel laughed sharply. "As much as I appreciate the sentiment, do you really think you could stop her? Her and all those – I don't know – ninjas she's got working for her?" Laurel twined her fingers through David's. "I have great faith in you, David, but I doubt you're very good at stopping bullets."

David sighed. "I just hate feeling so powerless. It's one thing to take my own life in my hands" – he chuckled ironically—"I'm a crazy teenager; we do that kind of stuff all the time." He sobered and was silent for a few moments. "But it's something else completely to have you in danger, and Chelsea, and Ryan, and all the other kids at the party. Things got really real tonight, Laurel. I was scared." He laughed. "No, I was terrified."

Laurel looked down at her lap and twisted the tail of her shirt with her fingers. "I'm sorry I got you involved," she mumbled.

"It's not that. I love that you got me involved." He took both of her hands and held them until she looked up at him. "I love being a part of your world. And despite almost dying last year, that was the most exciting thing that's ever happened to me." He laughed. "With the possible exception of tonight." He lifted her hands to his lips and kissed each one. "I love what you are and I love *you.*"

Laurel smiled weakly.

"I just think we need help."

"We have help," Laurel insisted. "I've had faerie sentries watching my house for six months."

"But where were they tonight?" David asked, the volume of his voice rising. "They weren't there. *Klea* was there. Like it or not, she saved us and I think that earns her some trust."

"So you want me to drive back and tell her everything? Tell her I'm a faerie and the real reason Barnes was after me?" Laurel asked hotly.

David took her hands and pressed them together between his. It was something he always did to help her calm down. She focused on their joined hands and took several long breaths. "Of course not," David said softly. "There's no reason for her to know anything more than she knows now. I just think you should trust her enough to accept some assistance. Not guards," he said, before Laurel could protest, "but if she wants to keep an eye on us when we're not at your house, is that such a bad thing?"

"I guess not," Laurel mumbled.

"We put a lot of people in danger tonight, Laurel. Now, I know we're going to be more careful in the future, but in case something like this happens again, don't you want" – he lifted the gun, which was looking all too safe tucked into its holster—"another line of defence?"

"But is this really the best way? She just armed two minors, David. Do you have any idea how illegal that is?"

"But it's for our own good! The law wouldn't understand any of this. We have to take matters into our own hands." He paused. "You weren't worried about the law when Tamani killed those trolls last year."

Laurel was silent for a long time. Then she straightened up and looked him in the face. "Have you ever shot someone, David?"

"Of course not."

"Ever pointed a gun at someone?"

He shook his head.

"Watched someone get shot?"

He shook his head soberly now, and very slowly.

"I've done all three," Laurel said, thumping her fingers hard against her chest. "After we escaped from Barnes, I had nightmares almost every night. I still have nightmares sometimes."

"I do too, Laurel. It scared the hell out me."

"*Barnes* scared the hell out of you, David. You know what scares me in my nightmares? Me. I scared the hell out of *myself*. Because *I* picked up that gun and *I* shot someone."

"You had to."

"Do you think that matters? I don't care why I did it. The fact is that I did. And you never forget that feeling. That moment when the gun kicks back in your hand and you see blood appear on the person across from you. You never forget it, David. So excuse me if I don't share your excitement at having another one forced on me."

David was silent for a long time. "I'm sorry," he whispered again. "I didn't think." He paused, then let out a frustrated sigh. "But you don't really understand, either. You have faerie sentries and potions. I don't have anything. Can you at least see why I feel more comfortable having some kind of defence?"

"A gun makes you feel big and powerful, does it?" Laurel shot off.

"No! It doesn't make me feel powerful or more like a man, or whatever other stupid things people say in the movies. But it makes me feel like I'm doing something. Like I'm helping in some way. Is that so hard to understand?"

Laurel started to speak, then closed her mouth. He was right. "I guess not," she mumbled.

"Besides," David said with a tentative grin, "you know what a technology whore I am. Microscopes, computers, guns – I love them all."

It took a few seconds, but she smiled back wanly. "That certainly is true. I remember you turning all CSI Lawson on me when I bloomed last year." They both laughed – the kind of laugh that doesn't make you feel happy but at least makes you feel better.

Chapter Seventeen

They pulled into Laurel's driveway and, after a moment's hesitation, threw open their doors and ran for the house. As soon as they were inside, Laurel turned and pushed the door shut – a little too hard – and the slam echoed through the dark house.

"Laurel?"

David and Laurel both jumped, their eyes turning towards the railing where Laurel's mom peered down at them with sleepy eyes.

"Is everything OK? You slammed the door."

"Sorry, Mom. It was an accident. We didn't mean to wake you."

She waved their concern aside. "I was up. Some animals have been fighting behind the house, dogs or something. Every time I drift off to sleep, it starts over again. I came down and made myself a cup of tea and things are quiet again. Hopefully for good this time."

David and Laurel exchanged glances. She doubted very much that there were any *dogs* fighting behind her house.

"Did you have fun?"

"What?" Laurel said, confused.

"The party. Was it fun?"

Laurel had almost forgotten. "Yeah," she said, with forced cheerfulness. "It was awesome. Ryan's house is totally gorgeous. And huge," she added, hoping she didn't sound too off. "You can go back to bed," she said quickly. "David and I are going to watch a movie now. Is that OK?"

"I guess," she said with a yawn. "Keep it down though, all right?"

"Yeah, sure," Laurel said, pulling David towards the rec room.

"Dog fight?" David asked sceptically after they heard her mom's door click shut.

"I know," Laurel said, her voice worried. "The trolls have been busy tonight." She peeked out through the blinds, peering into the darkness. She knew she wouldn't be able to see anything, but she tried anyway. Guilt surged through her. She didn't even want to consider the number of both humans and faeries she had put in danger tonight.

David came up behind her and wrapped his arms around her waist, pulling her against him.

"Please don't," she whispered.

He looked at his hands at her sides, then pulled them away and crossed them over his chest, his face confused.

"No, no," she said soothingly, "it's not you, it's my blossom." She groaned. "It hurts so much." Now that the stress of the night was really over, the jabbing pain in her back was all she could think about. She fumbled with the knot on her sash, trying to get it undone, but her hands kept shaking. Tears built up in her eyes as she yanked on the sash, wanting nothing more than to get her injured petals free.

"Let me," David said softly.

She gave up and stood still while David's soft fingers worked out her hurried knots. He unwound the sash, pushed her shirt up in the back a little, and helped smooth her petals upward. Laurel clenched her teeth and sucked in a quick breath. It was almost as bad letting them loose as binding them down. Laurel pressed the palms of her hands against her eyes as she forced herself not to whimper. "Do you see any damage?" she asked.

David didn't answer. She turned to look at him. His face wore an expression of pained horror.

"What?" Laurel asked, her voice a whisper.

"It looks like he got a fistful of petals. Tore them straight out. There's just some ragged edges."

Laurel's eyes widened and she looked over her left shoulder, where the familiar light blue petals should have been floating. Over her right shoulder her blossom was intact, but on the left side, nothing remained. The enormous petals were just... gone. A strange but overwhelming sense of loss crashed over Laurel. Tears streaked her face almost before she knew she was sobbing. She turned and buried her face in David's shirt and let all the despair, terror, and pain of the night finally rise to the surface.

He gently wrapped his arms around her back, carefully spaced so he didn't touch her blossom. His chest was warm, chasing away the chill of fear and the cold weather alike, and his cheek brushed her forehead, gritty after a few days of not shaving. There was no place in the world she would rather have been at that moment.

"Come here," he whispered, pulling her towards the couch. He lay on his side and she snuggled against his chest, her head resting on his shoulder. Only when

Laurel was breathing smoothly again did he speak. "Quite a night, eh?"

She groaned. "I'll say."

"So what do we do?"

Laurel grabbed his hand. "Don't leave."

"Of course not," David said, pulling her closer.

"Everything will be fine when the sun comes up," Laurel said, half trying to convince herself.

"Then I'll stay all night," David replied. "My mom will understand. I'll just tell her we fell asleep watching a movie."

Laurel yawned. "Wouldn't be very far from the truth. I'm exhausted."

"Besides, I'm not ashamed to admit I really don't want to go back out there tonight."

"Pansy," Laurel said, giggling at her lame plant joke for a few seconds before a large yawn overcame her. David could never really understand how hard it was to be awake and active this late at night. She felt like a sieve, constantly being drained of energy without anything to fill her back up. At this point she was running on sheer willpower.

"Go to sleep," David said soothingly, his hands warm on her shoulders. "I'll be right here," he promised.

Laurel snuggled into his chest and let herself relax. In

spite of the pain and her lingering fear, sleep came quickly. But with it came dreams of trolls with knives, and humans with guns, and Jeremiah Barnes.

Laurel woke with the sun and tried not to disturb David, but he was a very light sleeper. He opened his eyes, looked at her, and closed them again. A few seconds later they popped open again.

"I'm not dreaming," he said, his voice gravelly.

"You wish," Laurel said, trying to straighten her shirt. "I can't even imagine what I must look like." Her blossom still ached, but at least the pain wasn't stabbing any more. She gave up trying to pull her shirt down; it just made her blossom hurt.

David grinned at her bare midriff and his hands skimmed the sides of her waist, then travelled farther up her back, where he gingerly stroked the undamaged petals on the right side of her blossom. Laurel wondered if he realised just how much she could feel them; as if they were an extension of her skin. Sometimes he touched them idly, almost unconsciously. Other times she would feel his hand linger where the petals were wrapped tightly under her clothes. It felt a little strange to have him touch her like that. Intimate. More than holding hands. More than kissing, even.

"It's going to be gone soon, isn't it?" he said, more than a tinge of regret in his voice as he studied the large flower.

She nodded, craning her neck to look back at the blue blossom. "It should be gone in another week or two," she said. There was a distinct *lack* of regret in her voice. "Maybe less, after last night."

"Is it really such a bother?"

"Sometimes."

David's hands stroked one of the longer petals on the blossom from base to tip, then brought it briefly to his nose and inhaled. "It's just so... I don't know... sexy."

"Really? But it's so... plantish."

"Plantish?" David said with a laugh. "Is that a technical term?"

Laurel rolled her eyes. "You know what I mean."

"No, I don't. You have this thing on your back that is prettier than any flower I've ever seen. It smells amazing and is so smooth and cool to the touch. And," he added, "it's magical. What could possibly not be sexy about that?"

She grinned. "Maybe, if you put it that way."

"Thank you," David said, licking his finger and drawing himself a point on an imaginary chalkboard.

"But only because it's not yours," she countered.

"It's kind of mine," he said suggestively, pulling her tight against him.

"Only because I share," Laurel said.

He kissed her softly and stared down at her face just long enough to make Laurel squirm a little. "Did your mom call?" she asked, changing the subject to shift his focus away from her.

David shook his head. "Not yet, but I'd better go. In fact," he said, glancing at the display on his phone, "I don't have any messages, so my mom must not have missed me yet. If I hurry, she might not even realise I didn't make it home last night." He stretched. "And I'm really not much of a fan of your early mornings. I could use a couple more hours of sleep before work."

"How late are you supposed to work?"

"Just from noon to five. Don't worry." David was part of the stock crew at the drugstore where his mom was the pharmacist. Being the top dog's kid definitely had its advantages. He had a very flexible schedule and only worked about two Saturdays a month, with an occasional Sunday thrown in. Of course, Laurel had similar advantages and only had to work at her parents' stores when she needed a twenty. Or more.

"I don't suppose there's any way to keep your mom from going out at night?" Laurel asked.

David rolled his eyes in her direction. His mom was rather famous for being the life of the party.

"I was just asking."

"Do you still have Klea's card?" David asked.

Laurel found something interesting to look at on the floor. "Yeah."

"Can I see it?"

Laurel hesitated, then pulled it out of her pocket. She'd memorised it already. *Klea Wilson*, it proclaimed in bold, black letters. Then a number underneath. No job description, no address, no picture or logo. Just her name and number.

David had his cell phone out and was adding the number to his contacts. "Just to be safe," he said. "In case you lose this or something."

"I won't lose it." *Although I might throw it away on purpose.* Something about Klea made her uneasy, but she couldn't put her finger on it. Maybe it was just those stupid sunglasses.

"By the way," Laurel said tentatively, "I think I should go out to the land today. Tomorrow, at the latest."

David stiffened. "How come?"

"They need to know what happened," Laurel said, not meeting his eyes.

"You mean Tamani needs to know what happened?"

"And Shar," Laurel said defensively.

David pushed his hands into his pockets and was silent. "Can I come?" he finally said.

"I'd prefer that you didn't."

His head popped up. "Why not?"

Laurel sighed and ran her fingers through her hair. "Tamani always gets weird when you're around, and quite frankly, I think you get weird too. I need to sit down and have a serious talk with them about this Klea woman and I don't need the two of you trying to get at each other's throats while I'm doing it. Besides," she added, "you have to work."

"I could get out of it," he said stiffly.

Laurel looked up at him now. "You don't need to. I can do this alone. And it's not like you have anything to worry about. I'm with you. I love *you*. I don't know what else I can say to convince you."

"You're right, I'm sorry." He sighed and wrapped his arms around her, then pulled back and looked at her. "I'll be honest with you – I don't like it when you go out to see him. Especially alone; I'd rather be with you." He hesitated. "But I trust you. I promise." He shrugged. "I'm just the stereotypical jealous boyfriend, I guess."

"Well, I'm flattered," Laurel said, pushing up on her toes for a kiss. "But I'm just going to talk." She wrinkled her nose. "And clean. I should at least air out the house; no one's been inside it for months."

"Are you going to drive?"

"Well, I was going to fly," she said playfully, pointing to her back, "but apparently it doesn't actually work that way."

"I'm serious."

"OK," Laurel said, not sure where he was going with this. "Yes, I'm going to drive."

David's face was tight. "What if they follow you?"

Laurel shook her head. "I can't imagine they would. I mean, it's daylight, for one thing. And it's almost all highway. And really, if they followed me all the way to the land, they'd have a rude surprise waiting for them."

"That's true," David said, his brow furrowed.

"I'll be careful," Laurel promised. "I'm protected here, and I won't stop until I get there."

David pulled her close. "I'm sorry I worry so much," he said. "I just don't want anything to happen to you." He paused. "I don't suppose you'd consider taking the…um… thing Klea gave us?"

"No," Laurel said sharply. "That's enough. Out!" she said, shooing him towards the front door. "Out!"

"OK, OK," David said, laughing. "I'm leaving."

Laurel grinned and pulled him close for a kiss. "Bye,"

she whispered. He slipped out the door and she locked it behind him.

"I didn't think I actually had to *tell* you, no sleepovers with David. I thought that rule was pretty obvious."

Laurel jumped, then turned to look up at her mother leaning over the banister. "Sorry. We fell asleep watching the movie. Nothing happened."

Her mom laughed. "Your hair got that way just from sleeping?"

Laurel's fatigue and stress rolled together with the mental picture of how she must look, and suddenly everything seemed funny. She laughed, then snorted, and laughed harder. She tried in vain to stifle her giggles.

Her mom came the rest of the way down the stairs, her expression halfway between exasperation and amusement.

"I must look *so* bad," Laurel said, running her fingers through her hair. It was still a little crunchy from the hair spray she'd decided to use last night.

"Let's just say it's not your finest moment."

Laurel sighed and opened the fridge for a soda. "We really did just fall asleep."

"I know," her mom said with a smile. She busied herself crushing chewable vitamin tablets with a mini mortar and pestle. "I came down to check on you at two."

She sprinkled the vitamin powder on the soil around the African violets – a trick she'd learned years ago from a man who grew marijuana indoors, ironically. Laurel watched her mom and realised that neither of them had said anything awkward or mean. At least not yet. For a few minutes everything seemed normal. Laurel didn't know whether to enjoy it while it lasted or lament the fact that it happened so rarely.

"Sorry," Laurel said again. "I'll make sure to kick him out next time."

"Please do," her mom said teasingly.

They both turned when they heard her dad whistling as he came down the stairs. He greeted them both and dropped a kiss on his wife's cheek in exchange for a cup of coffee.

"Are you guys both working today?" Laurel asked.

"Is it Saturday?" her mom said wryly.

"No rest for the wicked," her dad said with a grin. He looked at her mom. "And we are very, very wicked." They laughed and for a moment Laurel felt like they had gone back in time to before she blossomed last year. Before anything was weird; back when they were normal.

Her smile melted away when she realised her dad was studying her with a strange look. "What?" she said as her dad walked over.

"What happened to your blossom?" her dad asked, concerned. "You're missing petals!"

The *last* thing Laurel wanted this morning was a family discussion about her blossom. "They just fall out sometimes," she said. "Tying them down every day isn't super good for them. I was wondering—"

"Do you need to stay home from school when you bloom so this doesn't happen?" her dad asked, interrupting her.

Laurel saw her mom's eyes widen.

"No, of course not," Laurel protested. "I've totally got this under control. It's fine."

"I guess you would know," he said reluctantly. He went back to sipping his coffee, but he studied her over the rim of his mug.

"Since you guys will be at work," Laurel said, pulling the conversation back on track, "do you mind if I go out to the land?"

Her mom gave her a sidelong look. "How come?" she asked.

"I need to do some cleaning," Laurel said, trying to hold a neutral face. "When I came back from… when I was there in August the place looked pretty bad. I really should go fix it up so some hobo doesn't decide to live there," she said, laughing awkwardly.

"I thought *they* kept stuff like that from happening," her mom said.

"Well, yeah, probably, but I'm not going to ask a bunch of sentries to be my maids."

"I think that's understandable," her dad said, jumping in. "And the place probably could use a good cleaning." He looked at her mom. "Does that sound OK with you?"

Her mom mustered up a tight smile. "Sure. Of course."

"Thanks," Laurel murmured, looking away. Part of her wished she hadn't asked.

Chapter Eighteen

Laurel sat in her car for several minutes, just staring at the cabin. *Her* cabin, or very nearly. She'd been here often enough in the last year – on her way to and from Avalon, as well as the times she'd come to see Tamani last fall. But she hadn't been inside since moving to Crescent City almost a year and a half ago. Where the lawn wasn't blanketed in two seasons' worth of leaves, it grew long and shaggy and the bushes had grown high enough to cover half of the front windows. Laurel sighed. She hadn't thought about the yard when she packed her cleaning supplies. The most obvious solution was to bring David next time, along with a lawn mower and hedge trimmers, but that would be painfully awkward at best.

Another day; she certainly had enough to do for now. She popped the trunk, picked up a bucket full of sponges, rags, and other cleaning supplies she'd packed that morning, and lugged it towards the front door.

The door squeaked on its hinges as she walked into the cabin. It was weird to walk into a totally vacant house; houses were meant to be filled with stuff and people and music and smells. The wide front room that took up most of the bottom floor seemed gaping now. A room full of empty.

Laurel set the bucket down on the kitchen cabinet and walked around to the sink, turning the water on. After a short gurgle a stream of copper-stained water poured out of the spigot. Laurel let it run for a moment and soon the water slipping down the drain was clear. She smiled, strangely comforted as the sound of running water filled the room and echoed off the bare walls.

She circled the downstairs, unlocking and opening all the windows, letting the crisp autumn breeze flow through the house, cleansing it of the stale, stuffy air that had been trapped inside for months. The window to the right of the front door wouldn't open, and Laurel struggled with it for a few seconds.

"Let me get that for you," a quiet voice said from just behind her.

Even though she'd been expecting him, Laurel jumped. She moved aside and let Tamani spray something from a small bottle on each side of the window before lifting the sash easily. He turned to her with a grin. "There you go."

"Thanks," she said, smiling back.

He said nothing, just shifted a little to lean up against the wall.

"I'm here to do some housecleaning," Laurel said, gesturing to the bucket of supplies.

"I see that." He looked around the empty room. "It's been a while since anyone was in here. Ages since I was."

They stood for long seconds in a cloud of silence that felt awkward to Laurel but didn't seem to bother Tamani in the least.

Finally, Laurel stepped forward to hug him. His arms twined around her back, instantly finding the lump of her bound blossom, and he jerked back as if shocked. "Sorry," he said hastily, crossing his arms across his chest. "I didn't know."

"It's OK," Laurel said, her hands hurrying to the knot at her waist. "I was going to undo it as soon as the windows were open." Her petals sprang up as soon as they were released and Laurel didn't bother to suppress her sigh of relief. "This is one of the best parts about being here," she said lightly.

Tamani started to smile, but his eyes fixed on the blue and white petals. "What the hell happened?" he asked, stepping behind her.

"Um… that's the other reason I'm here," Laurel admitted. "The cleaning was what I told my parents to get them to let me come."

But Tamani was hardly listening. He was staring, aghast, at her back, his hands clenched into fists. "How?" he whispered.

"Trolls," Laurel said quietly.

His head jerked up. "Trolls? Where? At your house?"

Laurel shook her head. "I was dumb," she said, trying to downplay just how bad the situation had been. "I went to this party last night. They found us and ran our car off the road. I'm fine, though."

"Where were your sentries?" Tamani demanded. "They aren't just there to guard your house, you know."

"I think they might have been… occupied with other things," Laurel said. "When we got home, Mom said something about dogs fighting in the back."

"You could have been killed!" Tamani exclaimed. He glanced at her back again. "It looks like you almost were."

"A… woman found us, just in time. She chased off the trolls."

"A woman? Who?"

Laurel handed Klea's card to Tamani.

"Klea Wilson. Who is she?"

Laurel relayed the story of the previous night, with several interruptions from Tamani asking for clarification here, more details there. By the time she was done, she felt like she'd relived the entire ordeal. "And then she made us take the guns and we left," she finished. "It was so weird. I have no clue who she is."

"Who—" Tamani paused and paced a few steps. "There's no way—" More pacing. Finally he stood still, his arms crossed over his chest. "I've got to talk to Shar about this. This is… problematic."

"What am I supposed to do?" Laurel asked.

"Stop going out at night?" Tamani suggested.

Laurel rolled her eyes. "Besides that. Should I trust her? If I'm in trouble and the sentries aren't around—"

"They should *always* be around," Tamani said darkly.

"But if they're not, if I see this woman again… do I trust her?"

"She's a human, right?"

Laurel nodded.

"Then no, we don't trust her."

Laurel gaped at him. "Because she's human? What's that supposed to say about David? Or my parents?"

"So you want to trust her?"

"No. I don't. Maybe. I don't know. Tell me not to trust her because she hunts non-humans or because she gave us guns. But you can't just decide that she's not trustworthy because she's a human. That's not fair."

Tamani held his hands out in frustration. "It's all I've got, Laurel. I have nothing else to judge her on."

"She did save my life."

"Fine, I'll take away one strike." He walked over and leaned against the wall beside her.

Laurel sighed. "Why is this happening now?" she asked, frustration creeping into her voice. "I mean, it's been almost a year since Barnes, and nothing. And then in one night, bam! Trolls, Klea, more trolls at my house. All at once. Why?" Laurel asked, turning her head to look at Tamani.

"Well," Tamani said hesitantly, "there hasn't exactly been nothing for the last year." He looked apologetic. "We didn't think you needed to know about every troll that passed through Crescent City and glanced your way."

"There have been others?" Laurel asked.

"A few. But you're right: This is the best organised, most carefully targeted attack I've had any report of."

"I can't believe there were others," Laurel said in disbelief. "I really don't have any control over my life."

"Oh, come on. It's not like that. Most of them never made it within a half mile of your house. The sentries took care of them. No big deal."

Laurel scoffed. "'No big deal.' Easy for you to say."

"It was under control," Tamani insisted.

"How about last night? Was last night under control?"

"No," Tamani admitted. "It wasn't. But nothing like that has ever happened before."

"Then why now?"

Tamani smiled wearily. "It's a good question. If I knew, it might answer some of my questions as well. Like why the trolls have stopped sniffing around here lately, or how Jeremiah Barnes figured out the gate is on this land, or who's really giving orders to who in this fiasco. It's one of the many things we're still trying to figure out."

Laurel was silent for a moment. "So what do I do?" she asked.

"I don't know," he said. "Take things slow, I guess. Be careful and try to avoid getting into a situation where this Klea person might come around again."

"Oh, trust me, I will."

"For the moment, though, I think that's all you can do. I'll talk to Shar. We'll see if we can figure anything else out. OK?"

"OK."

"Thanks for coming to tell me," he said. "I really appreciate it. And not just because I get to see you. Though it's a nice bonus. Oh," he said, reaching into his pack. "I have something for you. Jamison gave it to me." He handed her a large cloth sack. Laurel took it and peered into it for a second before laughing.

"What is it?" Tamani asked, confused.

"Powdered sugarcane. I make potion vials out of it and I'm almost out." She shook her head. "Now I can break a hundred more vials," she said ruefully.

"Things still not working?" Tamani asked, trying to hide his concern.

"No," Laurel said lightly, "but they will. Especially now that I have a ton more of this," she added with a grin.

Tamani smiled before his eyes slipped to the side, focusing on something just over her shoulder.

"What?" Laurel said, craning her neck to look self-consciously at her petals.

"Sorry," he said, apologising again. "It's so beautiful and I hardly got to see it last year."

Laurel laughed and spun, showing off her bloom. By the time she got back around, Tamani was conscientiously studying Laurel's bucket of cleaning stuff. Laurel thought about the conversation she and

David had about how sexy he thought her blossom was. If it was sexy to David…

No more spinning.

"So what is all this?" Tamani asked, covering the awkward moment.

"Just cleaning stuff. Glass cleaner, floor cleaner, multipurpose cleaner." She pulled out a pair of rubber gloves. "And these, so none of it gets on me."

"So… can I help?"

"I only brought one pair of gloves, but" – she pulled out a feather duster—"you can dust."

"How about I clean and you dust?"

"It's just dusting," Laurel said with a laugh. "You don't have to wear a ruffly apron or anything."

Tamani shrugged. "Fine. It's just weird."

"Why's it weird?" Laurel asked as she filled her bucket with warm, sudsy water and donned her gloves.

"This is Ticer work. It's weird to see you doing it. That's all."

Laurel laughed as she ran her sponge over the dusty countertops. "I thought you were getting uncomfortable because it's 'women's work'."

"Humans," Tamani muttered derisively, shaking his head. Then, cheerily, "I've scrubbed many a room in my day."

They worked in silence for a time, Tamani clearing cobwebs from several of the corners, Laurel scrubbing at the counters and cabinets in the kitchen.

"You really should let me bring you some cleaning supplies from Avalon if you're going to do this very often," Tamani said. "My mom knows a M— ah, Fall who makes the very best stuff. You wouldn't need the gloves."

"You were going to say *Mixer*," Laurel teased.

"I'm a soldier," Tamani said, his voice taking on an exaggerated formality. "I am surrounded by uncouth sentries from dawn to dusk. I apologise for my vulgar behaviour."

Laurel looked up at him, watching her with a playful, almost taunting, smile. She stuck out her tongue, which made him laugh. "Well, if it's not an inconvenience, faerie cleaning supplies would be nice," she said. "How is your mom?"

"Good. She would like to see you again."

"And Rowen?" Laurel asked, evading the question his statement implied.

Tamani smiled broadly now. "Had her first performance at the equinox festival; she was adorable. She held the train for the faerie playing Guinevere in the *Camelot* retelling."

"I bet she was beautiful."

"She was. You should come to a festival one of these days."

The possibilities loomed large in Laurel's mind. "Maybe someday," she said with a smile. "When things aren't so... you know."

"There's no place in the world safer for you than Avalon," Tamani said.

"I know," Laurel said with a quick glance out the window.

"What are you looking for?" Tamani asked.

"The other sentries."

"Why?"

"Don't you get tired of knowing there's always someone listening to you?"

"Nah. They're polite. They'll give us our privacy."

Laurel snorted in disbelief. "Admit it, if it was Shar and some strange girl, *you'd* spy."

Tamani's face froze for a second before his eyes darted to the window too. "Fine," he admitted. "You win."

"It's one reason I don't know that I could ever live in this cabin again. Never really being alone."

"There are other advantages," Tamani said not-so-teasingly.

"Oh, I'm sure," Laurel said, not taking the bait. "But privacy isn't one of them."

They cleaned silently for a while longer. At first, Laurel wished she had thought to bring a radio or something. But Tamani didn't seem to mind the silence, and soon Laurel realised that it wasn't really silent at all. The breeze winding through the trees and wafting through the windows was a sound track all its own.

"Is it hard?" Tamani asked suddenly.

"What?" Laurel said, looking up from the window she was polishing.

"Living a human life? Now that you know what you are?"

Laurel was still for a long time before she nodded. "Sometimes. What about you? Isn't it hard living in the forest so close to Avalon, but on the wrong side of the gate?"

"It was when I started, but I'm used to it now. And I really am close. I go back a lot. Plus, I have friends – faerie friends – who are with me all the time." He paused for a few seconds. "Are you happy?" he whispered.

"Now?" she replied, her voice equally low as her hands clenched the paper towels.

Smiling sadly, Tamani shook his head. "I know you're happy now. I can see it in your eyes. But are you happy when we're – when you're not here?"

"Of course," Laurel said quickly. "I'm very happy." She

turned and rubbed hard at the window.

Tamani's expression didn't change.

"I have every reason to be happy," Laurel continued, forcing her voice to stay calm. "I have a great life."

"I never said you didn't."

"You're not the only person who makes me happy."

A tiny nod and a grimace. "I'm quite aware of that."

"The human world isn't as dreary and bleak as you like to believe. It's fun and exciting and" – she searched for another word—"and…"

"I'm glad," Tamani said. He was close by her shoulder now. "I wasn't asking to prove some kind of a point," he said earnestly. "I really wanted to know. And I hoped you were. I – I worry about you. Needlessly, I'm sure, but I do nonetheless."

Embarrassment flooded through her and she tried to relax her stiffened spine. "Sorry."

"Well, you should be." Tamani grinned.

Laurel shook her head with a laugh.

Out of the corner of her eye she saw him lift his hand towards her, then he let it drop and attempted to subtly push his hands into his pockets.

"What?" Laurel said.

"Nothing," Tamani said, turning and starting to cross back over to the opposite side of the room.

"The 'faerie dust'?" Laurel asked, remembering last year as well as earlier that summer in Avalon.

Tamani nodded.

"Let me see." She'd been too late in Avalon, but now she had a perfect opportunity.

"You got mad at me last year."

"Oh, please. Don't make me responsible for all the stupid things I did last year." She grabbed his wrist and pulled his hand into hers.

He didn't resist.

His hand was lightly brushed with a fine, glittery powder. She held his arm at an angle so the pollen caught the sun and glimmered. "It's so pretty."

Only then did Tamani's hand relax. A playful grin crossed his face and he lifted a hand and rubbed a finger across her cheek, leaving a light, silvery streak.

"Hey!"

His swift hands shot out and he drew a line across her other cheek. "Now you match."

His hand reached out once more – aiming for her nose – but she was ready this time. Her fingers closed around his wrist, blocking him. Tamani looked down at his hand, a good three inches away from her face. "I'm impressed."

He brought his other hand up so quickly, Laurel didn't

even see it before it touched her nose. She swatted at his hand as he laughed and continued trying to paint stripes and she tried, usually unsuccessfully, to block him. He finally managed to grab both of her hands and held them down to her sides, pulling her against his chest. Her smile melted away as she looked up at him, their faces only a few inches apart.

"I win," he whispered.

Their eyes locked and Tamani slowly moved forward. But before his face could reach hers, Laurel dropped her head, breaking eye contact. "Sorry," she murmured.

Tamani just nodded and let her go. "Were you going to try to get the upstairs today too?" he asked.

Laurel looked around at the half-clean downstairs. "Maybe?"

"I'll stay and help, if you want," he offered.

"I would like you to stay," Laurel said, her words answering more than just the simple question. "But only if you want to."

"I do," he said, his gaze unwavering. "Besides," he added with a grin, "you didn't bring a ladder. How will you get all the way to the ceiling without my help? You're practically a sapling."

They worked for the next three hours, until they were both tired and dusty, but the house was mostly clean. At the very least, it would be an easier job the next time Laurel attempted it.

Tamani insisted on carrying the bucket when he walked her back out to her car. "I'd ask you to stay, but I really would be more comfortable if you were home by sunset," he said. "Especially after last night. It's just better that way."

Laurel nodded.

"And be careful," he said sternly. "We watch out for you as much as we can, but we're not miracle workers."

"I will be careful," Laurel promised. "I *have* been careful." She stood for a few moments, and this time it was Tam who stepped forward first, his arms twining around her, holding her tight, his face against her neck.

"Come back soon," he murmured. "I miss you."

"I know," Laurel admitted. "I'll try."

She slid in behind the wheel and adjusted the mirror so she could see Tamani standing with his hands in his pockets, watching her. A small movement caught her eye and she studied a thick tree at the end of her yard. It took a moment to make out the tall, slim faerie standing half behind it. Shar. He said nothing to make his presence known – he just glared.

Laurel shivered. He wasn't glaring at Tamani. He was glaring at *her*.

Chapter Nineteen

L aurel pulled open the heavy double doors in the front of the school on Monday morning, anxious to see David. Between her trip to the land and a last-minute visit David had to make to his grandparents, they hadn't seen each other all weekend.

Her smile faded when she got to her locker and found it deserted. She and David drove in together about half the time, but when they didn't, they always met here before class. And after class.

And between classes.

But today, he was nowhere to be seen. She would have assumed he was just running late, but he hadn't called to say so, as he had in the past. Laurel tried to reason away her concerns. It wasn't exactly a regular occurrence for David to miss the first bell, but still, it did happen sometimes. She slowly retrieved her Spanish book, trying to look like she was busy instead of like a girl who had nothing better to do than hang out at her locker, waiting for her boyfriend.

She procrastinated until thirty seconds before the final bell, then sprinted to make it into Spanish on time.

She rushed out of class right as her teacher released them only to find the space in front of her locker empty again. Fear pounded through her and she hurried to the front office, wishing for the millionth time that she had a cell phone. Her parents could certainly have afforded one for her, but her mother steadfastly maintained that she didn't need one until she left for college.

Parents.

"Can I use the phone real quick?" Laurel asked the secretary. The secretary plunked a cordless down on the counter in front of her. Laurel dialled David's cell number and her tension rose as it rang, once, twice. On the fourth ring his voice mail picked up. It beeped for her to leave a message, but what was she supposed to say? *I'm worried. Please come to school?*

She hung up without saying anything. She considered ditching and driving around town looking for him, but besides the futility of that, she had chemistry next. If he did just show up super late, at least if she was in class she'd know immediately.

Chemistry class had never lasted so long. While her teacher rattled on about polyatomic ions, Laurel's mind was flipping through progressively worse and worse scenarios. David killed by trolls. David taken and tortured by trolls. David taken by trolls and used as a trap for her so *she* could be tortured. By the end of the class they all seemed not only believable but probable.

Laurel ran over to the social studies hallway, where Chelsea was just stepping out of history. "Have you seen David?" Laurel asked.

Chelsea shook her head. "I always assume he's with you."

"I can't find him," Laurel said, trying to keep her voice from shaking.

"Maybe he's sick," Chelsea suggested – Laurel had to admit – rationally.

"Yeah, but he's not answering his cell. He always answers his cell."

"He might be sleeping."

"Maybe," Laurel said. She returned to her locker and pulled out her American literature textbook. She looked at the cover and suddenly the thought of reading anything someone wrote a hundred years ago seemed like the most pointless thing in the world. She put it back and grabbed her bag instead. She just had to see if he was at home. It wouldn't take that long – she probably wouldn't even be counted absent if she hurried back. She was just reaching out to swing her locker door shut when Chelsea tapped her shoulder, startling her.

"There he is," she said, pointing down the hall. David was walking towards her, a smile on his face and sunglasses hiding his eyes. Laurel was running before she could stop herself. She slammed into David and wrapped her arms around him, squeezing as hard as she could.

"Well, hello," David said, looking down at her questioningly.

After an hour spent visualising his demise, David's casual tone made hot anger bubble up in her chest. She grabbed the front of his shirt in both fists and shook him a little. "You scared me to death, David Adam Lawson! Where the hell have you been?"

David glanced down the hall towards the front doors. "Let's get out of here," he said, not answering her question.

"What do you mean?"

"Let's go somewhere, have some fun."

She glanced around before saying quietly, "Ditch?"

"Oh, come on. You have literature this hour. You're getting, what? An A plus, plus? Let's go!"

She looked up at him, one eyebrow raised sceptically. "You want to take off and ditch class to go 'have some fun'? Who are you and what have you done with my boyfriend?"

David just smiled. "Come on," he said earnestly. "Just this once."

"OK," she said. She was so relieved to see him, it didn't really matter where he wanted to go. She was game. "Let's do it!"

"Great," David said, grabbing her hand. His gait was as close to skipping as Laurel had ever seen. "Come on!"

She had to admit that his excitement was infectious. She found herself laughing along with him as they raced out to his car.

"Where are we going?" she asked as she clicked her seat belt.

"It's a surprise," David said, a mischievous glint in his eye. He pulled out a long strip of cloth. "Close your eyes," he said softly.

"You're kidding me, right?" Laurel said in disbelief.

"Come on, now," David said. "You trust me, don't you?"

Laurel looked up at him, his sunglasses reflecting her own face back at her. "What's up with the shades?" Laurel asked. "I can't see your eyes in those things."

"That's the point, isn't it?"

"What, preventing your girlfriend from seeing your eyes?"

"Not you specifically." He grinned. "Anyway, I think they're pretty sweet."

"I think it would be pretty sweet if I could see your eyes, David."

Without hesitation, he slipped off the sunglasses and looked at her, his soft blue eyes open and earnest. All of Laurel's worries dissipated and she turned to let him blindfold her. "I trust you," she said.

Once the blindfold was in place, Laurel sat back in the passenger seat and tried to pay attention to each turn David was making, determined to keep track of where she was. But after about five minutes it became obvious that he was going in circles, so she gave up. Soon the car bumped against a kerb and came to a stop. After a few seconds her door opened and David gently helped her out, one hand at her waist and the other on her shoulder to stabilise her.

"David," Laurel said tentatively, "I hate to be a spoilsport, but I hope we're someplace safe. After the other night... well... you know."

"Don't worry," David said, his mouth close to her ear.

"I've brought you to the safest place in the world." David removed the blindfold, and for a moment the sunlight was blinding as it filtered down through the leaves, giving everything an ethereal glow. They were standing in a small clearing ringed by the very last of the autumn flowers – orange gloriosa daisies, touches of purple coneflowers, and some blue Russian sage. In the middle, on a patch of thick, green grass, was a blanket with a couple of couch pillows and several bowls of sliced fruit. Strawberries, nectarines, apples, and a bottle of sparkling cider with beads of condensation that glinted in the gentle sunlight. Laurel smiled and turned around, to confirm her suspicion – just past the edge of the trees, she could see her own backyard. Safest place in the world, indeed.

"David! This is beautiful!" Laurel said breathlessly, stretching up on her toes to kiss him, glad they were just out of sight of the house, in case either of her parents came home for lunch – which they usually didn't. "When did you do this?"

"There was a reason you couldn't find me this morning," he said sheepishly.

"David Lawson!" Laurel gasped with mock sternness. "What is the world coming to when Del Norte's star student is skipping his classes?"

He shrugged, then grinned. "Some things are more important than my GPA."

After a brief hesitation, Laurel asked, "Did I... forget some special occasion?"

David shook his head. "Nope. I just thought that we've both been under so much stress lately that we haven't really had any good together-time."

Laurel reached her arms around David's neck and kissed him. "I think this is definitely going to make up for it."

"That's the idea," he replied. "Have a seat." She sat cross-legged on the blanket and he dropped to the ground behind her. "One more thing," he said, his hands slipping around her waist, just under her shirt. Laurel smiled as he worked at the knot in her sash, but he eventually managed it and pushed her shirt back so her blossom could splay out behind her. "Much better," David said. He poured them each a glass of cider and they lay propped up on the pillows, with Laurel snuggled against David's chest.

"This is awesome," Laurel said lazily. David held up a slice of nectarine; she laughed as he avoided her hands and held the fruit towards her face. She tilted her head back and opened her mouth. She leaned forward at the last second, her teeth biting lightly at his fingers. Then she let his hand go and pressed her mouth against his lips instead. His fingers trailed over the bare skin, now showing between the top of her jeans and the hem of her shirt, caressing her softly, gently, tentatively. Even after a year he always touched her that way, as if it was a privilege he wasn't entirely convinced he had earned.

He tasted like apples and nectarines, and the smell from the grass had seeped into his clothes. Laurel often noticed the biological differences between the two of them, but today they seemed the same. With the smell and taste of nature all around him, David could almost have been a faerie.

"How is your blossom?" David asked, stroking it very gently.

"It's OK now," Laurel said. "The first couple of days it still ached, but I think it's going to be fine." She craned her neck, trying to see the damaged side. "I hate the way it's healing, though. The ends are dry and brown. It's really not very pretty."

"But it was some major damage," David said. He kissed her forehead. "It will grow back next year and will be as beautiful as ever."

"Wow, next year," Laurel said. "I can hardly even imagine next year. Sometimes it feels like this year will never end."

"And last year – doesn't it seem like ages ago? So much has happened." David laughed. "Would you have imagined a year ago that we'd be lying here today?"

Laurel just smiled and shook her head. "I thought I was at death's door last year."

"What do you think we'll be doing next year?"

"This same thing, I hope," Laurel said, snuggling against him.

"Well, other than that." He lay back, lacing his fingers together to support his head. Laurel rolled on to her side, her stomach pressed against his ribs. "I mean, senior year next year. We'll be picking colleges and stuff."

Laurel's heart sank and she looked away from him. Ever since Chelsea had brought up the SAT tests the thought of her education and future had been a little hard to think about. "I don't think college is in my future."

"What? Why not?"

"I imagine they'll want me at the Academy full-time," she said, a little despondently.

David propped his head up on his elbow so he could look at her. "I always figured you would study at the Academy off and on – maybe full-time eventually – but that doesn't mean you can't go to college."

"What would be the point?" Laurel shrugged. "It's not like I'm going to have a career someday. I'm a faerie."

"So?"

"They'll want me to do... faerie stuff." She gestured vaguely with her hands.

David pursed his lips. "What does it matter what *they* want? What do *you* want?"

"I... don't really know, I guess. What else would I do?"

"You're way more than just a faerie, Laurel. You have this opportunity to do something most faeries never get to do. To live like a human. To make that choice."

"But they'll never see any of that as important. The only thing that matters to anyone in Avalon is that I learn how to be a Fall faerie – and that I inherit the land."

"It doesn't matter what *they* think is important. You're the one who decides what's important. Same with anything in life. The value you give it is the only value it has." He paused. "Don't let them convince you that humans aren't important," he said, his voice barely a whisper. "If you think we're important, then we are."

"But what would I do?"

"What did you want to do before you found out you were a faerie?"

Laurel shrugged. "I hadn't decided on just one thing. I thought about being an English teacher or a college professor." She grinned. "For a while I thought about being a nurse. I don't think I've ever told anyone that."

"How come?"

She rolled her eyes. "My mom would just die if I ended up working in a hospital." She looked up at David. "I've always kind of wanted to be in a position where I could help people, you know?"

"What about being a doctor?"

She shook her head. "That's the thing – I don't think I'm really that interested in medicine… or teaching, either. But teachers and nurses help people, so I thought maybe that's what I'd do. But I really don't know."

"Well, whatever you decide to do, you should do it. But it should be what *you* want."

"Sometimes… sometimes I don't think I have control over my life any more. I mean, do I have the option of not attending the Academy? It's the role I've always been intended for."

"What are they going to do? Drag you kicking and screaming back to Avalon? I kinda doubt it."

Laurel nodded slowly. He was right. Maybe she could stay.

But will I want to stay?

For now, all she wanted was to enjoy David. He looked like he was about to say something else, but she cut him off with a kiss, her arms wrapping around his neck. "Thank you for this," she murmured against his mouth.

"It's just what I needed. You always seem to know exactly what I need."

"My pleasure," David said, smiling softly. The air around them was full of the scent of pine and fruit, damp earth and the soft aroma of Laurel's blossom. Everything was perfect as he kissed her again, his lips always so soft, so gentle. Now his hands were in her hair as Laurel raised one knee up to rest against his thigh, their bodies snug together like well-fitting puzzle pieces. She never wanted this to end.

David pulled his face back and studied her, staring until Laurel giggled self-consciously. "What?"

David's mouth, usually so quick to smile, stayed serious. "You're so beautiful," he whispered. "And not just because of what you look like. Everything about you is beautiful. Sometimes I'm afraid this is the most awesome dream ever, and I'm going to wake up someday." He chuckled. "And quite frankly, you being a faerie isn't exactly helping."

They both laughed, the sound filling the glade. "Well," she said coyly, "I guess I'll have to prove to you just how real I am." She pressed herself close against his chest and lifted her head to kiss him again.

Chapter Twenty

Laurel sprawled down on her bed with a smile. It had been such a great day – and a break she really needed. With a contented sigh she spread her arms out and something sharp hit her elbow. She glanced over at a familiar-looking square of ribbon-bedecked parchment. A nervous jolt shot through her and she hoped this wasn't an early summons to come back to the Academy for the month-long winter break in December. Much as she had enjoyed her summer in Avalon, she didn't want to spend the rest of high school being summoned to the Academy every time she had a break from school. She had a life!

Hesitantly, she pulled the ends of the ribbon and opened the folded square. A thrill of excitement replaced her dread.

You are cordially invited to attend the festival of Samhain to usher in the New Year. Should you choose to attend, please present yourself at the gate on the morning of November 1st.

Formal dress is requested.

Then, scribbled in boyish script at the lower right hand corner of the invitation, was a note.

I'll escort you. Tam

Nothing else.

She touched the signature at the bottom. It said so much and yet so little. There was no closing; not "Love, Tam" or "Your Tam". Or even "Sincerely, Tam". But he had signed it Tam, not Tamani. Maybe it was in case someone else opened the invitation. Or maybe he had noticed that she only called him Tam when they were having a particularly close moment.

And maybe it meant nothing at all.

Besides, that was the least of her concerns. How was she going to make this work? She couldn't tell David. Not after the way he had reacted last time she'd gone to see Tamani. Suddenly she wondered how much today was inspired by the long Saturday she'd just spent at the land.

Telling David she wanted to go spend another entire day in Avalon – escorted by Tamani – probably wouldn't sit well with David right now.

But a festival in Avalon! It was a chance she couldn't pass up. She'd want to go even if Tamani couldn't be there.

She didn't like lying to David, but in this case, maybe it was for the best. There were some things it was just better if your boyfriend didn't know. Besides, David was fascinated with Avalon. It seemed almost selfish to tell him where she was going when he couldn't come. The faeries would never let a human enter Avalon. Maybe it really *was* better all around if he just didn't know.

The more Laurel thought about it, the more anxious she felt about the whole thing. She pushed the invitation under her pillow and, in an effort to distract herself, sat down at her desk, pulling out her sugar-glass components. When the first vial shattered – as if on cue – Laurel sighed. She started again.

November first was a Saturday; David would probably be working. That was helpful, at least a little. But her social life was fairly limited. If she wasn't at home, in school, or at work, she was always with David. Well, and sometimes Chelsea.

Chelsea! She could say she was doing something with

Chelsea. Her brilliant idea fizzled almost as soon as it came into being. Chelsea didn't even lie for herself; she certainly wouldn't lie for Laurel.

Still, Laurel couldn't bear the thought of missing the festival. She didn't have any clue what it might be like, but she knew exactly what she would wear. It was the perfect opportunity to wear the dark blue gown she'd picked up near the end of her stay in Avalon. Though she had felt a little guilty taking it at the time, now it seemed like kismet.

Smiling in anticipation, Laurel put down her diamond tube and surveyed her work. She hadn't given a conscious thought to the mindlessly repetitive task since the first vial shattered in her hand.

There, lined neatly at the top of her desk, sat four perfectly formed sugar vials.

That Friday, Laurel sat at the kitchen counter, toiling over her Spanish homework. There were only about six weeks until finals, and conjugating verbs in the past imperfect remained a complete mystery. Her petals hung limply behind her; two had already fallen out, and Laurel's relief managed to crowd out her disappointment. It felt dangerous to be in bloom while trolls were stalking her. There hadn't been any more scares in the last few weeks, but then, she and David had been extremely careful. They rarely hung out anywhere except at Laurel's house, and even at school Laurel kept her full kit in the bottom of her backpack and carried it around at all times.

She'd been working extra hard on her Avalon studies as well. This week's success with the sugar-glass vials had renewed her confidence; unfortunately, it had been dwindling again as her attempts at potion brewing continued to fail. She hadn't even managed to make another vial since Monday. And now she'd run out of ingredients for the monastuolo serum, which left her mixing fertilisers or insect repellents – not exactly the kind of thing that would come in handy against a troll. But she couldn't stop practising, not when so many people were depending on her to get things right.

With tonight being Halloween, Laurel's stress level was ratcheted up a notch. She didn't like the idea of a bunch of people running around in masks. What was to keep trolls from terrorising the town? On top of that, her mom and dad had volunteered for a Halloween programme where the kids went trick-or-treating at local businesses. Laurel would have felt much more comfortable with them being home, where she – and, more importantly, her faerie sentries – could keep an eye on them. But that would require telling them about the trolls, which was unlikely to go over well. Particularly seeing as how Laurel's mom was already in perpetual shock over the existence of faeries. No, it was better that they were blissfully ignorant. Besides, the trolls weren't after her parents; they were after her.

As if sensing her thoughts, Laurel's mom came downstairs and grabbed the coffeepot, filling her travel mug with dark, hours-old coffee. "I gotta head back to the store," she said, her eyes studiously avoiding Laurel's blossom – or what was left of it. "I won't be back till late. You're having friends over tonight to help hand out candy, right?"

"In about half an hour," Laurel said. That had been her brainchild. She couldn't protect everyone, but at least she could keep Ryan and Chelsea safe. Not that Laurel really felt the trolls represented much of a danger to them, but something had Laurel feeling universally paranoid tonight.

"Have fun," her mom replied, popping the lid on to her mug. She took a sip and made a face. "Ugh, this is terrible. Well, the candy's in the top cupboard." She gestured vaguely.

"Great! Thanks for picking that up." Laurel smiled, probably trying a little too hard, but it was better than not trying at all.

"No problem. And there should be plenty, so you can eat some too." She hesitated, and her eyes met Laurel's. "I mean, not you specifically. Obviously you don't eat it. But, you know, David and Chelsea and – I gotta go." She breezed past Laurel, fleeing the awkwardness. It was always like that; things would be good for a while, then something would remind Laurel's mom just how strange life had truly become. Laurel sighed. Moments like these always depressed her. The disappointment was just starting to wash over her when her mom cleared her throat from behind Laurel's right shoulder.

"Um," she said tentatively, "you seem to be falling apart." She was looking down rather strangely at three more petals that had fallen out while Laurel was doing her homework. Her mom paused for a second and looked like she would turn and head out the door, but then she changed her mind and leaned down and picked up a petal. Laurel sat still and held her breath, trying to figure out if this was a good thing or not. Her mom held the long petal – bigger than any other she'd ever seen on a regular plant, Laurel was sure – and then lifted it towards the window, watching the sun shine through it. Another pause and then her mom looked over at her. "Can I… do you mind if I take this with me to the store?" she asked, her voice quiet, almost timid.

"Sure!" Laurel said, cringing as her voice filled the room – too bright, too cheery.

But her mom didn't seem to notice. She nodded and tucked the petal carefully into her tote. She glanced down at her watch and sucked in a loud breath. "Now I really am late," she said, whirling towards the door. She took two steps, then stopped and turned. As if breaking through an unseen barrier, she rushed back and hugged Laurel. Really hugged her.

It was too short – only a few brief seconds – but it was *real*. Without another word, her mom strode out, her heels clicking on the wood floor as she opened the door and shut it hard behind her.

Laurel sat on her stool, smiling. It was a small step, and by tomorrow it might not mean anything, but she was willing to take it for what it was worth. She could still feel her mom's hand on her back, the warmth of her cheek, the faint lingering smell of her perfume. Familiar, like a long-lost friend coming home.

The front door swung open suddenly, startling her out of her reverie, and Laurel crumpled a page in her book, barely managing to bite off a scream. She ducked behind the island in the kitchen and heard soft footsteps heading towards her. Had a troll managed to get past the warding around her house? Jamison had said it would block all except the strongest trolls, but it wasn't foolproof.

Laurel thought of her sentries outside. Where were they? The footsteps stopped at the base of the stairs. He was between her and the back door. Laurel took a quick moment to reach up and grab a knife from the block on the counter.

The butcher knife. Awesome.

Maybe she could surprise him, get him with the butcher knife somehow, and get to the back door before he could catch her. It was a big risk, but she didn't have any other choice. If she could just make it out the back door where the sentries could see her, she would be safe. She snuck around to the kitchen doorway and raised the knife in front of her chest. The footsteps were coming closer.

David's familiar form stepped around the corner. "Whoa!" he cried, jumping back with his hands held out in front of him.

Laurel froze, the butcher knife still clutched in both hands as shock, fear, relief, and mortification crashed over her all at once. With a grunt of disgust she slammed the knife down on the counter. "What is *wrong* with me?"

David stepped forward and pulled her to him, rubbing his hands up and down her arms.

"It's my fault," he said. "I'm early. I saw your mom backing out of the driveway and she told me to just go in. I should have thought, and knocked, or—"

"It's not your fault, David. It's mine."

"It's *not* your fault, it's – it's just everything. The trolls, Halloween, Klea…" He ran his hands through his hair. "We're both totally wound up."

"I know," Laurel said, leaning forward and wrapping her arms around his waist. Forcing herself to change the subject, she said, "I had a good moment with my mom just before you got here."

"Oh, yeah?"

Laurel nodded. "I've been waiting for things to get better for almost a year. Maybe… maybe they're starting to."

"It will work out."

"I hope so."

"I know so," David said, his lips trailing down her face and behind her ear. "You're too beautiful for anyone to stay mad at too long."

"I'm serious!" she said, her breath quickening as his lips caressed the side of her neck.

"Oh, I'm serious too," he said, his hands sliding up the skin on her back. "Very, very serious."

She laughed. "You're *never* serious."

"Serious about you," he said, his hands coming to rest at her hips.

She melted against him and his arms went around her back for a few seconds before he pulled away.

"What?" she said.

He pointed at the floor. Two petals were lying on the carpet. "We should probably pick those up before Chelsea and Ryan get here," he said teasingly.

"No kidding. The whole thing will be gone by tomorrow. Thank goodness."

"We could try to get them all rubbed off right now," David said, cocking his head towards the couch.

"As nice as that sounds," Laurel said, tapping her fingers gently against his chest, "Chelsea and Ryan will be here any minute."

"They won't be shocked – they make out at school, like, constantly," he said with a grin.

Laurel just looked at him with one eyebrow raised.

"Fine." He kissed her once more, then walked into the kitchen and opened the fridge. "Can't you keep anything stocked in here except Sprite? Some Mountain Dew, maybe?"

"Sure, 'cause that would be a *great* colour for my eyes and hair," Laurel said sarcastically. "Besides, the caffeine would make me sick."

"I didn't say *you* had to drink it," David replied, opening a can of Sprite and handing it to her. "Just keep it around in case somebody else wants it." He opened his own can and slid on to a stool at the bar. "Chelsea isn't going to expect us to dress up to hand out candy or anything, is she?" he asked, wrinkling his nose.

"No, I checked to make sure," Laurel replied. "No one's dressing up except me."

"You're dressing up?" David asked sceptically.

"Yep. I'm pretending to be a human."

David just rolled his eyes. "Walked right into that, didn't I?" He looked down at her crumpled Spanish book. "Studying?" he asked. "It looks like your book is taking it pretty hard."

"I was, till I got distracted trying to kill you with the butcher knife."

"Oh, yes, that was fun. We must do it again sometime."

Laurel groaned and leaned her head into her hands. "I could have killed you," she said.

"No way," David said with a grin. "I was totally prepared." He reached behind him and pulled out the black gun.

Laurel jumped off her stool. "David! You brought your gun into my house?"

"Sure," he said, completely nonchalant.

"Get it out of here, David!"

"Hey, hey, come on," he said, quickly stowing the gun in a concealed holster at the small of his back. "It's not like I've ever done it before. Your house is safe... well, as safe as anything is these days. But" – he glanced around the room as if he expected someone to be there, listening—"we're having Chelsea and Ryan over tonight. And you freaking out about Halloween is making me freak out a little bit too. I wanted to be ready in case... just in case. Honestly, I thought it might make you feel a little more secure. Obviously I was wrong."

He looked up and met Laurel's eyes, her glare warring with his apologetic but determined gaze. She faltered first. "I'm sorry. I just hate those things."

He hesitated "If you really want me to, I'll take it out to the car."

What he said about being ready did make sense. But her hatred of the gun won out. "I would appreciate that," she said quietly. The shrill chiming of the doorbell made Laurel jump. "They're here," she said, frustrated. "Just keep that thing out of sight for now," she ordered. "I don't want to see it again."

She got as far as the kitchen doorway before David grabbed her arm. "Your blossom," he whispered. "I'll get the ones on the floor."

"Crap. Be right there!" Laurel yelled towards the front door. She unwound the sash from her wrist and hurriedly replaced it around her waist. She just had to get the limp petals out of sight; she could steal away to the bathroom later and do a more graceful job.

David disposed of the petals she'd left on the floor while Laurel opened the front door to Chelsea and Ryan with a smile she hoped didn't look too fake. "Hey, guys."

They were wearing silly grins and neon headbands, complete with glowing eyes bobbing over their heads at the ends of long springs.

Laurel raised an eyebrow. "Impressive," she said dryly.

"Not as impressive as that," Chelsea said, pointing over Laurel's shoulder.

"What?" Laurel said, whipping her head around, suddenly panicked that her petals were sticking up. As soon as she did, something snapped on to the sides of her head and she rolled her eyes upward to see her own set of googley eyes, swaying in and out of view. "Thanks," she drawled sarcastically.

"Aw, come on," Chelsea said. "They're fun!"

Laurel turned to Ryan, eyebrow raised.

"Don't look at me," he said. "This was all Chelsea's idea."

"OK, I'll wear them," Laurel said with a conspiratorial

grin. "As long as you brought a set for David, too."

Chelsea held up a fourth headband.

"Perfect." She pulled Chelsea in and peered out at the dusk as she shut the door behind Ryan.

Chapter Twenty-one

The morning air was cold and sharp, the sun merely a bright pink shadow working its way up the cloudy eastern horizon. Laurel shrugged into her jacket on the front porch and pulled her keys out of her pocket, trying to make as little noise as possible.

"Where are you going?"

Laurel shrieked and dropped her keys. So much for stealth.

"Sorry," her dad said, poking his head out the front door. His hair was sticking out every which way and he looked groggy – he never had been one for mornings. "I didn't mean to startle you."

"It's OK," Laurel said, bending to pick up her keys. "I'm just going to Chelsea's." She could have told her dad where she was actually going, but it was easier this way. Less chance of David accidentally finding out.

"Oh, that's right, you told us that last night. Why so early?"

"Chelsea's got a date with Ryan tonight," Laurel said, the lie rolling off her tongue. She wondered if this was getting too easy. "We'll need all the time we can get."

"Well, get going, then. Have fun," her dad said with a yawn. "I'm going back to bed."

Laurel hurried to her car and backed out as quickly as she could without drawing attention to herself. The sooner she was out of town, the better.

In the end, she'd decided not to tell David. She hated lying but didn't know what else to do. After last night he'd be too worried; he'd insist that she skip it.

Or accompany her with that stupid gun of his.

She hated that she now knew he carried it around with him. Logically she couldn't blame him – he didn't have even the rudimentary defences that she did – but several times last night she had seen him start to reach for the hidden holster when someone knocked on the door. Which, being Halloween, had happened every few minutes. It was better if she just didn't tell him where she was going. They were both too wound up.

She hadn't come up with a good excuse for Chelsea,

so she wouldn't tell Chelsea anything at all. With luck, David would never miss her and Chelsea wouldn't be consulted. She'd leave the festival early, if she had to. And not just to get back before David got off work; she didn't want to be anywhere but safe in her house when night fell.

There was no traffic on the way to Orick, but Laurel still kept a sharp eye on the sides of the road and her rearview mirror, watching for any sign she was being followed. She pulled into Orick's lone gas station and, after studying the parking lot, ran inside and hurried into the bathroom. She opened her backpack and pulled out the dress. She hadn't worn it except to try it on; now, as she slipped the rustling fabric over her head and adjusted it around her slim body, a thrill of excitement rushed through her. Her final few petals had fallen out during the night, and her back was smooth and ivory, a tiny scarlike line down the middle, just like last year. After peeking out of the bathroom to make sure the convenience store was still mostly empty, Laurel darted back to her car, her skirts swishing around her ankles and flip-flop-clad feet. From there it was only minutes to the end of the cabin's long driveway. She parked her car behind a large fir, concealing it from the main road.

Tamani was waiting for her, not at the edge of the tree

line, but right up in the yard of the small cabin. He was leaning against the front gate, a long black cloak hanging from his shoulders, his knee-length breeches tucked into tall, black boots. Her breathing quickened at the sight of him.

Not for the first time, Laurel wondered if coming today had been a mistake. *It's not too late to change my mind.*

As Laurel approached, Tamani stood motionless, his eyes following her. He didn't speak until she stopped in front of him, close enough that he could have reached out and pulled her to him if he tried.

"I wasn't sure you would come," he said, his voice breaking a little, as if he hadn't spoken in a long time. As if he had stood out in the cold all night, waiting for her.

Maybe he had.

She could leave. Tamani would forgive her. Eventually. She looked up at him. There was something wary in his demeanour, like he could sense she was on the verge of turning back.

A gust of wind burst through the trees and brushed Tamani's hair across his eyes. He lifted one hand and tucked the long strands behind his ear. For just a second, as his forearm crossed over his face, his eyes dropped, scanning the length of her from head to toe – something he almost never did. And in that split second, something felt different. Laurel wasn't sure just what.

"To Avalon?" Tamani beckoned towards the trees as his hand pressed, gently, against the small of Laurel's back. She was approaching the point of no return; some part of her sensed it.

She looked at Tamani; she looked at the trees.

Then she stepped forward and crossed the line.

The streets of Avalon were teeming with faeries. Even with Tamani carefully guiding her, it was a little difficult to wade through the crowd.

"What exactly do you do at a festival?" Laurel asked, ducking around a tight circle of faeries conversing in the middle of the street.

"It depends. Today we're going to the Grande Theatre in Summer to see a ballet. Afterwards we'll all gather on the common green where there will be music, food, and dancing." He hesitated. "Then everyone will stay or disperse as they choose and the revelries will continue until everyone is satisfied and returns to their usual pursuits. This way," he said, pointing up a gentle hill.

As they climbed, the coliseum slowly came into view. Unlike the Academy, which was mostly stone, or the homes of the Summer faeries, which were glass, the walls of the coliseum were living trees, like the one where Tamani's mother lived. But instead of being round and hollow, these black-barked trees were stretched and flattened, overlapping one another to form a solid wooden wall at least fifty feet high topped with dense foliage. Bolts of brightly coloured silk, brilliantly painted murals, and statues of marble and granite adorned the walls almost haphazardly, lending a festive atmosphere to the massive structure.

Laurel's awe was dampened when they found themselves near the end of a long line of faeries waiting to enter the coliseum. All were smartly dressed, though Laurel didn't see anyone else in clothing as fine as hers. Dressed wrong again. She sighed and turned to Tamani. "This is going to take ages."

Tamani shook his head. "That's not your entrance." He pointed to the right of the line and continued guiding her through the crowd. They came to a small archway in the coliseum's walls, about fifty feet from the main entrance. Two tall guards in deep-blue uniforms stood on either side of the door.

"Laurel Sewell," Tamani said quietly to the guards.

One glanced at Laurel before his eyes swung back to Tamani. For some reason he looked up and down Tamani's arms before speaking. "*Am fear-faire* for a Fall?"

"*Fear-gleidhidh,*" Tamani corrected, glancing

uncomfortably at Laurel. "I'm Tamani de Rhoslyn. Hecate's eye, man, I said this is Laurel *Sewell.*"

The guard straightened a little and nodded at his partner, who opened the door. "You may pass."

"*Fear-glide?*" Laurel said, knowing even as the phrase came out of her mouth that she was butchering it. She remembered Jamison's explanation of *Am fear-faire* earlier in the summer, but this was something new.

"It means I'm your… escort," Tamani said, furrowing his brow. "When I gave him your human surname, I assumed he'd realise who you were and not make a fuss. But he clearly never trained at the manor."

"The manor?" How did every conversation with Tamani turn into a crash course in faerie culture?

"Not now," Tamani replied gently. "It's not important."

And indeed, as Laurel surveyed the interior of the expansive coliseum, all questions evaporated from her mind and she gasped in delight.

The coliseum walls had been grown around a steeply inclined depression in the top of the hill. She stood now on an expansive mezzanine, an outgrowth of tightly woven branches that extended from the coliseum's living walls. Except for three ornate golden chairs on a dais at the centre of the mezzanine, all the seats were wooden, cushioned in red silk and complete with armrests that grew seamlessly from the floor. They had clearly been arranged with attention to view rather than the most efficient seating capacity.

Fifty feet away, Laurel saw faeries crowding through the main entrance and descending into the ground floor, which was little more than a grassy hillside. There was no seating below the mezzanine, but faeries crowded together amicably, jostling to get as close as they could to the biggest stage Laurel had ever seen. It was draped in silky white curtains that glittered with thousands of crystals that swung gently in the breeze, casting rainbows over the entire theatre. From above, sunlight poured through a thin canopy of gauzy material that billowed and waved with the wind. It softened the glare of the sun without blocking out its beneficial rays.

And everywhere she looked Laurel saw shimmering diamonds, swatches of golden silk, elaborate tapestries celebrating the history of Avalon. Dark corners were lit with gold orbs like the one Tamani had used on Laurel more than a year ago, after she'd been thrown in the Chetco. Here and there, wreaths of flowers or piles of fruit adorned randomly distributed pillars of wood or stone.

Laurel took a deep breath and began walking forward, wondering where to sit. After a few seconds, she looked back, sensing Tamani was no longer with her. He remained by the archway, looking as though he intended to stay there.

"Hey!" she said, striding back to him. "Come on, Tam."

He shook his head. "It's just for the show. I'll wait for you here, and we'll go to the revelries afterwards."

"No," Laurel said. She walked to his side and laid a hand on his arm. "Please come with me," she said quietly.

"I can't," Tamani said. "It's not my place."

"I say it's your place."

"Take it up with the Queen," Tamani said sardonically.

"I will."

Alarm filled his voice now. "No, Laurel. I can't. I'll just cause trouble."

"Then I'll stay here with you," she said, slipping her hand into his.

Tamani shook his head again. "This is my place. There" – he gestured to the red silk seating at the lip of the mezzanine—"is yours."

"Jamison will be here, Tam. We'll both insist you be allowed to sit with me. I'm sure of it."

Tamani's eyes flitted back and forth between Laurel, the Fall faeries milling around the mezzanine, and the crush of Spring faeries pouring through the main entrance. "Fine," he said with a sigh.

"Thank you!" Laurel said, pushing impulsively up on to her toes to kiss his cheek. As soon as she did, she wished she hadn't. She pulled back a few inches and couldn't seem to go any farther. Tamani turned his head to look her full in the face. He was so close, their noses almost touched. His breath caressed her lips, and she felt herself leaning towards him.

Tamani turned his face away. "Lead on," he said in a voice so quiet Laurel barely heard him.

So Laurel led Tamani down the steps of the mezzanine, and this time he followed. But the nervous, almost frightened Tamani following her was a stranger to Laurel. His cockiness was gone, his confidence sapped; he looked like he was trying to disappear into his cloak.

Laurel stopped and turned to him, her hands on the sides of his arms, not speaking until he finally raised his eyes to hers. "What is wrong?"

"I shouldn't be here," he whispered. "I don't belong here."

"You belong with me," Laurel said firmly. "I need you with me."

He looked down at her, an edge of fear in his eyes that she'd never seen before. Not even when Barnes shot him. "It's not my place," he insisted again. "I don't want to be that faerie."

"What faerie?"

"The kind who latches on to a girl above his station, consumed by ambition like a common animal. That's not what I'm doing; my oath to you, it's not. I just wanted to meet you afterwards. I didn't plan this."

"Is this because you're a Spring faerie?" she asked sharply. The buzz of the crowd kept their conversation relatively private, but she lowered her voice just the same.

Tamani refused to meet her gaze.

"It is! Not only do *they* think you're a second-class – oh, excuse me, *fourth*-class citizen – *you* think you are too. Why?"

"It's just the way things are," Tamani muttered, still not looking at her.

"Well, it's not the way they should be!" Laurel hissed. She grabbed both of Tamani's shoulders and forced him to look at her. "Tamani, you are twice the faerie of any Fall faerie in the Academy. There's no one I would rather have by my side in all of Avalon." She gritted her teeth before continuing, knowing it would hurt him, but it might be the only thing he would listen to. "And if you care about me half as much as you claim, then it should matter way more to you what *I* think than what *they* think."

The eyes staring into hers darkened. A long moment passed before he nodded. "OK," he said, his voice still quiet.

She nodded but didn't smile. It wasn't a smiling moment.

He trailed behind her, his black cape swirling around his feet. Now he brooded silently but with a determined air.

"Laurel!" came a familiar voice. Laurel turned to see Katya, resplendent in a silk dress that accentuated her figure. Pale pink petals matching the shade of her dress stood out over Katya's shoulders. Her light blond hair lay perfectly around her face, and she wore a sparkling silver comb over her left ear.

"Katya," Laurel smiled.

"I hoped you might come to this!" Katya said. "It's the very best festival to come to all year long."

"Is it?" Laurel asked.

"Of course. The start of the New Year! New goals, new studies, new class placements. I look forward to it all year long." She twined her arm through Laurel's and pulled her towards the far end of the mezzanine. "I think Mara's finally going to be elevated to journeyman tomorrow," she said with a giggle. Her eyes flitted over to where the dark-eyed Fall stood in a stunning purple dress with a neckline cut far lower than Laurel would have ever dared in public. Like Katya, Mara was in bloom, a modest, six-pointed star resembling a narcissus flower setting off the colour of her dress.

Laurel looked back to make sure Tamani was following and gave him a quick smile when he met her eyes.

"You brought him?" Katya said in a whisper.

"Of course," Laurel said at full volume.

Katya smiled, only a little tightly. "Silly of me. You certainly need a guide. You've never been to one of these. I should have thought. I'll see you after the show, OK?" Katya waved happily, then turned and disappeared into a small group of faeries, most of whom Laurel recognised from the Academy. A few of them were staring at her unashamedly. She had been so busy looking at the scenery that she hadn't noticed the faeries in the mezzanine stealing long looks at her and Tamani. It took her a moment to realise why.

Katya and Mara weren't the only ones in full bloom. The blossoms dotting the mezzanine were small and unassuming compared with those Laurel had seen this summer, tending towards single colours and simple shapes, like hers. But they were all in bloom; every single female Fall.

Except her.

Laurel thought about the temperature in Avalon; it was a little bit cooler than when she had been there in the summer, but only just. She wondered how the faeries' bodies knew when to bloom. Was it the angle of the sun? The slight changes in temperature? It did make sense that Avalon's temperate weather would delay autumn blooming – and maybe prolong blossoming – but for how long? Laurel made a mental note to find out more about blossoming when she was in Avalon next summer. Until then, she could only conclude that something was different between Avalon and Crescent City. Two days earlier, two degrees higher, and maybe she wouldn't have felt so out of place.

Lifting her chin resolutely, Laurel walked to the edge of the balcony. She touched Tamani's arm and looked down at his hands. Sure enough, at some point he had pulled on a pair of black velvety gloves. Even he had noticed. Refusing to dwell on it, Laurel looked at the main floor below her, turning her attention from the decorations to the faeries themselves. Their apparel was much plainer and Laurel didn't see many sparkles of jewellery, but the Spring faeries looked completely happy. Hugs were shared, children were caught up in embraces, greetings exchanged, and even from her spot so far above, peals of laughter found their way to Laurel's ears.

"Are they all Spring faeries?" Laurel asked.

"Most of them," Tamani said. "There are a few Summer faeries who are too young to perform, but most of the Summer faeries are involved in the show."

"Is…" She hesitated. "Is Rowen down there?"

"Somewhere. With my sister."

Laurel nodded, not knowing what else to say. She hadn't considered that accompanying her meant Tamani wouldn't be able to sit with his family. A familiar guilt filled her. It was too easy to believe that Tamani lived only for her, that his life did not exist at all except where it intersected her own. To forget that there were other people who loved him.

The buzz of the crowd changed abruptly, and the faeries below the mezzanine all looked up with an air of anticipation.

Laurel felt Tamani's hand around her arm and suddenly he was half escorting, half dragging her to a seat several rows farther away from the centre of the mezzanine. "This should be the Winter faeries," Tamani whispered. "Jamison, Yasmine, and Her Majesty, Queen Marion."

Laurel's throat tightened as she turned away from Tamani, her attention – like all the other faeries – on the archway at the top of the mezzanine. She wasn't sure whether she was more surprised that there were only three, or that there were as many as three. She'd only ever considered Jamison and the elusive Queen before.

An entourage of guards in sky-blue uniforms came through first; Laurel recognised them from the last time she'd seen Jamison. They were followed immediately by Jamison himself, dressed in deep-green robes with his usual twinkling smile. He was escorting a young girl who looked about twelve, her smooth, ebony skin and carefully arranged ringlets setting off an extremely formal gown of pale purple silk. Then the entire coliseum seemed to breathe in all at once as the Queen entered.

She was wearing a shimmering white dress with a train of glittering threading that curled up from the ground in the soft breeze. Her hair was jet black and streamed down her back in soft waves that reached just past her waist. A delicate crystal crown balanced atop her head with strings of diamonds attached that fell into her curls and glimmered in the sunlight.

But it was her face Laurel focused on.

Pale green eyes surveyed the crowd. Although Laurel knew the face would be considered beautiful by any fashion magazine's standards, she couldn't get past the pursed lips, the tiny furrow between her eyes, the slight lift of one eyebrow as if she were loath to acknowledge the deep bows that everyone around her had dropped into.

Including Tamani.

Which left Laurel alone standing straight up.

She hurried to bow like everyone else before the Queen saw her. It apparently worked; the Queen's gaze fluttered over the crowd without pausing, and within seconds, the Fall faeries had resumed their upright stances and their buzzing conversations.

Marion turned with a whispering flutter of her gown and walked to the dais, where three ornate seats sat in prominence over the others. Laurel watched Jamison take the little girl's hand, helping her up the steps and into a fluffy chair at the Queen's left. Laurel caught his eye and he smiled and whispered something to the little girl before turning and approaching them. The crowd didn't stop talking or laughing as Jamison passed by, but they subtly shifted out of his way, clearing a path.

"My dear Laurel," Jamison said, his eyes, now green to match his robes, sparkling. "I'm so happy you've come." He clapped Tamani on the shoulder. "And you, m'boy. It's been too many months since I've seen you. Overworking yourself at that gate of yours, I imagine."

Tamani smiled, shedding some of his brooding air. "Indeed, sir. Laurel keeps us busy with her mischief."

"I imagine she does," Jamison said with a grin. The sound of stringed instruments being tuned filled the vast coliseum. "I had best take my seat," Jamison said. But before he turned he lifted his hands to Laurel's face, gently framing her cheeks with his fingers. "I'm so glad you were able to join us," he said, his voice a quiet whisper. Then he was gone, the rich green of his robes rustling away through the crowd.

Tamani nudged Laurel towards seats on the far end of the large balcony, where Katya was waving at them.

"Who's that little girl?" Laurel asked, craning her neck to watch Jamison hand something to the girl before taking his seat.

"That's Yasmine. She's a Winter faerie."

"Oh. Will she be the Queen someday?"

Tamani shook his head. "Doubtful. She's too close in age to Marion. Same thing happened with Jamison and Cora, the late Queen."

"There's only three Winter faeries in all of Avalon?"

"Only three. And often fewer." Tamani smiled. "My mother was the Gardener for both Marion and Yasmine. Yasmine blossomed just months before my mother retired. Very few Gardeners have the honour of tending two Winter faeries." He tilted his head towards the young Winter faerie. "I got to know Yasmine a little before she was sent to the Winter Palace. Sweet thing. Good heart, I think. Jamison is very fond of her."

Just then a small but elaborately dressed faerie stepped out from behind the massive curtains that stretched across the stage. The crowd hushed.

"Get ready," Tamani whispered in her ear. "You've never seen *anything* like this."

Chapter Twenty-two

The curtains opened to reveal an exquisite forest scene with bright beams of multicoloured lights shining down in soft circles. Laurel realised that there was no way to dim the light in the coliseum – and no need either. Everything on the stage seemed to glow from within – brighter, clearer, more real even than Laurel's immediate surroundings. She was riveted; surely this was Summer magic at work.

Two faeries knelt in the middle of the stage, their arms wrapped around each other, and soft, romantic music drifted up from the orchestra. They looked pretty much like regular ballet dancers, the man with perfect, mocha-coloured skin, well-defined arms, and closely cut hair, the woman with long, lean limbs, her auburn hair pulled tightly back. The couple rose and began dancing on soft, bare feet.

"No toe shoes?" Laurel whispered to Tamani.

"What are toe shoes?"

OK, no, obviously, Laurel thought. But she could see how it was ballet nonetheless. The movements were flowing and graceful, with long stretches and lifts worthy of any human con tortionist. Though for principal dancers in such an important show, they did seem a little ungraceful. Their feet plodded a bit and their movements felt very heavy. Still, they were quite good. It took a few minutes into the pas de deux before Laurel realised what seemed so out of place.

"What's up with the beard?" she asked Tamani. The male dancer was wearing a black beard that blended in with his costume, but as Laurel watched, she realised it trailed almost down to his waist.

Tamani softly cleared his throat and for a second Laurel thought he was going to avoid her question entirely. "You have to understand," he finally whispered. "Most of these faeries have never seen a real human. Their idea of what a human looks like is almost as distorted as what humans think of faeries. Faeries are" – he searched for the right word–"intrigued by the idea that humans grow fur on their faces. It's very animalistic."

Laurel suddenly realised that she had never seen a faerie with a beard. The idea simply hadn't occurred to her. She thought about how Tamani's face was always smooth and soft – without the gritty hint of stubble that David's usually had. She'd never actually noticed before.

"The dancers who are playing humans also move less gracefully, to show that they are animals, not faeries," Tamani continued.

Turning her attention back to the play, Laurel watched the dancers rise and fall with just that hint of plodding. Knowing now that it was deliberate, she appreciated the talent it must take – to gracefully portray a lack of grace. She banished to the back of her mind a handful of angry thoughts about perpetuating stereotypes. Those would have to wait.

Two more bearded dancers entered the stage, and the woman tried to hide behind her partner. "What's happening?" Laurel asked.

Tamani pointed to the original couple. "That's Heather and Lotus. They're secret lovers, but Heather's father there" – he pointed to an older faerie with a bushy brown beard shot through with grey—"orders her to marry Darnel instead. The human custom of parents arranging marriages is ridiculous, by the way."

"Well, they don't any more. At least not where I come from."

"Still."

Laurel watched as the two men departed and Heather and Lotus came together for a mournful duet. The music was like nothing Laurel had ever heard before and she felt tears building up in her eyes for these star-crossed humans who danced so beautifully to the orchestra's woeful refrain.

The lights illuminating the stage brightened and Lotus leaped on to a rock, casting his arms wide in an elaborate proclamation. "What's happening now?" Laurel asked, tugging on Tamani's shirt in her excitement.

"Lotus has decided that he will prove himself to Heather's father by retrieving a golden apple from the Isle of Hesperides. Also known as Avalon," he added with a smile.

The stage cleared, and the set shimmered for an instant before morphing into an enormous flower garden with blooms of every imaginable colour covering the perimeter of the stage. Laurel gasped. "How did they do that?"

Tamani smiled. "Much of the set is an illusion. This is why Summer faeries are in charge of our entertainment."

Laurel leaned forward, trying to study the new scenery, but she didn't have much time before the faux glade was filled with dancing faeries in bright, multicoloured costumes. She saw instantly just how obviously ungraceful the "human dancers" had been. The company of faeries whirled through elaborate choreography with a grace that would have put Pavlova to shame. After a few minutes of the incredible corps, a rather tall faerie in a sheer, clinging gown entered from stage right. The company of faeries dropped to their knees, allowing the female faerie to take central focus for her solo. Laurel had been to professional ballets in San Francisco, but nothing prepared her for the raw talent and grace of this principal dancer.

"Who is that?" she breathed to Tamani, her eyes riveted on the stage.

"Titania," Tamani responded.

"*The* Titania?" Laurel asked breathlessly. His arm was snug around Laurel's back as their heads pressed close so they could whisper, but Laurel hardly noticed.

"No, no. I meant she's *playing* Titania."

"Oh," Laurel said, a little disappointed that she wasn't going to get to see a legendary faerie perform. In the middle of Titania's beautiful arabesque, a male faerie – with no beard this time – entered from stage left. The faerie corps twittered and dropped into low bows on the floor of the stage.

"Is that Oberon?" Laurel asked, thinking of the faerie king often paired with Titania in faerie lore.

"See, you're catching on," Tamani said with a grin.

The faerie playing Oberon began his own solo, his movements brash, daring, almost violent, but with the same controlled grace of the faerie playing Titania. Soon the two were dancing together, each trying to outdo the other as the music rose stronger, louder, until with a surge of brass, Titania tripped on her own feet and sprawled on to the ground. With a wave of her hand, and angry, stomping steps, she and some of the faerie corps exited the stage, chased by Oberon's faeries.

"Why are they angry with her?" Laurel asked.

"Titania is a very unpopular figure in history," Tamani responded. "She was a Fall faerie – and Unseelie at that – who became Queen during a time when there were no Winter faeries. Oberon was born soon after and took over as King, when he was only twenty years old – almost a child, in terms of royalty, and still not soon enough for most people's taste. Titania was responsible for the disastrous mess in Camelot."

"The trolls… destroyed it, right?"

"That's right. And the aftermath led to his death just as he was proving to be one of the greatest kings in Avalon's history. So Titania is generally blamed for that loss."

"That seems unfair."

"Perhaps."

The stage cleared again and returned to a forest scene. Lotus rushed in, pursued by Heather, who hid behind the trees every time Lotus turned around. They rushed about in confusing circles until two more figures entered the stage: Darnel, and a very pretty female faerie.

"Now I'm confused again," Laurel said as the female faerie tried to cling to Darnel and he kept pushing her away.

"That's Hazel. She is in love with Darnel. Darnel is chasing Heather, who is chasing Lotus, trying to stop him from the dangerous trip to the Isle of Hesperides. Hazel is trying to convince Darnel to just be happy with her."

Something clicked in Laurel's head as the lovely Hazel tugged forlornly on Darnel's coat and he cast her aside. "Wait a second," she said. "This is *A Midsummer Night's Dream*."

"Well, it's what would eventually become *A Midsummer Night's Dream*. Like most of Shakespeare's best plays, it started out as a faerie story."

"No way!"

Tamani shushed her gently as a few Fall faeries glanced their way. "Honestly," Tamani continued, his voice low and soft, "did you think he came up with *Romeo and*

Juliet all by himself? A thousand years ago it was Rhoeo and Jasmine, but Shakespeare's version is a passable retelling."

Laurel's eyes stayed locked on the four faeries dancing their dizzying chase. "How did Shakespeare come to know the faerie stories?" She glanced up at Tamani. "He *was* human, wasn't he?"

"Oh, yes." Tamani chuckled quietly. "He lived in a time when the rulers of Avalon still kept an eye on human affairs. They were impressed by his plays about the kings – Lear and Richard, I believe. Deadly dull stories, but his writing was magnificent. So the King had him brought here to give him some fresh story lines for his beautiful words. And they hoped he would correct some of the errors in faerie mythology. *A Midsummer Night's Dream* was his first play after coming to Avalon, followed soon after by *The Tempest*. But after a while he resented that the King would not let him come and go as he pleased. So he left and didn't come back. And as revenge, he didn't put any more faeries into his plays. He made them all human and claimed them as his own."

"Is that really true?" Laurel asked in wonder.

"That's how I learned it."

The scene returned to the flowered clearing where Puck – a Fall faerie of remarkable skill, Tamani informed

Laurel – was instructed by Oberon to create a potion that would make Titania fall in love with the first creature she saw, in payment for her mishandling of Camelot. And since he was a benevolent king, he also tried to help the humans. "After all," Tamani explained, "he couldn't let them actually enter Avalon and take a golden apple, but he didn't want to send them home with nothing to show for their pains."

Laurel nodded and turned her attention back to the ballet. The story continued in a familiar manner, now that she knew what play it was – Lotus and Darnel both chasing after Hazel, Heather being left loverless, and everyone dancing in intricate, frenzied patterns that made Laurel's head whirl.

Then the scene changed back to the faerie bower and, after Puck placed his potion in Titania's eyes, a huge, hulking beast came lumbering in. Laurel couldn't tell if the beast was an illusion or an elaborate costume. "What's that?" she asked. "Isn't he supposed to be a man with a donkey head?"

"He's a troll," Tamani said. "There is no greater disgrace among the fae than to fall in love with a troll. It just doesn't happen without serious derangement – or some kind of magical compulsion."

"What about the part where all the men are putting

on a play? That's where the guy is supposed to come from."

"Shakespeare put that part in by himself. There's no weird play in the original story."

"I always did think that was the lamest part of the story. I thought it should end when the lovers wake up and are discovered," Laurel said.

"Well, it does," Tamani said with a grin.

Laurel watched silently for a while as the dancers continued the story and everything began to be set right. Just before the final scene, Titania came back on and danced the most beautiful solo Laurel had ever seen to the sad strains of a soft lament. Then she spun and swooned at Oberon's feet, offering him her crown.

"What just happened?" Laurel asked when the dance was over. She couldn't bear to ask during the solo – it was too lovely to take her eyes off of even for a second.

"Titania begs forgiveness of Oberon for her misdeeds and concedes her crown to him. That means that she admits she was never truly the Queen."

"Because of Camelot?"

"Because she was a Fall faerie."

Laurel frowned as she considered this. But the scenery changed quickly to the clearing where the lovers awoke from their enchanted sleep and danced a joyful double pas de deux, and were joined by the full corps at the end. When they stepped forward for their bows, the audience on the ground floor seemed to rise as one to applaud the company. Tamani rose from his seat as well and Laurel jumped up to join him, clapping so hard her hands began to sting.

Tamani placed a firm hand on her arm and pulled her downward.

"What?" Laurel said, pulling her arm away.

Tamani's eyes darted back and forth. "It's not done, Laurel. You don't stand for anyone below your station. Only your equals, or your superiors."

Laurel glanced around. He was right. Nearly everyone in the balcony was clapping enthusiastically, faces lit with broad, beautiful smiles, but no one was standing except her and Tamani. She raised an eyebrow at Tamani, turned her face back to the stage, and remained on her feet as she continued clapping.

"Laurel!" Tamani said sternly under his breath.

"That was the most incredible thing I've ever seen and I am going to express my appreciation as I see fit," Laurel said flatly, continuing to clap. She shot a quick look at him. "Are *you* going to stop me?"

Tamani sighed and shook his head, but he stopped trying to get her to sit down.

Slowly the applause faded and the dancers ran gracefully off the stage, where the scenery had melted into stark whiteness. About twenty faeries in bright green lined up at the back.

"There's more?" Laurel asked as she and Tamani took their seats again.

"Fire dancers," Tamani said with a broad smile. "You'll love these."

A deep boom from a large kettledrum sounded. At first, it was just a slow, steady beat. The green-clad faeries moved forward as one, taking slow, marching steps in time with the drums. As each line reached the front of the stage, they raised their hands, sending beams of multicoloured light skyward. A second later, enormous showers of sparks exploded above the crowd – almost eye level with the balcony – beautiful, vivid colours in rainbow hues that made Laurel blink against their brilliance. It was better than any fireworks display she'd ever seen.

A second drum began to sound in a quicker and more intricate rhythm than the first, and the faeries onstage changed with it. Their dance turned acrobatic, faeries flipping and leaping to the front of the stage instead of walking. A third drum started, then a fourth, and the performers' pace and motions grew frenetic with the beat.

Laurel watched, transfixed, as the fire dancers performed, twisted, and tumbled with remarkable skill. Each time they reached the front of the stage, they put up another light show. Rays of light fell like raindrops over the audience, and spinning balls of fire careened through the coliseum, trailing bright sparks that faded into glistening jewels before extinguishing themselves. Laurel was torn, watching first the acrobats, then the fireworks, wishing she could watch both at the same time. Then, when the beat of the drums became so fast Laurel couldn't figure out how the faeries kept up, they all tumbled to the front of the stage, releasing the fireworks from their hands all at once, creating a curtain of sparkles that dazzled almost as brightly as the sun.

With her breath catching in her throat, Laurel rose to her feet, applauding the fire dancers with as much enthusiasm as she had the ballet dancers. Tamani rose silently beside her and didn't say a word this time about her standing.

The fire dancers took their final bows and the applause began to die away. The Fall faeries in the balcony rose and started making their way to the exit; Laurel could see the Spring faeries below her doing the same thing.

Laurel turned to Tamani with a smile. "Oh, Tam, that

was incredible! Thank you so much for making sure I got to come." She looked back at the empty stage, concealed now behind its heavy silk curtains. "This has been the most amazing day."

Tamani took Laurel's hand and laid it on his arm. "The celebration has scarcely begun!"

Laurel looked up at Tamani in surprise. She dug in her small bag for a few seconds, glancing at the watch she'd brought with her. She could spare another hour or so. A smile spread across her face as she looked at the exits again, with eagerness this time. "I'm ready," she said.

Chapter Twenty-three

"That was amazing," Laurel said again as she and Tamani lounged on pillows beside low tables heaped with fruits, vegetables, juices, and dishes of honey in a dizzying array of colours. Music filled the air from a dozen directions as faeries across the green lounged, and danced, and socialised. "I had no idea theatre could be like that. And those fireworks at the end! Those guys were incredible."

Tamani laughed, much more relaxed now that they were spread out in a meadow where the faerie classes mingled a little more freely. "I'm glad you liked it. I haven't been to a Samhain celebration in several years."

"Why not?"

Tamani shrugged, his mood turning sombre. "I wanted

to be with you," he said, not meeting her eyes. "Coming to festivals didn't seem as important when it meant leaving you behind the gates. Especially considering the revelries at sundown."

"What revelries?" Laurel asked, half distracted as she dipped a large strawberry in a dish of bright blue honey.

"Um... well, you'd probably find it rather distasteful."

Laurel waited, her attention piqued now, then laughed when he didn't continue. "Keep going," she prodded.

Tamani shrugged and sighed. "I think I told you last year: Pollination is for reproduction, and sex is for fun."

"I remember," Laurel said, unsure how that related.

"So at big festivals like this, most people... have... fun."

Laurel's eyes widened and then she laughed. "Really?"

"Come on, don't people ever do anything like that in the human world?"

Laurel was about to tell him no when she remembered the tradition of kissing at midnight on New Year's Eve. Though, granted, it wasn't really the same thing. "I suppose." She looked at the crowds around her. "So nobody cares? Aren't most of these people married?"

"For starters, you don't get married in Avalon. You get handfasted. And no, most of them aren't. In Avalon, the main reason to get handfasted is to raise seedlings.

Typically faeries aren't ready to do that until they are" – he paused, considering—"eighty, maybe a hundred years old."

"But—" Laurel cut off her own question and turned her face away.

"But what?" Tamani prodded gently.

After a moment of hesitation she turned to him. "Do faeries ever get handfasted young? Like... like at our age?"

"Almost never." He seemed to know what she was asking, though she couldn't bring herself to be completely forthright; his eyes bored into her until she had to turn away. "But that doesn't mean they aren't entwined. A lot of people have committed lovers. Not a majority, but it's common enough. My parents had been entwined for over seventy years before their handfasting. Handfasting is a little different from human marriage. It is not just a sign of a committed romance but an intention to form a family – to create a seedling and become a societal unit."

Laurel giggled, trying to dissipate the tension that enveloped them. "It's so weird to think of faeries having kids when they're a hundred years old."

"That's barely middle-aged, here. After we reach adulthood, most of us don't change much until we're a hundred and forty, a hundred and fifty. But then you age fairly quickly – at least by faerie standards. You can go from looking like a thirty-year-old human to looking like a sixty- or seventy-year-old human in less than twenty years."

"Does everyone live to two hundred?" Laurel asked. The thought of living for two centuries was boggling.

"More or less. Some faeries live longer, some shorter, but not usually by much."

"Don't they get sick and die?"

"Almost never." Tamani leaned over and touched the tip of her nose. "That's what you're for."

"What do you mean?"

"Not you specifically – Fall faeries. It's like having the world's most perfect… shoot, what do you call them? Hostels?" He sighed. "Help me out; where people go when they're sick."

"Hospitals?" Laurel suggested.

"Yeah." Tamani shook his head. "Wow, it's been a long time since I lost a human word like that. I mean, we all speak English, but human-only lingo really is like another language sometimes."

"You weren't speaking English earlier, to those guards," Laurel observed.

"You really want another history lesson today?" Tamani teased.

"I don't mind," Laurel said, savouring a spear of perfectly ripe nectarine. Harvest time never seemed to end in Avalon.

"Those were Gaelic words. Over the years we've had a lot of contact with the human world, through the gates. *Am fear-faire*, for example, is basically a Gaelic word for 'sentry', but we borrowed it many years ago, when the humans we encountered still spoke Gaelic. These days it's mostly a formality."

"So why *does* everyone speak English? Aren't there gates in Egypt and Japan, too?"

"And in America, lest ye forget," Tamani said, smiling. "We've had some contact with your Native Americans as well as with the Egyptians and Japanese." He laughed. "In Japan, we had extensive contact with the Ainu — the people who lived there before the Japanese arrived." He grinned. "Though even the Ainu never quite comprehended how long before *them* we were there."

"Hundreds of years?" Laurel guessed.

"Thousands," Tamani said solemnly. "The fae are far older than humans. But humans have reproduced and spread much faster than us. And they are just plain heartier. Certainly more capable of surviving extreme temperatures. It's only with the help of Fall faeries that our sentries manage to survive the winters at the gate on Hokkaido. Because of that, humans have come to dominate the world, so we have to learn to live among them, at least a little. And language is a big part of that. We have a training facility in Scotland, where, as you know, they speak English. Every sentry with dealings in the human world must train there, at least for a few weeks."

"So you and Shar trained there?"

"Among others." Tamani was growing increasingly animated, speaking without the hesitation that always clouded his behaviour when he set foot in Avalon. "Covert operations are usually performed by Sparklers, and *very* rarely a Mixer will need an ingredient that doesn't grow in Avalon. The manor is built around the gateway, in the middle of a sizeable game preserve, so it guards the gate as well as forming a safely controlled connection to human affairs. It was acquired centuries ago, in much the same way we're working to acquire your land."

Laurel smiled at Tamani's enthusiasm. He clearly knew more about the human world than other faeries, not simply because he lived there but because he'd spent his life studying humans.

And he did it so he could understand me. He'd dedicated literally years to understanding the person she would become as a human. She'd sacrificed her memories and left Avalon at the former Queen's bidding and Tamani had followed her in more ways than one. It was a startling realisation.

"Anyway," Tamani concluded, "the manor has been our main connection to the world outside Avalon for centuries, so it's only natural that we would speak the language of the humans who live nearby. But even the experts at the manor get some things badly wrong, so I guess I can't feel too bad about forgetting a word here and there."

"I think you do great," Laurel said, running one finger along Tamani's arm.

Almost instinctively, Tamani reached up and covered her hand with his own. Laurel's eyes fixed on that hand. It looked so harmless sitting there, but it meant something and Laurel knew it. She looked up, and their eyes locked. A long moment of silence stretched out between them, and after a few seconds Laurel pulled her hand out from under Tamani's. His expression didn't change, but Laurel felt bad nonetheless.

She covered the awkwardness of the moment by pouring herself a drink from the first pitcher she saw and taking a big swallow. It tasted like liquefied sugar as it coursed down her throat. "Oh man, what is this?" she asked, peering down at the ruby-red liquid in her glass.

Tamani glanced over. "Amrita."

Laurel studied it dubiously. "Is it like faerie wine?" she asked, already feeling the drink going to her head.

"Kind of. It's nectar from the flowers of the Yggdrasil tree. They only bring it out at Samhain. It's a traditional way to toast the New Year."

"It's *awesome*."

"I'm glad you approve." Tamani laughed.

Laurel sighed. "I am stuffed." Only the food in Avalon ever pushed Laurel to eat to discomfort. And she had just reached that point.

"All done then?" Tamani asked, hesitation creeping back into his tone.

"Oh, yes. Totally done," Laurel said, smiling and settling down a little more into the pile of pillows.

"Would you…" He paused and looked out into the middle of the meadow. "Would you like to ask me to dance?"

Laurel sat up abruptly. "Would I like to *ask* you to dance?"

Tamani looked down at his lap. "I apologise if I was too forward."

But Laurel scarcely heard him in her anger. "Even at a festival you can't just ask me?"

"Is that a no?"

Something in his tone turned Laurel's frustration into sorrow. It wasn't Tamani's fault. But she hated that even with her, he felt bound by the ridiculous social customs. She raised her chin and pushed back her indignation. She didn't want to punish *him*. "Tamani, would you like to dance?"

His eyes softened. "I'd love to."

Laurel looked out at the dancers and hesitated. "I don't really know how," she said tentatively.

"I'll show you… if you want."

"OK."

Tamani stood and offered her his hand. He had relinquished his cloak hours ago but still wore the black breeches and boots, paired with a loose white shirt with the strings loosened in the front, accentuating his tanned chest. He looked like a hero out of a movie; Wesley from *The Princess Bride* or Edmond Dantès from *The Count of Monte Cristo*. Laurel smiled and took his hand.

They wandered closer to a group of musicians; most were playing stringed instruments Laurel could not have named, but she did recognise the woodwinds – flutes and panpipes and something like a simple clarinet. Tamani led her skilfully through dance steps she almost seemed to remember, her feet moving with a grace she didn't know she had. She bounced and kicked and skipped along with the other couples and, even if she wasn't quite as graceful as everyone else, she could have held her own at a similar gathering of humans. She danced another song, and another, until she had lost track of how long they'd been dancing. The sweet-smelling meadow grew more and more crowded as others left their meals to join in the dance, and soon Laurel was awash in a sea of lithe limbs and graceful bodies, rolling and swaying and even crashing to the rhythm of the Summer faeries' intoxicating music, gauzy clothing fluttering in the temperate air of Avalon's eternal springtime.

Tamani guided Laurel under his arm in a long string of spins until her head whirled and she collapsed against his chest, laughing and breathing hard. It took her a moment to realise how tightly she was pressed against him. It was different from being close to David; for one thing, Tamani was much nearer to Laurel's height. Standing so close, their hips met snugly.

She felt his arm tight at her back, holding her in. He would probably let go if she pushed away, but she didn't. His fingers ran through her hair, then cradled the back of her neck, tilting her face back. He let his nose rest softly against hers and his breath was cool against her face as her fingers curled against the bare skin between the laces of his shirt.

"Laurel." Tamani's whisper was so quiet she wasn't completely sure she'd heard it at all. And before she could think to protest, he kissed her.

His mouth was so soft, gentle, and tender against hers. The sweet taste of him melted into her. The dancing around them became a leisurely waltz as the earth seemed to slow in its orbit, then stop, just for her and Tamani.

Just for a moment.

The illusion shattered as Laurel turned her head, breaking contact, and forced herself to walk away. Out of the green, away from the dancers. Away from Tamani.

Angry, confused feelings spun through her as she walked out of the clearing. Tamani followed but said nothing.

"I should go," she said vaguely, not turning to face him. And it wasn't an empty excuse. She wasn't sure just how long she'd been dancing, but probably too long. She had to get back. She headed in what she guessed was the general direction of the gate, hoping she would start to recognise her surroundings. She waited, optimistically, for Tamani's hand to touch her waist, gently guiding her in the right direction as he had so many times before.

No such luck.

"You could at least apologise," Laurel said. Her mood

had turned sullen and she wasn't quite sure why. Her head was a mess of confusion.

"I'm not sorry," Tamani said, his tone not apologetic in the least.

"Well, you should be!" Laurel said, turning towards him for just a second.

"Why?" Tamani asked, his voice annoyingly calm.

Laurel turned to face him.

"Why should I be sorry? Because I kissed the girl I'm in love with? I love you, Laurel."

She tried not to go breathless at his words, but she was completely unprepared for them. He had made his intentions known – very bluntly, at times – but he'd never told her straight out that he loved her. It made their flirtations seem too serious. Too consequential. Too close to being unfaithful.

"How long am I supposed to sit back and just wait for you to come to your senses? I've been patient. For *years* I've been patient, Laurel, and I'm tired." He gently held both of her shoulders, leaning over just a little to look her full in the face. "I'm tired of waiting, Laurel."

"But David—"

"Don't talk to me about David! If you want to tell me to back off because *you* don't like it, then say that. But don't expect me to worry about David's feelings. I don't care about David, Laurel." He paused, his breath loud, heavy. "I care about you. And when you look at me with that softness in your eyes," he said, fingers pressing just a little more firmly, "and you look for all the world like you want to be kissed, then I'm going to kiss you, David be damned," he finished quietly.

Laurel turned away, her head aching. "You can't, Tam."

"What would you have me do instead?" he asked, his voice so raw and vulnerable it was all she could do to keep looking at him.

"Just... wait."

"For what! For your parents to die? For David to die? What am I waiting for, Laurel?" he asked, his voice plaintive.

Laurel turned and started walking again, trying desperately to leave his words behind. She topped a steep hill and instead of seeing a slew of faerie homes, she looked out on to a pure white beach with sapphire-blue waves lapping at the shore. Something was off about that – it didn't *smell* like the ocean – but she couldn't turn around, Tamani was behind her. So she kept going, her feet slow in the glittering, crystalline sand.

She crossed her arms over her chest as she stopped. She'd reached the water. There was nowhere else to go. The wind blew at her hair, throwing it back from her face.

"I don't like having you so far away," Tamani said after a long pause. His voice sounded normal again, without the bitter edge. "I worry. I know you've got guards, but... I liked it better when you were at the land. I don't like trusting other faeries with your life. I wish... I wish I could come out and do it myself."

Laurel was already shaking her head. "It wouldn't work," she said firmly.

"You don't think I could do a good enough job?" Tamani asked, looking at her with a seriousness Laurel disliked.

"It wouldn't work," she repeated, knowing her reasoning was very different from Tamani's.

"You just don't want me in your human world," Tamani said quietly, his words carried to her on the light breeze.

The truth of the whispered accusation stung, and Laurel turned away from him.

"You're afraid that if I was part of your human life you might actually have to make a real decision. Right now you have the best of both worlds. You get your *David*." He spoke the name scornfully, anger creeping into his tone. It was better than the pain she heard in his voice before. She almost wished he'd just yell. Anger was so much easier than sadness, hurt. "And then you come out here and have me whenever you want me. I'm at your beck and call, and you know it. Do you ever consider how that makes me feel? Every time you leave – go back to him – you tear up my emotions all over again. Sometimes…" He sighed. "Sometimes I wish you would just stop coming around." He let out a frustrated growl. "No, I don't actually want that, but, I just… it's so hard when you leave, Laurel. I wish you could see that."

A tear slipped down Laurel's cheek, but she rubbed it away, forcing herself to remain calm. "I can't stay," she said, happy that her voice was solid, strong. "If I come here… *every time* I come here… I have to leave, eventually. Maybe it would be better for you if I stopped coming back at all – easier."

"You have to come back," Tamani said, concern laced through his voice. "You have to learn to be a Fall faerie. It's your birthright. Your destiny."

"I know enough to get me through for a while," Laurel insisted. "What I need now is practice, and I can do that from home." Her hands shook, but she folded her arms across her chest, trying to hide it.

"That's not the plan," Tamani said, his voice just short of a reprimand. "You have to come back regularly."

Laurel forced herself to speak calmly, coolly. "No, Tamani. I don't."

Their eyes met, and neither seemed able to look away.

Laurel gave in first. "I have to go. It's better for me to be in my house after dark. I need you to take me to the gate."

"Laurel—"

"The gate!" Laurel ordered, knowing she couldn't bear to hear whatever he was going to say. Somehow she'd spoiled their whole day, and now all she wanted was to end it.

Tamani stiffened, but there was defeat on his face. Laurel turned away from it. She couldn't look. He put his hand at her back and prodded her forward, his fingers at her waist, guiding her from his position one step behind her.

When they reached the stone walls that surrounded the gates, Tamani made a hand signal to the guards standing at the entrance and one of them left at a run.

After a few seconds Tamani spoke. "I – I just want you to be safe," he said apologetically.

"I know," Laurel murmured.

"What about that Klea person?" Tamani asked. "Have you seen her again?"

Laurel shook her head. "I told you I wasn't sure if I could trust her."

"Does she know about you?" Tamani said, turning

sharply to face her. "Does she have any idea you're a faerie?"

"Yes, Tamani. I spilled everything to her the instant I met her," Laurel said sarcastically. "No, of course she doesn't! I've been very careful—"

"Because the second she finds out," he continued, talking over her again, "the *instant* she knows, your life is in jeopardy."

"She doesn't know," Laurel yelled, drawing the attention of the guards. But she didn't care. "And even if she did, then what? Is she going to change her mind and start trying to kill me instead? I don't think so." It was strange to be arguing the opposite side she'd taken with David a few weeks ago, but logic seemed to be slipping away. "I'm fine!" she said in exasperation.

Their heads both turned as the sound of footsteps approached – a group of guards. Tamani's head dropped and he stepped backwards, taking his place at Laurel's shoulder. But she could hear his breath heavy with frustration.

The group of soldiers parted to reveal Yasmine, the young Winter faerie.

"Oh," Laurel said, surprised. "I thought they would send... someone else," she finished lamely when the girl's soft green eyes turned to her.

Yasmine said nothing, just turned towards the wall.

"Can she open it by herself?" Laurel whispered to Tamani.

"Of course," Tamani said, his tone clipped. "It's not a skill. You just have to be a Winter faerie."

Sentries led them down the path to the four gates. Tamani followed silently behind Laurel, not touching her at all. Laurel hated being like this with him, but she didn't know what else to do. Her two worlds, two lives that she tried so hard to keep separate, were crashing together. And she felt helpless to stop it.

Chapter Twenty-four

Silent and brooding, Laurel and Tamani passed through the gateway. The familiar brigade of sentries greeted them. Shar stepped forward and glared at Laurel as he addressed Tamani. "We have a visitor."

"Trolls?" Tamani stiffened and pushed Laurel back towards the sparkling gate. "Laurel, back to Avalon."

Shar rolled his eyes. "Not trolls, Tam. Do you think we'd have let you through if there were trolls waiting?"

Tamani sighed and dropped his hands. "Of course not. I didn't think."

"It's the human boy. The one who was here last autumn."

"David?" Laurel said, her voice weak. *How did he find out?*

Shar nodded as Tamani's jaw stiffened. "I'll take her to him," Tamani said, stepping forward. "Where is he?"

"He's keeping his distance," Shar said, gesturing vaguely with his head. "Out by the house."

"I'll be back," Tamani said, wrapping his hand around Laurel's upper arm and pulling her in the direction of the cabin. As soon as they were out of sight of the gate, he dropped his arm.

"I want to talk to him," Tamani said, his voice low.

"No!" Laurel insisted. "You can't."

"I want to know what he's doing to help keep you safe," Tamani said, not meeting her eyes. "That's all."

"Absolutely not," Laurel said through clenched teeth.

"How much are you going to throw away over David?" Tamani asked, exasperated. "Me, obviously. But what else? Your life? Your parents' lives? Even David's life, so I don't come in and put a hitch in your little romance? I just want to talk to him."

"You want to intimidate him. Threaten his position. I *know* you, Tamani."

"I may as well, since he's here," Tamani growled, glancing up the path.

"I didn't ask him to come," Laurel said, not quite sure why she felt compelled to justify herself.

Tamani was silent.

"He shouldn't be off work yet. He shouldn't even know I'm here."

Tamani stopped abruptly and turned. "You lied to him?" His face was unreadable.

"I—"

"You *lied* to him to come out and see me?" Tamani laughed. "You lied for me. I feel special." His voice was sharp and harsh, but there was something else behind it. Appreciation. Satisfaction.

Laurel scoffed and started to walk away. "Don't even think that; it wasn't for you."

Tamani grabbed her arm and whirled her around so quickly she stumbled forward against his chest. He didn't try to embrace her, just held her arms as she stood sprawled across him. "Wasn't it? Tell me you don't love me."

Laurel's mouth moved, but she said nothing.

"Tell me," he said, his voice sharp and demanding. "Tell me David is all you need or want in your life." His face was close to her, his soft breath caressing her face. "That you never think of me when you're kissing him. That you don't dream about me the way I dream about you. Tell me you don't love me."

She looked up at him, desperation consuming her. Her mouth felt dry, parched, and the words she tried to force out wouldn't come.

"You can't even say it," he said, his arms pulling her in

now instead of holding her steady. "Then love me, Laurel. Just *love* me!"

His face was filled with a yearning she could hardly bear. She couldn't leave him again. Not like this – not now that he knew. Why couldn't she hide it better? Why did she keep coming back when she couldn't stay? It was hurting *him* more than it was hurting her. How was that love? Love wasn't supposed to be selfish.

His lips were on her face now, in her hair. It was as if every emotion he had stifled, every temptation he'd resisted, had burst forth like a roaring river. And the current threatened to carry her away.

She forced herself to open her eyes. It didn't matter what she felt – she couldn't be with him. Not now. As long as she lived in the human world anything with Tamani would only be halfway. She would hate it and – even though she knew he would disagree – eventually, he would resent her for it. She wasn't ready to leave her human life behind. She wanted to graduate from high school and decide for herself what to do after that. She had family and friends and a life to live – a life she couldn't live with Tamani. She closed her eyes again, forcing away the dream of him. It wouldn't be a dream; it wouldn't have a happy ending. She had to send him away.

It was now or never.

"I don't love you," she whispered, almost losing her nerve with his mouth against her neck.

"Yes, Laurel, you do," he whispered, his lips brushing her ear now.

"I don't," she said, her voice stronger now, finally accepting what had to be done. She put both hands on his chest and pressed back firmly. "I don't love you. I have to go back. And you are *not* coming with me."

She turned before she could change her mind.

"Laurel—"

"No! I said I don't love you. I... I hardly even know you, Tamani. A handful of afternoons, a trip to a festival – that doesn't equal love!" she insisted. She didn't know what else to do. He was right; leaving him with hope for their future every time she saw him was cruel. Unspeakably cruel. She had to make him believe it wouldn't happen. It would hurt less in the long run. "I'm going to see David," she said, hurling the last of her ammunition at him and turning before she could see his reaction. She wasn't sure she could bear it.

She walked towards the cabin, expecting Tamani to stop at any moment. But at the edge of the forest, he was still right on her tail. "Stop following me," she hissed.

"I don't think you're in any position to order me around," he said tersely.

They broke from the tree line together, Tamani just behind Laurel's left shoulder. Laurel's eyes met David's instantly… a second before he saw Tamani. His eyes went back to her again, full of hurt and accusation. He scooted off the trunk of her Sentra and started to walk towards his car.

"David!" Laurel called, lifting her foot to run.

Tamani's hand shot out and grabbed her wrist. He pulled her around and before she could protest, his lips came down hard against hers, his kiss urgent and demanding and full of a heat that swept Laurel up for two seconds before she pushed him violently away.

She looked towards David, hoping he had missed it.

He was staring right at them.

David's and Tamani's eyes met and locked.

Tamani still had a hold of Laurel's wrist. She yanked it away. "Go away," she said. "I want you to just go!" Her voice was starting to tremble. "I mean it!" she yelled. "Go!"

His face was tense, his jaw flexed as he stared at her. She could hardly stand to meet his eyes. They were an ocean of betrayal. They probed her, searching for the smallest sign that she didn't mean it. That spark of hope that never seemed to go out.

She refused to drop her gaze. It was better this way. Someday maybe... she couldn't even think about it. He had to go. He had to leave. It wasn't fair to keep going on like this.

Please leave, she thought desperately. *Please go before I change my mind. Go.*

As if hearing her silent thoughts, Tamani turned without a word and walked silently into the trees, disappearing before her eyes.

Laurel couldn't look away from the spot where Tamani had been just a second earlier. She knew she needed to. The longer she kept looking the harder things were going to be with David.

She ripped her eyes away. David was already at his car door.

"David!" she called. "David, wait!" He paused but didn't turn to her. "David, don't go."

"Why not?" he asked, his eyes locked on the driver's seat, refusing to look at her face. "I saw what happened. All that's left is for me to imagine what I *didn't* see."

"It wasn't like that," she said, guilt and shame pounding through her.

"Wasn't it?" He turned now and faced her, his expression flat. If he had looked sad, or even angry, she could have accepted that. But he looked neutral, like he didn't care at all.

"No," she said, but her voice was quiet.

"Then what was it like, Laurel? Because I'll tell you how things look from my point of view. You lied to me to come out and see him, to be with *him*!"

"I didn't lie," Laurel protested weakly.

"You didn't say the words, but you lied all the same." He paused, his jaw clenched, his hands tense on the car door. "I trusted you, Laurel. I have always trusted you. And just because you didn't actually tell me a lie doesn't mean you didn't break my trust." He looked up at her. "I got off work early because I was worried about you. I was afraid for you. And when your mom told me you were at Chelsea's I called her and she didn't have any idea what I was talking about. And you know what my next thought was? That you were dead, Laurel! I thought you were dead!"

Laurel remembered having the same thoughts about David on Monday and looked down at her feet, ashamed.

"And then I realised that there was one place – one *person*," he said scornfully, "who you would sneak off to go see. And I come out here to make sure you're safe and I find you kissing him!"

"I wasn't kissing him!" Laurel yelled. "He was kissing me."

David was silent, his jaw muscles working furiously. "Maybe this time," he said, his voice steely. "But I saw the way he kissed you, and I promise you, that wasn't the first time. Go ahead, deny it. I'm listening."

She looked at the ground, the car, the trees, anywhere but at those accusing eyes.

"I knew it. I *knew* it!"

He slipped into the driver's seat and slammed the door, his engine roaring immediately to life. He backed up quickly, just missing Laurel as she stood rooted to the ground, unable to move. He rolled down his window. "I don't…" He paused, the only sign of weakness he'd shown the entire conversation. "I don't want to see you for a while. Don't call. When… if I decide I'm ready, I'll find you."

Laurel watched him drive away, finally letting her tears come. For a second she glanced back at the trees, but there was nothing there for her either. She slid into her car and let her forehead fall against the steering wheel, sobbing. How had everything gone so wrong?

Laurel sat on her bed, her guitar on her lap, watching the shadows that danced across her ceiling. She'd been sitting there for two hours as the sun sank and the room darkened, playing random melancholy chords that – no matter how much she tried – were strangely reminiscent of the music she'd heard earlier that day, in Avalon.

This morning her life was good – no, great! Now? She had destroyed everything.

And it was her own fault. She had spent too long straddling the fence. She had let her attraction to Tamani get out of hand. It wasn't enough to be faithful to David physically, he deserved her emotional fidelity, too.

She thought of the look on Tamani's face when she told him she didn't love him; this wasn't fair to him, either. She had been hurting everyone, and now there were consequences.

The thought of living out the rest of her life – even the rest of the week – without David made everything inside her hurt. She imagined seeing him with another girl. Kissing someone else the way Tamani had kissed her today. She groaned and rolled on to her side, letting her guitar slide on to the bedspread beside her. It would be like the end of the world. She couldn't let that happen. There had to be a way to make things right.

But two hours of thinking hadn't given her any ideas. She just had to hope that he would forgive her. Eventually.

She tried to drift off to sleep. Usually it was easy, once the sun went down, but today all she could do was sit and watch the numbers change on her alarm clock as the darkness enveloped her.

8:22

8:23

8:24

Laurel went downstairs. Her parents always did inventory on Saturday nights and wouldn't be back for another hour at least. She opened the fridge, more out of habit than hunger – no way she could eat at a time like this. She closed the fridge and let herself blame David and Tamani a little. She didn't want to hurt either of them, she wanted them both to be happy. They were both important in her life. Why did they keep insisting that she choose between them?

A movement in the yard caught her eye, but before she could focus in on it the picture window shattered, sending shards of glass skittering across the floor as Laurel's scream filled the air as she dropped into a crouch, hands protecting her face. But as soon as she closed her mouth, the room was deathly silent; no shouts, no more rocks, not even footsteps.

Laurel gazed at the shards of glass littering the kitchen floor. Her eyes settled on the large rock that must have come through the window.

A piece of paper was wrapped around it.

Laurel reached out with trembling hands and unwrapped the paper. Her breath caught in her chest as she read the bright red scrawl.

In an instant she was on her feet, running for the front door. As she threw the door open she paused, peering out into her front yard. It looked calm – serene even – under the glow of the streetlights. Laurel studied every shadowed form, looking for tiny shivers of movement.

Everything stood still.

She looked at her car, and back down at the paper in her hand. Tamani was right – she kept trying to do everything on her own. It was time to admit she needed help. She turned and began running, not to her car, but to the tree line behind her house. She paused at the edge of the forest, not sure how far the warding reached. After a moment's hesitation she started to shout. "Help! Please! I need your help!"

She ran along the tree line to the other side of the yard, shouting her pleas over and over. But she heard nothing except her own words echoing back at her. "Please!" she shouted one more time, knowing she wouldn't get an answer.

The sentries were gone. She didn't know where or when, but if a single faerie had been in those woods, she felt certain they would have answered her call. She was alone.

Desperation coursed through her and she pressed the heels of her hands against her eyes, forcing herself not to cry. The last thing she could afford to do was fall to pieces. She ran to her car, sliding into the driver's seat, and slammed the door shut. She stared at her dark, empty house. It had protected her for months; even before she knew about the sentries and the powerful wards. But she couldn't stay. She had to leave the protection of the wards. She knew it was what the trolls wanted. But she didn't have a choice; there was too much at risk. Her hands were shaking, but she managed to jam the key into the ignition and start the engine, peeling out backwards, her tyres spinning on the asphalt as she jerked the car into first gear and kept a wary eye on her rearview mirror.

Driving the half mile to David's house felt like it took hours. Laurel pulled up in front and studied the familiar structure that was practically a second home to her.

She felt like a stranger now.

Before she could talk herself out of it, she got out of the car and sprinted up the front walk. She heard the front bell reverberate through the living room and tried to remember when she had last rung the doorbell at David's. It seemed so formal, so unnecessary.

David's mom answered the door. "Laurel," she said cheerfully. But her smile died away when she saw Laurel's face. "What's the matter? Are you OK?"

"Can I see David?"

David's mom looked confused. "Of course, come in."

"I'll stay out here, thanks," Laurel murmured, her eyes aimed at the ground.

"OK," David's mom said hesitantly. "I'll go get him."

It was a long wait before the door opened again. Laurel looked up – afraid it would only be David's mom. But it was David, his face stony, eyes flashing. He paused, took a deep breath, and stepped out on to the porch, pulling the door shut behind him.

"Don't do this, Laurel. I'm only here because my mom's home and she doesn't know what happened yet. But you need to—"

"Barnes has Chelsea."

The anger drained instantly from David's eyes. "What!"

Laurel handed over the note. "At the lighthouse. I know you're mad at me but—" Her voice cut off, her breathing sharp and painful, but she forced her fear back. "This is bigger than us. Bigger than *this*. I need you,

David. I can't do this alone."

"What about your sentries?" David asked, wary.

"They're not there! I called for them. They're gone."

David hesitated, then nodded and ducked back into the house. She heard him yell something to his mom, then he was back on the porch, lugging his backpack as he pulled his jacket on. "Let's go."

"Will you drive?" Laurel asked. "I have… something I have to do."

After grabbing her own backpack from her car, Laurel joined David in his car.

"We have to go get Tamani," David said, his voice hard.

Laurel was already shaking her head.

"Laurel, I don't care about you and him right now. He's our best chance!"

"It's not that; we don't have time. If I'm not at the lighthouse by nine, he's going to kill Chelsea. We have" – Laurel glanced at the car's clock – "twenty-five minutes."

"Then you go to the lighthouse and I'll drive out to the land and bring him back."

"There's not time, David!"

"Then what!" he yelled, his frustrated voice filling the car.

"I can do this," Laurel said, hoping she was telling the truth. "But first I have to stop by my mom's store."

Laurel banged on the front doors of Nature's Cure until her mom came out of the back room, where she always did her closing paperwork. "Laurel, what in the wo—"

"Mom, I need dried sassafras root, organic hibiscus seeds, and ylang-ylang essential oil fixed in water instead of alcohol. I need them right now and I need you to not ask questions."

"Laurel—"

"I don't have a single minute to waste, Mom. I promise I will tell you everything – *everything* – when I get home, but right now I beg you to please just trust me."

"But where are you—"

"Mom," Laurel said, grabbing both her mother's hands. "Please listen. Really listen. There's more to being a faerie than just having a flower on my back. Faeries have enemies. Powerful enemies, and if I don't get these ingredients from you and go take care of them right now, people are going to die. Help me. I *need* you to help me," she pleaded.

Her mom stood confused for a moment before nodding slowly. "I take it this isn't something for regular old human police?"

Tears welled up in Laurel's eyes; she didn't even know

what to say. She didn't have time to argue.

"OK," her mom said determinedly, walking down an aisle and peering at the small bottles that lined both sides. She quickly plucked the ingredients from the shelves and handed them to Laurel.

"Thanks," Laurel said, and started to turn.

Her mom stopped her with a firm hand on her shoulder. Laurel turned as her mom gathered her into her arms, hugging her tight. "I love you," she whispered. "Please be careful."

Laurel nodded against her shoulder. "I love you, too." She paused, then added, "And if anything happens, do *not* sell the land, promise?"

Her mother's eyes filled with fear. "What do you mean?"

But Laurel couldn't stop. She tried not to hear the desperation in her mom's voice as she followed her to the door. "Laurel?"

Laurel was already out the door and slipping into David's car. "Go," she commanded, trying to block out her mother's last yell.

"Laurel!"

Laurel looked back, her eyes fixed on her mother's white face as her father burst out of the bookstore, both her parents staring at the car as it drove away.

Chapter Twenty-five

"**D**id you get what you needed?" David asked as he headed towards the Battery Point Lighthouse.

"I got it," Laurel said, already pulling out her mortar and pestle.

"What are you making?"

"You just drive, and we'll see if I can avoid blowing up your car, OK?"

"OoOOK," David said, sounding less than confident. They drove silently, the scraping of Laurel's pestle playing a sinister duet with David's tyres humming against the asphalt. They drove to the south side of Crescent City and the clock on the dashboard marched inexorably forward.

8:43

8:44

8:45

They pulled into the deserted parking lot of the Battery Point Lighthouse and Laurel remembered coming here with Chelsea more than a year ago. She remembered Chelsea's bright smile as she explained all about the landmark she was so attached to. As they pulled into the parking spot closest to the island, a lump grew in Laurel's throat as she considered the possibility that she might not see Chelsea again.

At least, not alive.

Laurel shook the thought away and tried to grasp the slightly unfocused calm she had accidentally achieved when she made her first perfect sugar vials last week. She threw some hibiscus seeds in the mix and crushed them with determination, forcing herself to focus on happy memories with Chelsea, fighting not to let her fears intrude.

She was startled by David's hand on her arm. "Should we call the cops?" he asked.

Laurel shook her head. "If cops come, Chelsea will die. I guarantee it. The cops, too, probably."

"You're right." David paused. "What about Klea?"

Laurel shook her head. "I just can't make myself trust her. There's something – something wrong about her."

"But Chelsea…" His voice trailed off. "I just wish we had something else – someone else." His fingers tightened painfully on her arm. "Please don't let them kill her, Laurel."

Laurel shook in a dusting of powdered saguaro cactus needles and held the mixture up against the dim glow of a streetlight. It reflected the low beams just the way it was supposed to. "I'm going to do my best," she said quietly.

After pouring the mix into one sugar-glass vial, Laurel measured several drops of oil into a second vial, completing the monastuolo serum. It looked right; it *felt* right. She hoped it wasn't her desperation speaking. If it worked, Jeremiah Barnes and his new lackeys would go to sleep, and once Chelsea was freed they could go get Tamani. He would know what to do. Laurel stuffed the vials into her jacket pockets and started to open her door. They'd already wasted too much time just sitting here in the parking lot while she finished the potion.

"Wait," David said, his hand on her arm.

Laurel's eyes darted to the dashboard clock that was rushing through minutes far too quickly, but she stayed. David dug into his backpack and when he withdrew his hand, he held the small SIG SAUER Klea had intended for Laurel. Laurel focused on the gun for a few seconds, then looked up at David.

"I know you hate it," David said, his voice quiet and steady. "But it's the only thing we know for sure can stop Barnes. And if it comes down to his life or Chelsea's" – he laid the gun in Laurel's shaking hand—"I know you'll have the strength to make the right choice."

Laurel's hands were shaking so badly she could hardly wrap her fingers around the icy-cold grip, but she nodded and stuffed the gun into the waistband of her jeans, pulling her jacket down to conceal it.

They exited the car, both staring up at the lighthouse, where a spot of brightness shone out from the upper floor. Then she and David walked out to the path that led up to the lighthouse.

It was three feet under the ocean.

"Oh, no," Laurel said under her breath. "I forgot about the tide." She stared out at the lighthouse, about a hundred metres away across the churning water. She would make it – it wasn't that far – but the salt would work into her pores. It would sap her strength instantly and linger for at least a week.

Without speaking David scooped her up in his arms. He walked to the edge of the water and after the slightest hesitation, stepped in, his long, powerful legs striding easily through the frothy currents. He gasped as the bitterly cold water crawled up to his knees, his thighs, his hips, and after about a minute Laurel heard his teeth chatter for a second before he clamped his jaw shut. But he couldn't stop shivers from coursing through his body. Laurel tried to support as much of her own weight as possible, with her arms twined around David's neck, but even the wind was fighting them tonight, whipping against their jackets and through Laurel's long hair, stirring the seawater into choppy waves.

Right in the middle where the water was the deepest – up to David's waist – a large wave slapped at him and he staggered, almost dumping them both into the water. But with a small grunt of determination he found his footing again and slogged on.

It seemed like ages before David stumbled up the other side, on to the island with the small lighthouse. He put Laurel down gently before wrapping his arms around himself and breathing heavily.

"Thank you," Laurel said, her words seeming so insufficient.

"Well, I hear that getting hypothermia once a year is good for the soul," David said, his voice shaking as shivers racked his whole body.

"I—"

"Let's just go, Laurel," David interrupted. "They've got to know we're here."

Soon they stood in front of the door. It was ajar. Someone was waiting.

"Do we knock?" David whispered. "I'm not exactly up to speed on my hostage situation etiquette."

Laurel put a hand to her waist, checking to make sure the gun was still on one side, and the vials of potion on the other. "Just push it all the way open," she said, wishing her voice wasn't shaking so badly.

David complied.

It was dark.

"No one's here," David whispered.

Laurel's eyes searched the room. She pointed to a tiny needle of light that decorated the opposite wall. "They're here," she said, thinking back on Jamison's flytrap metaphor. "But we won't see them until we're in too far to get away."

Even so, they crossed the lower room slowly, then carefully opened the door to the stairs. Dim light spilled in from somewhere above. Laurel put her foot on the bottom step.

"No," David said, his hand on her shoulder. "Let me go first."

Guilt flooded through her. Even after everything she'd

done, he was still willing to put his life before hers. She shook her head. "He's got to see me first. Just to be sure."

They were less than five steps up when David gasped sharply. Laurel glanced back and saw that two trolls had come into the lighthouse behind them. These were not the dirty, unkempt trolls that had chased them from Ryan's home, however. They were both wearing clean black jeans and long-sleeved black shirts, and they were pointing shiny chrome handguns at David's back – not that they had any need for the guns. Laurel knew they could break her in two with ease.

One was bizarrely asymmetric – the left half of his body was withered and gnarled, but the right half would have looked at home on a world-class bodybuilder. The other troll's face looked remarkably human, but the bones in his shoulders were twisted and uneven, pulling one shoulder back and one forward, twisting his legs as well, so he moved with a strange, shuffling gait.

David looked up at Laurel with wide eyes, but she shook her head, faced forward again, and continued climbing. They reached the top of the stairs and were greeted by two more trolls, also armed. These looked more like the goons who had thrown Laurel and David into the Chetco last year, with drooping cheekbones, offset noses, and mismatched eyes. One even had a shock of red hair combed back from his fearsome face. But of course it couldn't be Barnes's old lackeys; Tamani had disposed of them. Laurel paid them no heed and turned the corner at the top of the stairs.

"Chelsea!" she gasped as her friend came into view.

Chelsea was blindfolded and trussed to a chair with a gun at her head. "Finally," she grumbled.

"I told you she'd come," said a gravelly, all-too-familiar voice. "Laurel. Welcome."

Laurel's eyes left Chelsea and travelled to the man who held the gun against Chelsea's temple. The face, the eyes that haunted her dreams – even more than a year later.

Jeremiah Barnes.

He looked the same – *exactly* the same. From his broad, football-player shoulders to his very slightly crooked nose, and those dark brown eyes that looked black from across the room. He was even wearing a rumpled white shirt and suit trousers that completed the eerie sense of déjà vu and made her feel like she was trapped in one of her own worst nightmares.

"Little Miss Noble. You even brought your old human friend to die with you. I'm impressed."

The trolls surrounding them chuckled. Trying not to draw attention to herself, Laurel flexed her hand, crushing the glass vials together in her pocket, letting the two elixirs mix. The glass jabbed into her hand and she forced herself to breathe normally as the serum reacted, burning her fingers as it became a hot steamy vapour that Laurel hoped Barnes wouldn't notice. She just needed a few minutes… if it worked. *Please work,* she begged in her head. "No one's here to die, Barnes. What do you want?"

Barnes laughed. "What do I want? Revenge, Laurel." He smiled dangerously. "How about this? I shoot you in the shoulder, so you know how it feels, then we go down to that old cabin and you show me where the gate is. Then, if you're not dead by that point, *maybe* I'll put you out of your misery."

"And what about my friends?" Laurel asked. She met Barnes's eyes, glare for glare. "*If* I agree," she said steadily, "what happens to my friends?"

The potion burned on her fingers and Laurel longed to pull her hand out of her pocket and rub the liquid away. But it was too risky. She gritted her teeth and continued staring at the hulking troll.

Barnes licked his lips and grinned. "I'll let them go."

It was blatantly obvious that he was lying, but Laurel played along. "Let them go now," she said, stalling for time, "and we'll go to the land."

"Right. I don't think so. You faeries are tricky bastards, especially when you're fighting a losing battle. Your friends go when – and only when – you've shown me the gate."

"No deal."

Barnes turned the gun on Laurel now.

She didn't even flinch.

"I don't think you're in any position to bargain," he said. "We're going to do it my way. I'll tie you up, toss you in my Hummer, and we'll go down to Orick. It's that, or you all die here tonight. Oh, and we can take care of that shoulder thing now," he said, lowering the gun so it pointed at her shoulder. Laurel closed her eyes and flexed her entire body, waiting for the impact.

"No," David said, yanking her backwards and stepping in front of her. "I won't let you."

Barnes laughed his harsh, almost wheezing laugh, making Laurel's skin crawl. After so long she still remembered that laugh with absolute clarity. "Won't let me? Like you can do anything about it, little boy," Barnes taunted. He gestured to the other trolls. "Get him out of here."

One troll grabbed Laurel by the shoulders to keep her still, then the redheaded troll closed his hand around David's arm, but David was ready. He spun, breaking the troll's grip, and swung his fist. It hit with a resounding *crack!* and the troll staggered back two steps.

Laurel watched in horror as David cradled his hand, then wound up to try again. She couldn't move – couldn't yell for him to wait, to be patient – without giving herself away. He'd saved her from Barnes's gun and now he would suffer instead of her.

"David?" Chelsea's voice sounded so small, so helpless, Laurel felt a lump grow in her throat.

The next troll was faster, kicking out one leg and catching David in the chest. Laurel grimaced and tried to pull away as she heard at least one rib crack under the impact of that foot, but the troll holding her maintained his iron grip. She glanced at Barnes; he was watching with an amused smile on his face, his gun still trained on her. She hated his smug smirk. Just looking at him made her a lot less upset about the gun she had tucked away.

"David!" Chelsea yelled again as a strangled groan escaped David's mouth.

"Chelsea, it's OK," Laurel called, but she could hear the terror in her own voice. "Please just hold still." To Laurel's relief, she stilled instead of trying to wiggle away from the thick, calloused fingers clenched at her neck.

The half-bodybuilder troll threw a punch at the

helpless, hunched David, but it was strangely slow and off centre, so it glanced off David's cheekbone – though still hard enough to split his skin. The troll spun awkwardly, stumbling and landing on the floor.

"Get up, you stupid oaf!" Barnes yelled as the other trolls grabbed David's arms, but the fallen troll didn't move. The one with the twisted shoulders pulled out a loop of rope and moved to secure him. David yanked his arm out of the troll's grasp and shoved him away; the troll fell to the floor as unconscious as the other.

"What the—" Barnes stammered, clearly confused. The redheaded troll forced David's arms back behind him and secured him, struggling, to the stair rail. David yanked at his arms, trying to free them, but he couldn't get loose. He looked desperately at Laurel, blood trailing down his face now, but she was studying the troll beside him. Slowly, so painfully slowly, the redheaded troll fell to his knees and collapsed on the ground. Then finally, the troll holding Laurel in place collapsed. A few seconds later David stood, tied securely to the railing, with four trolls at his feet.

Barnes swiftly switched his attention back to Laurel.

She had her gun out and pointed right at his head. "It's over, Barnes," she said, forcing back the hysteria that was threatening to erupt. "Put down your gun."

"Well, you're not the girl I met last year, are you?" Barnes studied her coolly. "You couldn't shoot me even to save your little vegetable friend back then. Now you've dropped all four of my guys." He grinned. "You're still waiting for me to fall, aren't you?"

Laurel said nothing, just focused on holding the gun steady.

"That stuff doesn't work on me," he said with a strange laugh. "Let's just say I made a deal with a devil and now I'm immune." He paused, meeting Laurel's eyes. "What now?" he asked, his expression still amused.

Laurel watched her perfect plan come crumbling down around her.

"I want answers," Laurel said, forcing her arms not to shake as she held the gun up, pointing at Barnes's chest. She knew she couldn't really trust whatever he might tell her, but she had to stall. Do something to give her time to think.

"Answers?" he said. "That's all you want? Answers are cheap. I'd have given them to you without the gun." He paused, looking at her with interest. "Ask me your burning questions, Laurel," he said mockingly.

"Where are my sentries? Did you kill them?"

He laughed. "Hardly. They're off chasing a red herring. A damn good red herring, if I do say so myself. They think they're saving you from me. They'll be back when they realise the trail of faerie blood is leading them nowhere."

"Whose blood?" Laurel said, her voice shaking now.

Barnes grinned. "No one… important."

"Why now?" Laurel asked, forcing thoughts of dead sentries out of her head. She couldn't do anything about that right now. "Why didn't you do this a month ago? Six months ago? Why now, and why Chelsea?"

He shook his head. "Your tiny world is so simple. You think there's me and my little band against you and your little band. But you're just a myopic little brat, a pawn, a *stooge*. When there are only a handful of players it's easy to arrange everything perfectly. But when you have numberless players, infinite factors, it takes time for everything to fall into place." He shrugged. "And besides, it was good sport. I wanted to take you right from your carefully barricaded home, but your sentries gave me some trouble. So I stopped trying to do it the hard way." He petted Chelsea's hair, his hand tightening around her neck as she tried to squirm away. "Chelsea here was so much less protected than you. It was easy to nab her. And you're too soft-hearted for your own good. I knew you'd come. So," he said, pressing his gun a little harder against Chelsea's head, "now we have an interesting bet.

Can you shoot the big, nasty troll before he shoots your little friend? Because let me tell you, Laurel, I think you might really shoot me. But can you do it before I shoot her?"

"Laurel, whatever he wants, don't give it to him," Chelsea yelled.

"Shut up, you little brat," Barnes said. He tightened his finger on the trigger, and Laurel took one step forward.

"Wait, wait, wait," Barnes said. "I'm not going to shoot her yet. I don't think this is quite interesting enough." Then with a movement so quick she scarcely saw it, Barnes released Chelsea's neck, pulled another gun from a hidden holster, and pointed it at David.

Laurel could hardly breathe as all hope of escape vanished.

"After getting cornered by you last year, I've learned to always carry more than one gun, Miss Sewell." He turned his attention back to her, firearms aimed expertly at Chelsea and David. "See, I suspect you might risk one friend's life to save yourself and your boyfriend here, but will you risk two friends' lives just to save yourself?"

Maybe she could bargain. She had to try; she had no other options. "OK," Laurel said, dropping her gun to the floor with a loud clatter. "I give up."

"Laurel!" David shouted. "Don't do it!" He continued to struggle against his bonds.

"There's no other way." She slowly raised her hands over her head just as a loud creak sounded from the stairwell.

Barnes shifted his guns, pointing one at Laurel and one at the top of the stairs. "I hear you!" he shouted. "You on the stairs; I know you're there."

Laurel held her breath but heard nothing.

Barnes sniffed the air. "I know you've got a gun," he shouted. "I can smell it. Now I'm gonna give you to the count of three to throw your gun up here on the floor. If I say three, I will kill them all. You hear me?"

A long pause.

"One."

David's breathing grew ragged.

"Two."

Chelsea began to squirm in her seat, and sobs she'd held back this whole time began to shake her shoulders. Laurel stared desperately at the gun on the floor in front of her, wondering if there was any way she could get to it.

Something clattered up the stairs.

An enormous gun slid across the floor, a ribbon of ammunition trailing from it. Barnes looked at the gun with obvious appreciation and slowly reached down, dropping one of his own firearms and switching it for the much bigger weapon.

"That's better," he said. "Now show yourself. Show yourself and maybe I'll let you live."

Nothing.

"Do I have to count again?" Barnes threatened. "'Cause I will."

Rapid staccato footsteps ascended the stairs. Laurel turned and shock filled her already frazzled nerves when she saw Klea's red hair appear around the corner.

Surprise registered on Barnes's face. "You? But—"

In the split second it took Laurel to blink, she heard the rip of Velcro; when she opened her eyes a wet red circle had blossomed in the centre of Barnes's forehead and the roar of gunfire was ringing in her ears. Barnes's face shot confusion at the room for the tiniest instant before the force from the bullet snapped his head backwards and he crumpled to the floor. The acrid smell of gunpowder filled the air and matching screams tore from Laurel's and Chelsea's throats. Seconds felt like hours as Laurel took a shuddering breath and Chelsea slumped in her chair.

"Now that's what I call cutting it close," Klea said ruefully.

Laurel turned towards David and Klea. Klea was gripping a familiar-looking gun, and Laurel could just see the tail of David's shirt scrunched up against the ropes to reveal his concealed holster.

"S-s-see, Laurel," David said, his teeth chattering from cold, or shock – probably both. "I knew carrying that gun would come in handy someday."

Laurel couldn't even move; her body was frozen with relief, fear, disgust, and shock. Her eyes couldn't leave the crimson pool slowly expanding under Barnes's head, his body crumpled in the grotesquely awkward angles of sudden death. And despite knowing the world was better for Barnes's departure from it, she hated knowing she was directly responsible.

She turned to Klea, staring at those ever present sunglasses. Her mistrust, her refusal to call her, suddenly seemed silly, paranoid. For the second time, Klea had saved her from the brink of death. And not just her, but her two best friends in the world. It was a debt she could never hope to repay.

And yet, despite that, something still held Laurel back. Something visceral that told her this was not a woman to be trusted.

"Take this," Klea said, her voice calm as she handed Laurel a knife. Disturbingly calm, Laurel thought, for someone who had just shot a man in the head. "Cut them free, then meet me downstairs. I have to flag my team in."

She turned without another word and headed down the stairs.

Laurel ran to David and began hacking at the ropes. They came away easily under the razor-sharp blade. "Don't say anything," she whispered. "Not to Chelsea yet, and especially not to Klea. I'll make up something." She touched his ribs gingerly. "And as soon as we get back to the car, I'll take care of your ribs and hand, OK? Let's just get the hell out of here."

He nodded, his face pale and twisted with pain.

Laurel hurried to the chair where Chelsea was tied and made short work of her ropes too. Chelsea's wrists were red where the ropes came free and Laurel wondered just how long Barnes had made her sit there, gun pressed to her head, waiting for them. Refusing to dwell on it, Laurel pulled the blindfold away from Chelsea's eyes.

Chelsea blinked against the light and rubbed her wrists as Laurel sliced at the ropes around her ankles.

"Can you walk?" Laurel asked gently.

"I think I'll manage," Chelsea said, staggering a little. She focused on David. "You don't look too good, either."

"You should see the other guys." David said, smiling wanly. He pulled Chelsea to him, hugging her with more force than Laurel thought his ribs should be subjected to right now. But she didn't blame him. "I'm just glad you're alive," he said to Chelsea.

Laurel wrapped her arms around both of her friends, easing back when David groaned. "I'm so sorry you got dragged into this, Chelsea. I never intended... I never meant to..."

"Never meant to what?" Chelsea asked, rubbing at the red marks on her neck. "Nearly get me killed? I certainly hope not. Please tell me *that's* not going to be an everyday thing now." She let out a breath. "What happened here?"

Laurel looked helplessly at David. "Well, um, you see... the thing is..."

"Here," Chelsea said, sitting down in the same chair they'd just untied her from and crossing her legs. "Let me just sit here while you think of a good lie." She waved her hand at the far side of the room. "Maybe you and David should go confer over in the corner so your stories match. 'Cause that would help. Or," she said, raising one finger in the air, "you could just tell me that every fall an enormous bluish-purple flower grows out of your back, because apparently you're some kind of faerie. And then you could explain how these – I think he said trolls? –

have been hunting you because you're hiding a special gate from them. Because personally, I find that the truth keeps life a lot simpler."

Laurel and David just stood there, slack-jawed.

Chelsea looked back and forth between them in confusion. "Oh, please," she finally said. "Did you honestly think I didn't know?"

Chapter Twenty-six

Klea rowed them across the water in a wide, flat-bottomed boat. "My guys are going to take care of everything here at the lighthouse," she said. "You two take your friend back to her car, then get yourselves home."

They lurched to a stop on the beach and a tiny grunt of pain escaped David's lips. The three friends unloaded and each girl took one of David's arms, trying to help him walk without letting Klea know just how hurt he was. Though Klea had saved their lives, they had agreed that she should know as little as possible about Laurel. That meant getting David away quickly so that Laurel could take care of him without anyone observing.

"Laurel," Klea called.

"Keep walking," Laurel whispered to David and

Chelsea. "I'll be right there." Then she turned and walked back to Klea.

"I'm sorry I didn't get here sooner."

"You got here right on time," Laurel replied.

"Still, if I had been two minutes later." She sighed and shook her head. "I'm glad I had some of my guys watching you tonight. I wish—" She paused, shaking her head. "I wish you had called me. Anyway," she continued before Laurel could respond, "how did you dispatch those other four trolls? I was amazed."

Laurel hesitated.

"I looked at those trolls. There are no broken bones, no gunshots, no wounds whatsoever. Out like lights, and I don't expect them to wake up for hours yet. Are you going to tell me what really happened?"

Laurel pressed her lips shut as she searched for a lie. But she came up blank. She was too tired to think of anything good. But she wasn't going to tell Klea the truth, either, so she said nothing.

"Fine," Klea said with a strange smile. "I get it, you have your secrets. You obviously don't trust me yet," she said, her voice soft. "But I hope one day you will. Really trust me. You're clearly not helpless, but I could help you so much – more than you know. Regardless," she said, turning her gaze back towards the lighthouse, "having actual specimens will be helpful. Very helpful."

Laurel didn't like the way Klea said *specimens*. But she remained silent.

Klea studied her for several long seconds. "I'll be in touch," she said firmly. "You've proven resourceful and I could really use your assistance in another, unrelated matter – but it can wait a bit." Before Laurel could respond, Klea spun on her heel and leaped lightly back into the boat, gripping the pole with strong hands.

Laurel stayed just long enough to watch Klea push off the sandy beach before turning and running to catch up with David and Chelsea. They had reached David's car by the time Laurel joined them. David groaned as he slipped into the passenger seat and Chelsea gripped Laurel's arm. "We have to get him to the hospital. His ribs have got to be broken and that cut under his eye might need stitches."

"We can't go to the hospital," Laurel said, digging in her backpack.

"Laurel!" Chelsea said, her face white. "David needs help!"

"Relax," Laurel said, unwrapping a tiny bottle of blue liquid. "Being friends with a faerie has its perks." She *loved* being able to say that in front of Chelsea. She unscrewed the top of the bottle and lifted out the dropper, then leaned over David, who was breathing loud, laboured breaths. "Open," she said softly.

David opened one eye and looked at the familiar bottle. "Oh, man," he said. "That's the most beautiful thing I've seen all night." He opened his mouth and Laurel squeezed two drops in.

"Now hold still," she said, letting one drop fall on to her finger. She gently rubbed it against the gash on his face. "All better," she whispered as she watched his skin knit back together.

She stood and turned to Chelsea. "Are you hurt anywhere?"

Chelsea shook her head. "He was pretty nice to me, considering..." But her eyes were focused on David. "Wait a second." She leaned over and studied the skin under his eye. "I could have sworn...."

Laurel laughed, and even David joined in quietly. "In a few minutes his ribs and hand will heal too."

"Are you kidding me?" Chelsea asked with wild, excited eyes.

It reminded Laurel of the way David had reacted when he first found out she was a faerie. She grinned and held up the blue bottle. "It's useful – David gets beat up by trolls on a regular basis."

David snorted.

"Why don't you fix your hand?" Chelsea asked.

Laurel looked down at the burns on her fingers and wondered how she had ever thought she could hide anything from Chelsea. It was hard to tell she was hurt because, unlike humans, her skin didn't turn red when it burned. The colour hadn't changed at all, actually. But tiny bubbles – *blisters*, she corrected herself – had formed on her palm and trailed down two of her fingers. She stared at her aching hand in wonder. She'd never had a blister before.

Well, not that she could remember.

"It's only for humans," she said softly. "I'd need something else." She hesitated for a moment. "Hey, Chelsea," she said slowly.

Chelsea and David both looked up at the serious tone in her voice.

Laurel took a deep breath. "I'm really glad you know I'm a faerie. It helps so much to not have to hide from the whole world. But anyone who knows is automatically in danger. So—"

"It's OK, Laurel," Chelsea said. "I'd rather know. You have to take the good with the bad."

"It's more than that," Laurel said. "Stuff like this seems to happen a lot, unfortunately. If you…" She paused and laid a hand on David's shoulder, glad he didn't shrug it away. "If you do this with us – join us, I guess – I can't promise your safety. I'm a dangerous person to be around, and this isn't just about you. This may put Ryan in danger too. I mean, think about tonight. I didn't tell you anything and you still got nabbed. So think – think really hard – before you decide that this is really what you want."

Chelsea looked up at her warily. "Well, I think it's a little late for that. I'm involved now whether I want to be or not, aren't I?"

"Well…"

David and Chelsea both looked up at her questioningly.

"I could—" Laurel took a deep breath and forced herself to say it. "I could make you forget everything that happened tonight."

"Laurel, no!" David said.

"I have to give her the choice," Laurel insisted. "I won't force her into this."

"You could make me forget?" Chelsea said, her voice soft and small. "Just like that?"

Laurel nodded, her chest aching at the thought of actually doing it.

"But it's my choice, right?"

"Your choice," Laurel said firmly.

Several tense seconds passed before Chelsea broke into a wide smile. "Oh man, I wouldn't trade this for anything in the world."

A relieved breath rushed out of Laurel and she sprang forward to throw her arms around Chelsea. "Thanks," Laurel said. Although whether she was thanking Chelsea for sharing her secret or for sparing her from having to use a memory elixir, Laurel wasn't quite sure.

They all loaded into the car – Laurel insisting on driving even though David's ribs were almost healed – and drove off towards Ryan's house, where Chelsea had been headed when Barnes took her. Chelsea's mom's car had been carefully pushed off to the side of the road a few yards away from a stop sign. It looked so quiet and unassuming. No one would ever guess the circumstances under which it had ended up there. Laurel got out with Chelsea and walked her to the car.

"It's kind of surreal," Chelsea said. "I'm going to get in this car and drive back to my everyday life like nothing happened. And no one except me will know that it's a whole new world." She hesitated. "Even though I figured the whole faerie thing out – last year, actually," she said with a giggle. "I do have a bunch of questions. If you don't mind talking about it, I mean."

"I don't mind," Laurel said, then smiled. "I *love* that you know, actually. I hate keeping secrets from you." She sobered. "But not tonight. Go home," Laurel said, placing one hand on Chelsea's shoulder. "Hug your family; get some sleep. Then call me sometime tomorrow and we'll talk. I'll tell you anything you want to know," she said earnestly. "Anything. Everything. No more secrets. I promise."

Chelsea broke into a big grin. "OK. It's a deal." She leaned forward and hugged Laurel. "Thanks for saving me," she said, her voice serious now. "I was so scared."

Laurel closed her eyes, Chelsea's curls soft against her cheek. "You weren't the only one," she said quietly.

After a long hug, Chelsea stepped back and turned towards her car. She stopped just before slipping into the car and looked at Laurel. "You do know I'm going to call you at, like, six in the morning, right?"

Laurel laughed. "I know."

"Just checking. Oh," she added, "and you'll tell me where you really were this summer, right?"

She should have known Chelsea wouldn't buy the wilderness retreat. She laughed and waved one more time as Chelsea closed the door and headed on her way, tyres crunching loudly in the quiet night.

While Laurel and Chelsea were talking, David had shifted himself over to the driver's seat. Laurel walked around to the passenger door and let herself in. They drove silently, streetlights periodically illuminating David's brooding features.

She wished he would say something. Anything.

But he didn't.

"What are you going to tell your mom?" Laurel asked, more to break the silence than anything.

David was quiet for a long time and Laurel started to think he wasn't going to answer her. "I don't know," he finally said in a weary voice. "I'm tired of lying." His eyes darted to her. "I'll come up with something."

David turned into the driveway, his headlights cutting across the house. He pressed the button on his visor and the garage door rose slowly to reveal two empty spots.

"Oh, good," David said with a sigh. "She's gone. With luck I won't have to tell her anything at all."

They climbed out of the car and stood there, avoiding each other's gaze for a long, awkward moment.

"Well, I'd better change," David said, pointing his thumb at the side door. "My mom trusts me a lot, but even she would wonder why I decided to take a swim in November." He laughed tensely. "Fully clothed, no less."

Laurel nodded and David turned away.

"David?"

He stopped, his hand on the doorknob. He looked

back at her but didn't answer.

"I'm going out to the land tomorrow."

David looked down at the floor.

"I'm going to tell Tamani that I can't come see him any more. At all."

He looked up at her. His jaw was tight, but there was something in his eyes that gave Laurel hope.

"I'll need to go back to Avalon next summer to attend the Academy, because that's important. Maybe more important, with Barnes dead. I don't like what he said... about things being bigger than him. I don't even know what the consequences of tonight might entail. I—" She forced herself to stop rambling and took a deep breath. "The point is, I'm going to stop trying to straddle both worlds. I live here. My life is here; my parents are here. You're here. I can't live in both places. And I choose this world." She paused. "I choose you. One hundred per cent this time." Tears threatened, but she forced herself to continue. "Tamani, he doesn't understand me like you do. He wants me to be something I'm not ready to be. Maybe I won't ever be ready. But you want me to be what *I* want. You want me to choose for myself. I love that you care about what I want. And I love you." She paused. "I – I hope that you'll forgive me. But even if you don't, I'm still going tomorrow. You told me I need to choose my own life, and I am. I choose you, David, even if you don't choose me."

He didn't look away, but he didn't say anything, either.

Laurel nodded despondently. She hadn't really expected instantaneous results; she'd hurt him too badly. She turned to head out to her own car.

"Laurel?" By the time she looked back he'd grabbed her wrist and pulled her to him. His lips found hers – so warm and gentle – as his arms snaked around her, holding her against him.

She kissed him back with abandon, all the fears of the evening rushing away and relief flooding through her body. Barnes was dead. And no matter what was going to happen tomorrow, tonight they were safe. Chelsea was safe. David was safe. And he was going to forgive her.

That was the best part.

He finally pulled away and ran one finger down the side of her face.

She laid her head against his chest and listened to his heart, beating steadily, as if only for her.

David lifted her chin and kissed her again. Laurel leaned back against the car, David following, his warm body pressed gently against hers.

Her parents could wait a few more minutes.

It was after eleven by the time Laurel dragged herself to her front door. She paused as she laid her hand on the doorknob. She could hardly believe that only that morning she had left to attend the festival with Tamani. Could it really have been just fifteen hours ago? It seemed like months.

Years.

With a long sigh Laurel turned the knob and let herself in.

Her parents were both sitting on the couch, waiting for her. Her mom jumped up as the door swung open, wiping tears from her face. "Laurel!" She rushed over and put her arms around her. "I've been so worried."

It had been a long time since her mom had hugged her like that. Laurel hugged back, squeezing hard, overwhelmed by a sense of security that had nothing to do with trolls or faeries. A sense of belonging that had nothing to do with Avalon. A love that had nothing to do with David or Tamani.

Laurel pressed her face into her mother's shoulder. *This is my home,* she thought fiercely. *This is where I belong.* Avalon was beautiful – perfect, really – magical and exotic and exciting. But it didn't have this – this acceptance and love that she found among her human family and friends. Avalon had never seemed so superficial, such an illusion, as right at this moment. It was time she let this be her real home. Her *only* home.

She heard her father walk up and as she felt his arms encompass them both Laurel was certain she'd made the right decision. She couldn't live in two worlds, and this world was where she belonged. She smiled up at her parents and sank down on to the couch. They sat on either side of her.

"So what happened?" her dad asked.

"It's kind of a long story," Laurel began hesitantly. "I haven't been completely honest with you, not for a long time."

And with a deep breath, Laurel began explaining about the trolls, starting all the way back at the hospital the previous fall. She explained why Jeremiah Barnes had never shown up to finish buying the land, and why he had tried to buy it in the first place. She told them about the sentries who had kept them safe. The true nature of the "dog fights" in the trees behind their house. She even told them about Klea; she left nothing out. When Laurel finished relaying the events of that night, her dad just shook his head. "And you did that all on your own?"

"Everyone helped, Dad. David, Chelsea" – she hesitated—"Klea. I couldn't have done it alone." Laurel paused and looked over at her mom.

She had risen from the couch and was pacing in front of the window.

"I'm really sorry I didn't tell you earlier, Mom," Laurel said. "I just thought that you dealing with the whole faerie thing was enough without throwing trolls into the mix as well. And I know it's going to take some time to accept this, too, but from now on, I'll tell you guys everything, I promise, if you'll just… if you'll just listen and still" – she sniffed, trying to hold back tears—"still love me."

Laurel's mom turned to her with a look Laurel couldn't quite decipher. "I'm so sorry, Laurel."

Whatever Laurel might have expected, it wasn't that. "What? No, I'm the one who lied."

"You may have kept secrets from us, but I think you could tell I wouldn't have listened. And I'm sorry about that." She leaned forward and hugged Laurel, and Laurel felt her spirits lift and fly in a way she had been certain she would never feel again. She hadn't realised just how hard it was, hiding so much from her parents.

Her mom sat back down on the couch and put an arm around Laurel. "When you told us you were a faerie, it was weird and unbelievable, but more than that, it made me feel completely useless. You were this amazing thing and had spent your whole life having all these faerie… guards, or whatever, watching out for you. You didn't need me."

"No, Mom," Laurel said, shaking her head. "I'll always need you. You were the best mom. Always."

"It made me so angry. I'm sure that was the wrong way to feel, but it's how I felt. I took it out on you. I didn't mean to," she added. "But I did. And the whole time," her mom continued, "you were afraid for your life and keeping this huge secret." She turned to Laurel. "I'm so sorry. I'm going to try – I've been trying."

"I noticed," Laurel said with a smile.

"Well, I'm going to try harder." She kissed Laurel's forehead. "When you left my store tonight, I was afraid I might never see you again, and I didn't even know why. And the only thing I could feel through the fear was the overwhelming regret that you didn't know how much I loved you. How much I've always loved you." She leaned her head against Laurel.

"I love you too, Mom," Laurel said, her arms tight around her mom's waist.

"And I love you both," Laurel's dad said with a grin, hugging them tightly together, smooshing Laurel in the middle. They all laughed, and Laurel felt the tension of the past year dissipating. It would take work – nothing fixed itself in one night – but it was a start. It was enough.

"So," her mom said after a minute, "you didn't tell us what actually happened in Avalon today." She was hesitant, awkward, but her tone sounded genuine.

"It was amazing," Laurel said haltingly. "The most incredible thing I've ever seen."

Laurel's mom patted her thigh and Laurel lay down with her head in her mom's lap. She ran her fingers through Laurel's long hair the way she had ever since Laurel was a little girl. And with both of her parents just listening, Laurel began to talk about Avalon.

Chapter Twenty-seven

Standing at the edge of the tree line had never felt so much like standing at the edge of a cliff. Laurel took several deep breaths and had a few false starts before she forced her feet to walk down the path that led into the forest behind her cabin.

"Tamani?" she called softly. "Tam?"

She kept walking, knowing that it didn't really matter if she called or not; he must already know she was here. He always did.

"Tamani?" she called again.

"Tamani's not here."

Laurel bit off a yelp of surprise as she turned towards the deep voice behind her.

It was Shar.

He looked at her steadily, his eyes the same deep green as Tamani's, his dark blond hair with green roots framing his oval face and just touching his shoulders.

"Where is he?" Laurel asked when she found her voice.

Shar shrugged. "You told him to go, so he went."

"What do you mean, he went?"

"This gate is no longer Tamani's post. He was mostly here to watch you, anyway, and now you're gone. He has a new assignment."

"Since yesterday!" Laurel cried.

"Things can move very quickly when we need them to."

She nodded. Granted, the whole reason she'd come was to tell him they needed to not see each other any more, but she wanted to explain, to make him understand. She didn't want it to end like *this*. The last words she'd screamed at him echoed through her head, reverberating with a sickening clarity. *I want you to go away. I mean it. Go!* She hadn't meant it, not exactly. She was angry and scared, and David was standing right there. She took a long, shuddering breath and rubbed her temples with her fingertips.

It was too late.

"What have you got there?" Shar said, interrupting her thoughts.

He was reaching for her hand, and it didn't occur to her to yank it away. Her thoughts swirled, centring on Tamani and how badly her words must have hurt him.

Shar studied the blisters. He looked up at her, his eyes narrowed. "These blisters are from a monastuolo serum. Have you treated it?"

"Too many things going on," Laurel mumbled, shaking her head.

"Come with me," Shar said, pulling on her hand.

Laurel followed, too numb to resist.

Shar led her to a clearing, where he picked up a pack that looked very similar to Tamani's. She hated being here without him. Everything she saw was a reminder of him. Shar pulled out a bottle of thick amber liquid and laid her hand on his lap, squeezing the bottle carefully to release one large drop of the cloudy solution.

"A little goes a long way," Shar said, rubbing the tender blisters carefully. The cooling effect was instant, even with the irritation of Shar's fingers on the sensitive skin. "When I'm finished, keep it uncovered and in the sunlight if you can."

Laurel stared at him. "Why are you doing this?" she asked. "You hate me."

Shar sighed as he squeezed another drop on to her hand, rubbing her blistered fingers this time. "I don't hate *you*. I hate the way you treat Tam."

Laurel looked away, unable to meet his accusing eyes.

"He lives for you, Laurel, and that's not some kind of figure of speech. He lives every day for you. Even after you moved to Crescent City, all he did every day was talk about you, worry about you, wonder what was happening, if he would ever see you again. And even when I told him I was sick of hearing about you, I could tell he was still thinking about you. Every moment of every day."

Laurel studied her blistered hand.

"And you!" Shar said, his voice getting a little louder. "You don't appreciate that at all. Sometimes I think you don't even realise he exists except when you're around him. Like the only part of his life that matters is the part you see." He looked up at her and placed her hand back on her own lap. "Did you know he lost his father last spring?"

"I did." Laurel nodded emphatically, desperate to defend herself. "I knew that. I—"

"That was the worst part," Shar continued, talking over her. "The worst *ever*. He was so distraught. But he knew it would be OK, because you were going to come see him. 'In May,' he told me. 'She's coming in May.'"

Laurel's chest felt hollow, empty.

"But you didn't come in May. He waited for you every day, Laurel. And then, when you finally showed up at the end of June, the second he saw you – the *instant* he saw you – you were forgiven. And every time you come and then leave – go back to your human boy – you shatter him all over again." He leaned back with his arms across his chest. "And honestly, I don't think you care."

"I do," Laurel said, her voice brimming with emotion. "I do care."

"No, you don't," Shar said, his voice still even and calm. "You *think* you do, but if you really cared, you wouldn't do it any more. You'd stop stringing him along like a plaything."

Laurel was silent for a few seconds, then she stood abruptly and started to walk away.

"I suppose you came to beg his forgiveness and give him a lot of pretty hopes before traipsing back to your little human boy again," Shar said, just before she was out of sight.

"As a matter of fact, no." Laurel turned, angry now. "I came to tell him that I can't do this two-worlds thing any more. That I have to stay in the human world and he has to stay in the faerie world." She stopped and sucked in a breath, grabbing hold of her temper. "You're right," she said, calm now. "It's not fair for me to breeze in and out of his life. And… and it has to stop," she finished lamely.

Shar stared at her for a long time, then a hint of a smile played at the corner of his mouth. "Laurel, that's the best decision I've ever seen you make." He leaned forward just a bit. "And I've been watching you since you were just a wee thing."

Laurel scrunched up her face. *Thank you, Big Brother.*

"Where'd you get the blisters?" Shar stood and crossed his arms over his chest.

Laurel rolled her eyes and turned away.

"This isn't a game, Laurel." Shar caught her wrist, and not gently. "There's only one reason for using a monastuolo serum, and 'for fun' is not it."

Laurel glared at him. "I ran into some trouble," she said shortly. "I handled it."

"Handled it?"

"Yes, I handled it. I'm not completely helpless, you know."

"Are you going to tell me what happened?"

"I dealt with it; it doesn't matter," she said, trying to pull her arm away.

"Maybe you didn't hear me, Laurel. I said this isn't a game. Do you think it's a game?" Shar demanded, his eyes hard and flashing. "A contest between you and the trolls? Because I suspect that this little 'problem' is the same troll who was hunting you last year. The same troll who knows the gate is here on this land. The troll who wouldn't think twice about murdering you and every faerie in the realm to get into Avalon. Your little *problem* is threatening our lives, Laurel."

She pulled away and crossed her arms over her chest, saying nothing.

"I have a daughter, did you know that? A two-year-old little girl, barely more than a seedling. I'd like her to have a father for at least the next hundred years, if you don't mind. But the chances of that happening are dropping precipitously right now because you have this animal-brained determination that you have to *handle* things yourself. So I ask you again, Laurel, are you going to tell me what happened?"

His voice hadn't gotten any louder, but Laurel felt her ears ring as though he'd shouted. It was more than she could handle. She rubbed her eyes with the heels of her hands, trying to stop the tears, but it didn't help; they came anyway. She'd screwed everything up. She'd let down everyone who'd had any degree of importance to her at all. Even Shar.

Shar's sharp whisper made Laurel's head snap up. He'd said something in a language she didn't understand, but he didn't seem to be addressing her. She forced back her tears, and her eyes flashed around at the trees surrounding her. But no one appeared and Shar was still focused on her.

Laurel nodded numbly. "OK," she said softly. "I'll tell you."

Shar watched Laurel leave the glade and climb into her car after she had finished telling him about Barnes. She'd answered all his questions.

All the ones she knew the answers to, anyway.

Shar waited, standing still against the tree until her car – its yellow signal blinking annoyingly – turned on to the highway.

"You can come out now, Tam," he said.

Tamani stepped out from behind a tree, his eyes fixed on Laurel's departing car.

"Thank you for staying put – even though you almost didn't," he added wryly.

Tamani just shrugged.

"She wouldn't have told me as much with you around. She needed to think you were gone. Now she's really told us everything."

"She didn't have much of a choice," Tamani said, his voice flat. "Not with the way you were interrogating her." He paused for a few seconds. "You were pretty hard on her, Shar."

"You've seen me be hard on someone, Tam. That wasn't hard."

"Yeah, but—"

"She needed to hear it, Tamani," Shar said sharply. "She may be your duty, but the gate is mine. She needs to know how serious this is."

Tamani tightened his jaw but didn't argue.

"I'm sorry I made her cry," Shar said grudgingly.

"So are we agreed on what needs to be done next?"

Shar nodded.

Tamani smiled.

"It'll take months, Tamani. This is a huge endeavour you're undertaking."

"I know."

"And she did come here to say goodbye."

"I know," he said, his voice soft. He turned now, to look at Shar. "But you'll watch her? You'll make sure she's safe?"

"I promise." He paused. "I'll assign more sentries to her house. If Barnes could get the whole crew away from her house last night, then there weren't enough. I'll make sure there's enough next time."

"Will there be a next time?"

Shar nodded. "I'm sure of it. Barnes was a twig, maybe

a branch, but weeds like this grow from the roots. I'm not too proud to admit that I'm afraid of what we're not seeing." He glanced at Tamani. "If I weren't so sure, I wouldn't let you do this at all."

They gazed up the path, towards the empty cabin with its overgrown yard and ageing exterior.

"You ready for this?" Shar asked.

"Yeah," Tamani said, a grin spreading across his face. "Oh, yeah."

Acknowledgments

The more I learn about publishing, the less credit I think authors deserve. For at least a million reasons, these are my champions: Erica Sussman, Susan Katz, Kate Jackson, Ray Shappell, Cristina Gilbert, Erin Gallagher, Jocelyn Davies, Jennifer Kelaher, Elise Howard, Cecilia de la Campa, Maja Nikolic, Alec Shane, and the countless people at HarperCollins and Writers House who have worked tirelessly to make this series a success.

A special thankyou goes to my personal knights in shining armour, my beyond amazing editor, Tara Weikum; agent-extraordinaire Jodi Reamer; and the most patient publicist in the world, Laura Kaplan. You three work so hard for me, and every moment is appreciated.

My friends, my wonderful friends, you all know who you are, and what you've done, and I promise not to turn you in for it: David McAfee, Pat Wood, John Zakour, James Dashner, Sarah Cross, Sarah MacLean, Sarah Rees Brennan, Carrie Ryan, Saundra Mitchell, R. J. Anderson, Heidi Kling, Stephenie, and the whole Feast of Awesome. Wow. You are amazing and have very questionable taste in friends, for which I am grateful. Betas Hannah, Emma, and Bethany, I am still going to send you guys stuff! And thank you to authors Claire Davis and William Bernhardt for helping me learn the craft. I'm still trying!

My family and family-in-law: No one has ever had such a supportive family, I am convinced. A huge thankyou to Audrey, Brennan, and Gideon; you are my sunshine, always will be. Last and above all, Kenny, you are there every step. And every misstep. It hasn't been easy, but you make it look that way.

See where it all began...

APRILYNNE PIKE

Laurel has always lived as an ordinary girl – but now
something is happening to her.
Something *magical*.

In this enchanting tale of magic, romance and danger,
everything you thought you knew about faeries
will be changed forever.

"A remarkable debut"
STEPHENIE MEYER

ISBN 978-0-00-731436-2